The Children of Resurrection Gardens

STONE WALLACE

The Children of Resurrection Gardens by Stone Wallace
©2017, Stone Wallace

Tell-Tale Publishing Group, LLC
Tucson, AZ 85737

Printed in The United States of America.

This "Little Shop of Horrors" is dedicated to the masters of the macabre, each an inspiration: Robert Bloch, Ray Bradbury, James Herbert, Stephen King, and Richard Matheson.

From Ghoulies
And Ghosties
And Long-Leggety Beasties
And Things That Go Bump in the Night,
The Good Lord Deliver Us!
- Old Cornish Prayer

PROLOGUE

A Halloween Tale

A coastal town in Massachusetts . . . some years ago

The haggard, crook-backed conjuring crone cast her one mobile eye over the small group of girls and leaned forward toward the flickering candle flame. The atmosphere in the room was perfect as the light from the candle cast shifting, ominous shadows against the wall. Her wretched face looked to be pulled from the very depths of a nightmare. Beneath her pointed hood and matted hair her skin had a greenish tinge and was as withered as dry parchment. Her few remaining teeth just visible under a prominent hooked nose were twisted and rotting, like time-worn headstones set within a dank, foul cavern.

Her words carried forth on ancient breath.

"The house still harbors its legend," she said, her words delivered slowly and with a tremulous inflection. "You all know the house. It stands at the very end of Dawson Road. What you do not know," she added, thrusting a sharp-nailed finger toward the girls, "is that at one time a graveyard stood on that spot. But the graveyard was old and desecrated and soon it was plowed under and the tombstones removed and discarded. And then a house was built on the property.

"Superstitions never die and for a long time no one would occupy the house. No one in town, that is." She pressed her index finger against her lips and said in a whisper, "*Shhhhh*, they all kept the secret. But people from other localities looking to settle in our town were tempted to buy the place at a cost too attractive to pass up. And then it happened. Soon after and continuing ever since. Tragedy befell every family that dared to take possession of that residence. There were unexplained accidents. Supposedly, occurrences of madness—and murder. The story goes that the spirits haunting the old graveyard became angry and vengeful at this defilement of their final resting place and that a curse fell upon the house and all who inhabited it. Eventually the house became empty, blackened by the evil that existed within those walls. Haunted by the ghosts who had made that house their new dwelling. No one would take possession of the house—not for any price. And especially not after one Halloween night when two teenage boys went into the house on a dare . . . and were never seen again. After that, the doors and windows were boarded and sealed, and not to keep things out, but to keep things *in*. Over the years, through time, neglect and decay, all the possessions and furnishings were destroyed; *all* except one—the mirror."

Each of the girls was captivated not only by the tale, but by the eerie shadings that played across the crone's wizened face, misshapen and malevolent shadows cast upon her features by the flickering candlelight.

A luminous beam of autumn moonlight filtered into the room through the open, curtainless window. The drying leaves still clinging to nearly barren branches rustled in rhythmic accompaniment to the late season gusts of wind, their distorted reflections twitching in silhouette against the walls.

An ideal atmosphere . . . for the telling of ghost stories.

Cassandra Springer, perfectly attired in her tattered "Grizelda the Witch" costume, her breath redolent of chewed garlic for effect, her features built up to exaggerated proportions through the generous application of green putty and further highlighted by special Halloween makeup, was wrapping up her annual "Ghosts and Goblins" party with her four remaining guests by the customary sharing of spooky tales. Sitting around the makeshift séance table were Amber and Ashley (the "too-cute" Anderson twins) as well as Josie Mainer and Rebecca Arnold, all of whom were listening in rapt attention.

"Yessss," Cassandra continued, drawing out the word with snakelike sibilance, "someone took the mirror. Snatched it from the attic before it could be destroyed. What that person did not know was that the mirror, too, was inhabited. Possessed by the spirit of a murderer who escaped an eternal hellfire punishment for her evil deeds. A woman who it is said made a deal with Satan just before her death that if he spared her an eternity in hell, she would serve him in the afterlife. The terms of the bargain were that she would bring many souls to him in exchange for her own. But any bargain with the devil comes with a catch. He demanded one hundred souls from her . . . and until that number was reached her spirit would be imprisoned within the glass of a mirror. Yes, *that* mirror. The one taken from a house already infested with evil. Not all the souls were collected. The Devil had not yet been paid his due. The only way to claim those souls is to lure a person toward the mirror, tempting them with the weakness of vanity. And from that another legend grew."

She started to chant . . .

"Bloody Mary, Bloody Mary

Lived in a house by the cemetery,

She didn't kill once and she didn't kill nice

She used her knife to slash and slice."

The room fell silent as a palpable chill was felt by all.

"Bloody Mary," too-cute Amber Anderson said in a gasp.

"Bloody Mary," Cassandra acknowledged balefully.

There were few tales that could raise shivers in a person as effectively as the legend of Bloody Mary.

But as everyone knew . . . it was just a story.

What everyone did *not* know (because it had been carefully hushed up through the years) was that there was a foundation of truth behind the legend just as horrifying as the oft-told Halloween tale. Many years ago there lived a woman who became the inspiration for the story of Bloody Mary, a woman named Mary Pemberton. And the atrocities committed by this evil woman made the crimes of Lizzie Borden seem tame in comparison.

The Pemberton family emigrated from England, landing on American shores late in the 1700s. Supposedly there was some distant connection to the British monarchy. Whether or not that was true, the Pemberton family presented themselves as people of means and the family quickly established itself among the citizens of the Massachusetts colony where they had chosen to settle. In fact, in the nineteenth century, it was Roger Pemberton who aided in the expansion of the village by lending money to merchants and small business proprietors—although it was always a mystery how Pemberton acquired his wealth. Some claim that he'd made his fortune through a profitable import business; others maintained that he had established connections on the west coast and secretly financed opium dens and brothels in San Francisco from which he earned substantial profits.

His only child, a daughter he and his wife Prunella named Mary, came to them late in life. Yet she remained a child of suspect heritage due to her odd features and peculiar shading of skin. The fact that Roger Pemberton had also done much trading in the West Indies also added to the suspicion regarding the child's true origin. Nevertheless, young Mary was fiercely protected by her parents . . .

or if truth be known, was made a virtual prisoner under their strict rules. She never attended school, and was forbidden to associate with children of the village. This alone made her an outcast in the community. Her companions—if such could be termed that—were the household servants. Her only other human contact was with the friends of her parents. And these were people possessed of a dark character. Perhaps because Roger's excursions to exotic locales introduced him to mysterious and forbidden rites, he and his wife developed an interest in witchcraft and Satanic worship, and actively indulged in the practice during full moon ceremonies attended by fellow devotees from throughout the state.

From a young age Mary was encouraged to both observe and participate in these rituals, through which she was exposed to unnamable obscenities. Both of Mary's parents were dead before she was out of her teens. They died within a week of each other. Mary's mother apparently became so distraught over her husband Roger's "accidental" fall down the staircase that her mind snapped and she ingested a bottle of rat poison. Mary found her mother writhing on the floor, screaming in agony, her body wracked with convulsions, and the girl stood quietly, calmly watching as slow death overtook the woman who may or may not have given her birth. Mary stood there until the servants came to urge her away from the terrible sight, her mother's corpse twisted, features fixed in a rictus of horror, a repulsive death grimace, and all the while she displayed not a shred of emotion. Her eyes were empty, devoid of emotion or compassion. Her similar comportment at the funeral gave rise to the suspicion that she might have had a hand in her mother's death, as Mary, as the sole heir, would inherit her family's wealth.

Following her parents' burial, she immediately fired the household staff, locked herself in the house and became a virtual recluse. But people in the village also reported seeing a woman dressed in black wandering about the cemetery on nights when the moon was full, a woman who some recognized as Mary Pemberton; even as those with more active imaginations took to exaggerating her appearance, claiming that she had transformed by moonlight into a hideous hag in a tattered dress, eyes red and pupils afire, her lips smeared with blood. What was not an exaggeration, however, was that soon afterward children were reported missing, not just from the village, but also from neighboring communities. And then, inexplicably, the parents of some of these children died under mysterious circumstances. No cause of death could be attributed, although it was reported that some were found with expressions of horror distorting their features, as if in their final moments they had gazed into the very countenance of Satan.

As a panic began to overtake the village it soon was decided that Mary Pemberton was the one responsible. Her peculiar behavior and nocturnal graveyard visits made her a prime suspect. A select group of men finally stormed the house and dragged Mary, screaming and cursing and struggling like a wildcat, off to a jail cell. But before Mary could stand trial, late one night, long after midnight, some of the villagers, fearful yet emboldened by alcohol, broke into the jail determined to perform their own brand of justice.

Mary was carted off into the woods, her body braced against a tree while a noose was slipped over her head. Before the rope could be pulled and her body left to swing under the branches, Mary Pemberton spoke. Her final words were considered so blasphemous that they were never recorded by any of those responsible for her "execution." But they were remembered . . . as a scream that echoed through the night . . .

"Suffer the little children to come unto me. Though you condemn my spirit to everlasting darkness, I will not rest. The children you

abuse; those that you hate and neglect, will have their day of reckoning!"

A house is never still in darkness to those who listen intently;
There is a whispering in distant chambers,
An unearthly hand presses the snib of the window,
The latch rises.
Ghosts were created when the first man awoke in the night.
 J.M. Barrie

CHAPTER ONE

A Graveyard Tale

Behind a tranquil facade, that of picket fences and trimmed hedges, a town may hold many secrets. Dark, perhaps tragic secrets, facts hidden and protected, never spoken of, even in shadowed whispers.

But even the most carefully guarded secrets can be exposed.

Made manifest, in unexpected, inexplicable—even terrifying ways.

Yes, the door behind which those secrets are concealed may be opened…

And that is when nightmare becomes reality.

* * *

A traveler driving north along the coastal highway would likely be unaware that the steep cliffs bordering a three-mile stretch of the Pacific Ocean housed the town of Clear Vista, a small, pastoral community overlooking Buchanan Bay. The name was appropriate, as this was precisely what the town of Clear Vista provided its citizens and visitors. A high, wide view of the seascape visible from the farthest point inland, beyond the town limits, where the land was open and uninhabited. Gulls were a common sight, flying in from the coast, gliding gracefully and carefree across blue, cloudless skies, urged on by the gentle sea winds.

Summer was an attractive time in Clear Vista. The climate was balmy, the heat of the season cooled by the refreshing breezes that drifted in from the bay. In autumn the temperatures were chilly, but the town grew even more picturesque as the leaves surrendered their hold from the trees and the landscape became a patchwork quilt of gold and red.

As a town itself, there was nothing especially unique about Clear Vista. A quaint, quiet community where everyone knew one another, but where people went about their business without interfering in their neighbor's affairs. Men met after work and on Saturdays congregated at the hotel beer parlor, where they would either engage in serious matches of shuffleboard or just sit around and bullshit. The womenfolk of Clear Vista were mostly housewives who took care of the domestic needs of their families. Occasionally they might treat themselves to a day of shopping or share a lunch with their friends at Katie's Coffee Shoppe and catch up on all the latest gossip.

The shops and stores along the main street did a steady business, maintaining the healthy economy of the town. The homes next to the main route were mainly bungalows, neat and trim, the yards kept tidy. The educational needs of the community were provided by a modern school conveniently nestled within the residential district, servicing elementary through secondary grades. In the center of the town was a nondenominational church, welcoming all faiths, which enjoyed good and regular attendance. For those with more traditional religious leanings there was the First Methodist Episcopal Church just a few blocks farther. Civic affairs were handled out of the Municipal Building which stood adjacent to the Clear Vista Police Department.

In short, a pleasant, average locality with little of particular interest to catch the eye of the casual observer who might decide to turn off the main highway and navigate the rise that curved onto the quarter mile of paved road leading into the town.

But if a traveler were to drive on just a little farther, less than two miles past the eastern boundary of the town along the narrow gravel road, he would come upon a peculiar "time capsule" incongruous with the outward contemporary charm of Clear Vista.

A dark and dreary tract of land known as Resurrection Gardens.

In the small town of Clear Vista, the dead outnumbered the living by three to one; the decedents resting beneath the soil or entombed in the dusty crypts of Resurrection Gardens. It was the town's one cemetery, a wrought iron fence-enclosed graveyard with a historic relevance to the community, a remnant of a time long past. The sole reminder of struggles and accomplishments, now marked by broken and weathered crosses, blessed monuments and tombstones upon whose worn sandstone surfaces were etched barely legible engravings, each a faded testament to the town's pioneers.

Back then the settlement had adopted the name of one of its founders, a man called Quentin Niles-Fenn, who led a group of sturdy and determined settlers west. His courage and tenacity did not falter before the trail's many hardships, but he fell ill and died of consumption shortly after his party reached their destination. In honor of the man whose vision and fortitude had brought them to a new opportunity in the west, the settlers named their community Fenntown. But as time passed and both expansion and modernization took hold, the name of the town was thought to be outdated. Quentin Niles-Fenn's legacy eroded as rapidly as the name scrawled upon his headstone. A much more appealing and colorful name was wanted for the town and Clear Vista was selected by unanimous decision.

It was rare for the citizens of Clear Vista to visit what had become known as the "old" section of the cemetery. The past was the past and except for a passing reference or for educational purposes, the graveyard was seldom acknowledged. It became of little significance even to the descendants of those whose bones inhabited the weed-infested plots. A visitor to the town, however, might find himself drawn to the wooded acres where trees as old as the land itself stretched their skeletal limbs over the forgotten graves as if in mute protection, their extensions thin and claw-like and somehow threatening in their form, as if prepared to suddenly grasp the unsuspecting if one dared to venture too close. There, sparse foliage rustled like the folds of a shroud whenever the sea wind from Buchanan Bay gusted inland. One might wander under the bent and twisted trees, never imagining a more welcoming landscape just yards distant, where the grass was green and manicured and the gently rolling hills were marked neatly and strategically by marble headstones and the mausoleums of the wealthy. The majority of graves in this area were occupied by the adults and senior residents of the community.

Toward the far edge of this bleak acreage was a subdivision of the cemetery. Here no fence encircled the property; neither upright crosses nor monuments or tombstones intruded upon the grounds. Each plot was recognized by a flat grave marker, crafted of granite, bronze, or brass. Flowers were placed in the vases supplied, singularly or in small bouquets, adding splashes of color to complement the lush verdure. The town council had voted that this ground must stay pure and free of any surface embellishments that would visibly identify it as a cemetery. The threat of vandalism (which had already damaged structures in the "old" graveyard) was one concern. It was also agreed that in view of the gloomy atmosphere that pervaded the "historical" section, an open, almost park-like setting would be less upsetting to those who would visit this site.

And that was a principal consideration.

For it was in this small portion of cemetery that the children of Clear Vista were consigned to the earth. Although there was no gate or sign to acknowledge it by name, the townspeople referred to this section as Heavenly Angels. The mortality rate among the children was uncommonly high for a community the size of Clear Vista. Over a short number of years no less than fourteen children had been buried there, their coffins laid deep under the soil. The children ranged in age from infant to teenager. Even babies were laid to rest in graves marked by small, simple sandstone engravings.

It is a sad fact that children die every day, succumbing either to illness or falling victim to an unfortunate mishap. But whether a death is natural or accidental, the passing of a child is always a traumatic occurrence—perhaps not for the child who, depending on one's belief, has either entered the peace of eternal sleep or moved on to the realm of a glorious afterlife—but always for the family left to deal with their despair. It has long been accepted that time is the best healer, and to some measure that is true. Eventually the grieving will cease, but the pain never completely goes away.

Neither does the blame, regret—or remorse.

A small corner of the northwestern quarter of the cemetery had its own grim significance. It was there that two open graves could be found next to one another, side by side, but situated several yards from the other burial plots, the result of a vague yet superstitious fear that the other children who shared the soil could be corrupted, as if a contagion permeated the very ground where the bodies were soon to rest.

These two graves were to hold the victims of a brutal tragedy.

It was autumn, the season of Halloween. And the celebration was just a week away. But there would be no trick-or-treating that year. No happy costumed children running door to door with their sacks and pails seeking candy. No little witches and princesses parading the streets. No goblins or ghouls haunting doorsteps . . .

For that was the year a very real "ghoul" appeared in Clear Vista. A boogeyman, whose stay in town was brief, left behind death and despair. A stranger, he carried with him an unspeakable evil.

The devil had come to Clear Vista and life in the seaside community would never be the same.

CHAPTER TWO

No one in town could say much about the man. Most had assumed he was just another nameless, faceless transient, a virtual non-entity using Clear Vista as a stopover on his way to the city, as was common for the community. There was nothing remarkable or even noteworthy about the stranger. He dressed well and looked respectable, but when citizens were later questioned by the local police about any specifics, most drew a blank. His age was hard to determine. His features average—plain, certainly nothing in his appearance or deportment to suggest he harbored such maleficence in his soul.

He had taken a room at the local inn, but even Mrs. Ella Porter, the proprietor, who would have had the most contact with the stranger, as generally she made that her busybody business, had little to offer. She had seen him only in brief spurts, had exchanged few words with him, and usually, she said, when she was busily occupied with some other duty. And, as with everyone else who had a passing contact with the stranger, she reiterated that there was nothing distinctive or even peculiar about the man who had signed the register "Ernest Shade."

"It's like I told you, he was always pleasant and soft-spoken," Mrs. Porter tearfully said to Police Chief Braden Powell, her speech quavering and slightly muffled as she filtered her words through the cloth she held against her mouth. Her show of emotion was a repeat performance, right down to her using that same cloth in which to drain the build-up of mucous from her nostrils.

Exaggerated? Likely. But her emotion was genuine, Chief Powell determined.

He had spoken with Mrs. Porter for nearly a half hour, his second interview with the woman, hoping that she might be more composed today and that this round of questions might spark something—*anything*—in the woman's memory that could give him a lead on the suspect, or provide a clue to his whereabouts, his probable destination.

If, in fact, he *had* left the town. That likelihood was debatable. The stranger had checked out of the inn, but none of Powell's witnesses had actually seen him leave Clear Vista. No one could say for certain that they had noticed if he'd even had a car. One day he had just appeared. Had he hitchhiked into town or arrived on foot?

Or maybe he had just materialized? Powell considered with grim humor.

The room the stranger had taken at the inn had been checked over thoroughly. Oddly, there were no fingerprints found on items usually tagged as evidence in similar cases, such as door handles and bathroom faucets. Of course this could be attributed to the room being cleaned after the stranger checked out. Mrs. Porter prided herself on being a meticulous housekeeper and generally she wiped these fixtures down herself after a room was vacated. But she said she couldn't recall if she'd done so this time. She admitted with no little embarrassment that it was likely she hadn't, since the room was so clean and orderly when she inspected it, it was as if it had never been occupied.

The second day of the investigation had proven to be as repetitive and futile as the first. Chief Powell puffed out a prolonged breath and walked back to his desk, pushing aside papers and seating himself on its edge while regarding the woman with a look of weary frustration.

But he couldn't blame her—any more than he could rebuke the other townspeople he had interviewed hour upon hour for their faulty and even conflicting memories. If that were so, he could also reproach himself. He too had seen the stranger one afternoon in the local diner—Gregg's Grill—sitting quietly by himself sipping a cup of coffee. But there was nothing about the man to raise suspicion and so Powell had not paid him any attention and dismissed him from his thoughts. He doubted now if he could pick him out of a lineup. Unless there was something openly questionable about a visitor to town—and those types could be counted on the fingers of one hand—Powell wasn't about to probe any stranger with questions and make one's stopover in Clear Vista an unpleasant experience.

It was scant consolation, but in light of this tragic occurrence the police chief now made a commitment that he would never again be so trusting of any passerby come to town.

What remained especially perplexing was that those few who could provide Powell with a more definite physical description differed in their recollections. They were never consistent. In fact, they were downright contradictory. Those witnesses might as well have been speaking about completely different people, as the man's build and facial characteristics always varied. He was tall, he was of medium height; he was thin, he had a paunch; prominent jaw line, jowly; round-faced, angular-featured; full head of hair, balding. Black hair, blond hair, reddish brown. And in each of these descriptions there remained nothing outstanding about the man's appearance that could provide a solid lead as to who he was.

Chief Powell had begun to wonder if he was chasing a shadow.

He dismissed Mrs. Porter and watched the heavyset woman waddle to the outer office, the cloth still pressed against her lips, just managing to squeeze her broad body through the narrow door frame. There would be no point in speaking with her again.

Powell breathed out a sigh, then stood up from the edge of the desk and walked briskly into the bathroom. His scalp had begun to itch; his damn psoriasis was flaring up again. He stood leaning with his elbows on the sink basin, staring at his reflection in the cracked filmy mirror. He grimaced as he studied the inflamed red lesions just beginning their insidious encroachment onto his forehead from under his hairline, along with more visible scaly dry patches starting to spread across his left temple and over his eyebrows.

"I'm turning into a fucking leper," Powell said miserably.

If there was at least one thing Powell was grateful for it was that his hair hadn't started to recede—though God knows why he'd been spared baldness with all that he'd gone through—otherwise his scalp might bear an uncanny resemblance to a strawberry patch in full bloom.

He'd struggled with plaque psoriasis for years, always triggered by stress and at one point reaching such severity that it affected his arms, legs, and a good portion of his lower torso. At the time he was undergoing his own personal tragedy and he'd aggravated the condition with a poor diet and surrendering to other excesses. But he'd since thought he had managed to get his condition under control. Gradually his skin began to clear up until he was left with only a few patchy reminders on his legs. But recently and inexplicably the psoriasis had returned, this time with embarrassing results as it was no longer blotching areas where Powell could conceal it, but was now visible on his scalp and face. He'd started to use prescription creams and a special psoriasis control shampoo, but had received only minimal results. It was a frustrating condition and Powell didn't know which was worse, the markings on his face or the damn near persistent burning itch. One thing he was sure of, the only thing worse than the irritation of psoriasis was the crotch rot he had contracted and endured in the army.

Powell turned on the faucet and fingered some cool water through his hair, gently trying to massage the itch from his scalp. But it would offer only temporary relief. He doubted his condition would improve until he started making some solid progress into his investigation. In fact, the pressure was certain to make it worse.

It wasn't that Braden Powell was a stranger to stress. In fact, he had been subjected to one of the greatest stressors to which a person could be exposed, military combat. Shortly after high school, uncertain of his future plans, he enlisted in the infantry and right from basic training was shipped over into the heat of battle in the hot, humid jungles of Vietnam. A shoulder wound sent him home after an eight-month (that seemed like eight years) tour of duty. He recovered from his injury and only on rare occasions did a sudden twinge of discomfort remind him of the day when he caught the bullet, as did three of his buddies who also returned home—zippered in body bags.

He managed to cope with the stress of that experience and even deal with the terrible vivid dreams he'd had for long months afterward. But he was younger and—it seemed to him now—a hell of a lot more resilient. Like most who had served in a war, the experience occasionally revisited him, graphic if often exaggerated details pulled from his subconscious, yet he stubbornly refused to capitulate to those negative memories.

Now he was fulfilling the role of Clear Vista's top cop. After he'd returned from overseas he'd been restless and moved away from his home in Clear Vista to enter the police academy. He'd never considered a career in law enforcement prior to seeing action; he'd always intended to seek some sort of passive pursuit. But he admittedly had lost much of his earlier idealism and possessed just the right amount of edge and cynicism to be effective as a police officer. Promotions followed so that by the time he made the decision to give up the crime and corruption of the big city and return to the quainter surroundings of Clear Vista, he could officially be appointed his hometown's new chief of police.

It was a nice title and his fellow citizens generally accorded him the respect his position deserved, but it also afforded him little challenge. At first he almost came to miss the excitement he'd frequently had to deal with on city streets, chasing down criminals and busting drug dealers, but as time passed he inevitably settled into the slow-paced routine of his job and it soon reached the point where he got so comfortable he didn't welcome disruptions to his day.

And that was another reason why the murder of the Loewen girls hit with such impact.

*   *   *

Although the skies were clear and blue and the sun high and reflecting its shimmering brightness off the placid surface of Buchanan Bay that afternoon in mid-October, it would be remembered as a time of darkness for the people of Clear Vista. A day that all agreed left a permanent blemish on the town and even deeper scars on its citizens.

The Loewen twins, eight-year-olds Heidi and Holly, had gone missing after a day of playing at the neighborhood park, where they had enjoyed an afternoon of chasing each other and scampering about in the tempting piles of orange and golden leaves. A twelve-year-old boy and his friend playing nearby on the monkey bars later told investigators that a tall man in a black suit with a big smile ("Kinda like a clown that you see in the circus, but creepier," one of the boys recalled), whom neither recognized, had stopped to talk to the girls and then took them both by the hand and walked away with them.

When the twins didn't come home for supper their parents became frantic and notified the police. A search was launched and early the following day, shortly after sunrise, the group's effort yielded grisly results. The two girls were discovered dead inside a caretaker's tool shed located at a far corner of the "old graveyard," their bodies lying next to each another as if in repose, in an eerie, shadowy tableau. Curiously, there had been no lock on that shed since the time the groundskeeper retired from his job.

Whoever had taken the children to the shed had himself brought along a padlock, placed it on the door, and secured the crime scene after committing his heinous act. Even more mysterious was that the gate to the cemetery had been locked—and was secured when the search crew came out to Resurrection Gardens to investigate. How could anyone have gotten into the graveyard—especially with two sure-to-be-frightened children who were likely to have put up some resistance?

The former groundskeeper, Caspar McGee, became an immediate suspect since he might still have had access both to the locked grounds and the tool shed. But Chief Powell had to release him after preliminary questioning. Caspar McGee didn't match the physical description of the suspect as provided by the boys. McGee was a short, scrawny, almost weedy man. The person the two boys described was tall and lean. And he didn't look old, like McGee.

Despite a thorough search of the area, no physical evidence was found outside of that padlock. The grass around the shed had been overwhelmed by weeds and was in such neglected condition that to attempt to discern tracks of any kind was futile. A forensics unit from the city of Breckridge arrived to do an analysis of the scene, but no fingerprints or other tell-tale evidence could be found. Whoever the abductor/killer was, he had covered his tracks well.

It was hoped that the coroner's examination might yield a clue.

The town threatened to erupt into panic and outrage. The mayor of Clear Vista, a fastidious former restaurant entrepreneur named Edward Warrington, saw that his community was sitting on a potential powder keg and on the afternoon of the day when the bodies were discovered he summoned Braden Powell to his office after the police chief's work was finished at the cemetery. Powell arrived late; he had wanted to conduct some interviews first so that he might have something to offer, some answers to the questions he knew he would be asked. But he didn't have much information to provide.

When he entered the office he quickly noted that not only the mayor but Keith Birdlong, the editor of the town newspaper, the Clear Vista *Chronicle*, and two other prominent businessmen, the unpleasant Walter Stromm (who owned the development firm, The Stromm Agency) and the meek Sid Franke, who represented the citizens' council, were present. Powell was always curious why Franke (pronounced Frank*ee*) had been elected to be the council's spokesperson. He was not a man of authoritative presence, especially when matched against the overbearing personality of Walter Stromm.

The office itself was bright as the early afternoon sunlight filtered through the large front window. The atmosphere inside the room was another story. Tension was palpable, further made evident by the grave look on the faces of the men. It was obvious that none of these men appreciated having been kept waiting, busy schedules and all. Preliminaries were kept brief and perfunctory. Mayor Warrington was walking with the aid of a cane. He'd suffered a leg injury a week earlier and clearly was uncomfortable both from the physical pain and what he perceived as an insult to his vanity, disliking how he had to hobble about with assistance. Still, he was on his feet when Powell came into the room. Once he motioned for Powell to take a seat he spared no time getting to the matter at hand.

Powell noted that just he and the mayor had taken chairs—Warrington, of course, seated officially behind his rosewood desk, which was bordered on either side of the wall by framed photographs of him shaking hands with or cozying up to various state and federal officials. The other men present stood next to the wall by the door, giving Powell the impression that if he decided to make a hasty exit he would first have to get by them. Although in Walter Stromm's case, it was more likely he just wanted to get this business dealt with so that he could move on to matters of much more professional relevance.

"How soon until you receive word from the coroner on the cause of death?" Mayor Warrington said immediately.

Powell examined the mayor with a look of tempered surprise. "The bodies were just sent to Breckridge this morning—"

Warrington spoke his words with measured impatience. "Did you inform him how important this is?"

Powell nodded. "Talked to him on the phone when I got back to the office. Said he'd start on the post-mortem as soon as the bodies arrive."

"Good. This has to be made a priority."

Warrington maintained the frown he'd worn since Powell walked through the door and began drumming his fingers on the desk. "Well, we have ourselves a situation brewing," he said, and he leveled his attention directly on his police chief.

Powell understood that the mayor—as well as the other gentlemen in the room—wanted him to give them an encouraging report that would help to suppress the dread and uncertainty that now clouded the town. But that was an unreasonable expectation. The bodies of the two girls had been found just hours ago. The few people he'd had the chance to talk to on short notice could tell him virtually nothing.

"Any lead on a suspect?" Walter Stromm asked bluntly.

Powell looked over his shoulder at the man. Stromm had dark, penetrating eyes shadowed by fierce bushy eyebrows that flared like wings at the sides, and he was glowering at the police chief.

Walter Stromm was without question the most important person in the room. His age was difficult to determine, the best estimate early to mid-fifties, but he had one of those faces that seemed always to be the age it was now, as if the clock at some point had just stopped. He was a big man both in size and influence. Much of the expansion in the town was due to his efforts—which consisted of purchasing and developing properties, particularly in the business district, where profits were naturally higher. Powell knew that there were many people in the community who disapproved of Stromm because they saw him as too progressive (a polite word for "avaricious"). They did not want to see Clear Vista turned into a metropolis. Their quiet, simple way of life shouldn't be sacrificed to commerce. Still, he was a powerful man whose demands usually got results. Powell had to wonder just how *genuinely* concerned Stromm was over what happened to the two little girls. It was more likely his emotions ran no deeper than his pocketbook. The murder of children was not good for business.

Stromm's own young daughter Margaret had died tragically in a hit and run some months before. Powell remembered how that had affected everyone in town—everyone it seemed except for her father. He'd actually looked impatient at the funeral service while his wife sat next to him torn up with grief. Stromm's manner had suggested he was anxious for the service to be over so that he could get on with some business deal he had pending, which in all likelihood was precisely the case. And which seemed to be the situation now.

"At this point we're looking into this transient who came into town a couple of days ago," Powell answered Stromm straightly.

Stromm squinted his beady eyes and he spoke gruffly. "Transient? I don't know about any transient."

Keith Birdlong gave a slow nod of his head. "No one paid him much attention. Why would they? Quiet fellow. Kept to himself. Came and went."

"You mean he's gone?" Stromm said with a suspicious arching of one of his bushy eyebrows.

"That's what we assume," Birdlong answered. "He hasn't been seen around town since…well, since those boys saw… if it *was* him yesterday at the park. Doesn't seem likely he would hang around knowing he'd have a lot of questions to answer."

"Well, what do you know about him?" Stromm questioned. "Certainly someone must be able to provide a description." He scowled. "What about those boys?"

"Can't say for certain it's the same person." Birdlong lifted a shoulder. "The people I've spoken with have all pretty much said this character was practically nondescript. From what they've provided…well, I don't think we could even make a compelling artist's sketch."

"Seems you might know more about this man than our police chief," Stromm remarked, casting a critical eye at Powell.

Birdlong glanced at Powell and looked a little sheepish. He wouldn't have spoken up had he known it would get such a response from Walter Stromm. Birdlong liked and respected Chief Powell and would never have deliberately put him in such an awkward position. Especially under these present circumstances where he knew Powell's every move would be closely scrutinized by the town.

Keith Birdlong was the youngest man in the room and, unlike the others, had not been born and raised in Clear Vista. He was originally from Chicago. Having graduated university with a journalism degree, he worked on a metropolitan newspaper before "discovering" Clear Vista during a winter vacation on the coast. Preferring the simple seaside life to the bustle and congestion of the city, he decided to invest in the *Chronicle* and take over as editor.

He was good-looking, radiated an aura of confidence and one might assume was quite the womanizer in his personal life, although he had not been seen squiring any of the eligible young ladies around town. For a very good reason. In truth, he had recently broken off a long-distance relationship with his male lover. Birdlong had pleaded with the man to join him in Clear Vista (keeping their relationship clandestine, naturally, in such a closed and close-minded community; the fellow would "officially" be hired on as an employee at the paper). His lover refused, and Birdlong dealt with his unhappiness and disappointment by absorbing himself in his journalistic endeavors. If anyone in town had suspicions about Birdlong's sexual orientation, it had never been made the subject of town gossip. It was more likely people just assumed he was a serious young man dedicated to his work.

"What have you been able to find out about this vanishing stranger?" Stromm demanded.

Powell checked his offense at Stromm's unwarranted insinuation that he was somehow being negligent in his duty. Stromm could be a rude, intimidating sonofabitch, but Powell understood this quality about the man and knew that to challenge him would lead to a confrontation that would only reflect badly on *himself.* And so he kept his voice composed and conducted himself professionally even though his right fist had begun to clench and unclench reflexively.

"He checked into the Clear Vista Inn and registered under the name of—" He reached into his shirt pocket and withdrew a small black book. He wet his fingers and thumbed through the pages. "Ernest Shade. Could be an assumed name. Likely is. I've put out a call on it."

"I don't suppose Ella was of much help," Stromm presumed.

"She was upset, agitated," Powell told him. "I plan to speak with her again, later today or tomorrow, once she's in a better frame of mind to talk—along with anyone else who might have had contact with this…Shade character."

"More like *shady* character," Warrington murmured dryly.

Stromm's voice was only a little gentler. "No one can tell you anything?"

"Not what I need," Powell said stiffly. "I still think Ella might give us our best lead…if I can only get her to remember."

"Ella Porter is too accommodating," Stromm said, his upper lip curled in the suggestion of a sneer.

While none of the men knew precisely what Stromm meant by his remark, no one spoke up in Mrs. Porter's defense. One simply didn't argue with Walter Stromm's viewpoint on *any* matter. And that included the mayor, who often consulted with Stromm on delicate community issues; such as the one which Clear Vista was now having to face. Of course there were those in town who suspected that Mayor Warrington performed primarily as Walter Stromm's "puppet on a string." It wasn't a secret that Stromm had put a lot of his own money—not to mention his considerable influence—into Warrington's mayoral campaign.

"Have any of you gentlemen considered that we might be jumping the gun with our suspicion?" Powell suggested.

All eyes in the room turned to the police chief.

"It might be a mistake assuming this stranger is our killer. We could be overlooking the possibility that the murderer might be in our very midst," he pointed out.

The mayor practically gasped. "Are you suggesting, Chief Powell, that one of our own people might be responsible for this tragic crime?"

"The only witnesses who saw that individual take away the Loewen girls were those two young boys," Powell said, holding his hands up and shrugging.

"Neither of whom recognized the man," Warrington reminded him curtly.

"Because they never got a good look at him," Powell returned. "The best that only one of them could say was that he had the grin of a clown." He shrugged. "I haven't spoken to anyone yet who's said this transient looks like Emmett Kelly." He subtly turned his eyes toward Keith Birdlong.

The young man nodded thoughtfully. "A clown's grin. That would be a telling feature on someone, you'd think."

"What you're suggesting is preposterous!" Stromm thundered. "I'm familiar with everyone in this town and I can state unequivocally that no closet killer lives among us. Believe me, *I* would be the first to have such suspicions."

Powell's disagreement with that comment came with a slight clearing of his throat, apparently noticed by no one except Stromm, who gave the police chief a critical glare.

Mayor Warrington spoke again, prefacing his words with a heavy breath. "Too much of a coincidence that this fellow comes to town, leaves a day or two later—supposedly…and two girls are dead, their bodies found in the caretaker's shed in the cemetery." His voice was firm with conviction as he said, "No, I think we can drop the idea that anyone other than this transient is the killer. My God, Powell, what you're suggesting would create more of a panic among our citizens than what we're looking at already."

Powell cast another furtive glance at Keith Birdlong. The young man at least looked as if he was open to the possibility that there could be a suspect other than this fellow who had passed through town. Powell could use an ally. But this time Birdlong didn't speak.

"And who among us would you suspect of such a crime?" Stromm asked the chief in an aggressive tone. His manner was becoming heated, made evident by the thin trickles of sweat that ran down his neck and into his collar despite the air-conditioned coolness of the office.

Powell ignored Stromm's browbeating attitude and purposely avoided responding to his question. He had no suggestions to offer and Stromm damn well knew it. He was merely presenting a theory. That was his job, what he was paid for by the town treasury. He couldn't discount any possibility. Nor rule out any potential suspect. Even if that included checking out Walter Stromm himself. Which he had to confess would give him great pleasure. Not that he had even a tiny suspicion that Stromm was the killer, but an in-depth investigation would surely uncover other juicy tidbits, primarily about the man's carefully concealed professional affairs.

Powell said, "We all want this killer caught." He added pointedly, "To have some peace restored to our town. I agree the mystery behind this stranger's appearance in town does present a case for him being our chief suspect. But I want to be sure. We *all* want to be sure."

Once again it was Stromm who dissented. "It's a waste of time that could better be spent getting a lead on who even you're now agreeing is likely the *real* killer, this transient." He glared at the police chief and spoke coarsely. "My God, man, what you've suggested…it's an insult to the good people of this community!"

Powell's jaws clamped so tight the muscles in his cheeks stood out. He thought bitterly, *the good people of this community whose properties help to keep you, Walter Stromm, a wealthy man.*

What's more, as the chief law officer of Clear Vista, Powell often knew more of what went on behind the scenes than Stromm, despite the "authority" the businessman believed he held over the town. Or—if Stromm was knowledgeable concerning some of these incidents, he chose to close his eyes to them—and surely for self-serving "practical" reasons.

But Powell wasn't naive nor motivated by greed or glory. He simply did his job. At times it was a terrible truth that he uncovered…and much to his despair and professional frustration he frequently was the only one who recognized it.

Mayor Warrington rose from behind his desk. He spoke in formal tones. "Gentlemen, of course we want this perpetrator apprehended—and quickly—and I'm sure Chief Powell will put out every effort to do so. Undoubtedly that will include working with the state police and other jurisdictions, since it's a sure bet this murderer is miles away by now. As we all agree, we *do* have a likely suspect and this is the avenue our police department should—no, *must*—be pursuing. In the meantime, I feel it's imperative we do whatever we can to reassure the citizens of this community." He turned to focus on the newspaper editor. "Keith, people here know what happened to those two unfortunate girls. I don't want your paper in any way to sensationalize the details or even prolong the coverage. Yes, report the facts, print updates as Chief Powell provides them, people will demand that, but…let the readers know we have every confidence this was an isolated incident and, though certainly caution must be maintained until this person is caught, that people should not let their fears overwhelm them. Emphasize that we can expect protection from our police force."

Powell grimaced inwardly. Police *force*? Hardly. Just him, two part-time shift officers and a young patrolman starting to get his feet wet. Not exactly a sterling representation of law enforcement. He'd never considered the small staffing a problem before. In fact, with how quiet and uneventful things usually were in town he often considered he was working with too much manpower.

He only hoped that this *was* an isolated incident. He didn't want to be dealing with a serial killer with only limited resources at his disposal.

"Most importantly," Stromm put in, sternly, and his attention went toward Powell, "I don't want even a suggestion of what our police chief said about the killer being right here in our community to get reported to the citizens."

Birdlong nodded vaguely and then he turned to Powell. "I'll need you to give me a statement. As the mayor says, something to reassure my readers."

"You know it's too soon for me to make any official statement," Powell argued.

Birdlong was sympathetic, but he also knew the newspaper game. "If this were the city we could probably hold off on that," he said. "But in a town this size we don't have that luxury. People want to know…and they want to know now."

"Surely there's something you can tell our citizens to help ease their apprehensions," Sid Franke finally spoke in a voice of trained neutrality.

Powell knitted his brow. "Sure. I can tell 'em whatever. But it won't necessarily be accurate. And it could come back to bite me on the ass."

It appeared that no one in the room was particularly concerned about Powell's ass getting chomped. This dilemma they were facing went beyond one's man interest. Unless of course your name happened to be Walter Stromm.

"I suggest we hold a meeting at the church this evening," Mayor Warrington stated. "It will give Chief Powell time to perhaps gather more information and see what the situation is with this…suspect, and decide the best way his office can present this information—along with his department's assurances—to the public."

Stromm nodded his head agreeably. "The church. Yes, good idea, Ed. And maybe Pastor Barber can provide a few words of comfort."

At first Powell couldn't be sure whether Stromm was being facetious. To his way of thinking, Stromm's only religion came from what was inside his wallet.

Birdlong sighed. "Of course any calm we might establish is going to shatter once the cause of death is released by the coroner. And I recommend that we release that information ASAP. Otherwise if we wait, it'll be just like ripping the scab off a sore."

The room went quiet. Birdlong had presented a telling point. But the mayor wholeheartedly disagreed.

"No. Stall with the results, if they come in," Warrington instructed Powell. "I don't want too much thrown at the people all at once. Let's see if we can give them some hope first."

* * *

That evening at a town meeting held at the Sea Haven Church, following solemn yet hopeful words from the pastor—over the shouts of concern and demands from those assembled—Powell made a bold declaration. He informed the townspeople that law enforcement in nearby locales had been put on alert and that the perpetrator of this heinous act would soon be apprehended and brought to justice. But the police chief knew he had spoken much too prematurely. With little information to go on and the likelihood that the killer had already vacated the vicinity and vanished into at least temporary obscurity, Powell feared he would have a long, uncertain road ahead of him in trying to solve this case.

And he doubted the people of the community would remain patient for long.

CHAPTER THREE

Two days after the discovery of the bodies of the Loewen sisters, Chief Powell found himself pacing the hexagonal tiled flooring outside the office of Sheffield County Coroner Dr. Rice Arborshaw. It was Dr. Arborshaw who had performed the autopsies on the two girls and he'd telephoned Powell to meet him at his office. That request would entail a forty-five minute drive to the Breckridge Medical Center and Powell was puzzled about why Arborshaw simply wouldn't present his findings over the phone. But Powell didn't question him, and told Arborshaw he'd be there as soon as he could.

He first had a couple more interviews to conduct that he knew would just be a waste of time. People were willing to come forward, Powell had no problem there. But from an informational point of view, what he'd been able to gather wasn't worth a teaspoon of spit. And because of those dead ends Powell was eager to receive the results from the coroner. Especially since there had appeared to be no physical markings on the bodies that could account for the cause of death. Conversely, Powell also dreaded hearing what Arborshaw had to say. For reasons as personal as they were professional the deaths of the two children greatly disturbed him.

Dr. Rice Arborshaw had served as County Medical Examiner for just under three years, but had come to his post with impressive credentials, including over twenty years on staff with the Los Angeles Medical Examiner's Office. A heart condition precipitated his move to Breckridge where he oversaw a less stressful workload. Powell knew him as a capable if somewhat remote individual, a man who likely spent more time in the company of the dead than the living. He may even prefer it that way.

Arborshaw was a small, about 5'3", slightly-built man with a narrow face, high and prominent cheekbones and a receding hairline. He looked to be about sixty years of age and had the appearance of an academic, replete with inquisitive, probing eyes, and a beak-like nose upon which were perched his spectacles. When he spoke he made it a point to look at the person from over the rim of his glasses, giving the impression that he might be studying him—or her—for future reference.

Powell was working on his third cup of coffee. He was growing impatient and at one point instinctively reached into his breast pocket for the pack of cigarettes he still kept there, even though he'd been trying to quit smoking since before this recent tragedy had occurred. Once more he managed to control the urge, though he didn't know how much longer he would be able to resist lighting up. With his craving for a Camel unfiltered intensifying, he considered yet another refill of coffee in substitution, but in a quick act of willpower he crushed the Styrofoam cup with a sharp flexing of his fingers and deposited it into the garbage pail. Powell glanced at the wall clock. He'd been waiting to see Arborshaw for going on forty-five minutes.

Finally, Arborshaw stepped from the hallway into the outer office. He greeted the police chief with just a nod. The men were familiar with each other and so a handshake between the two was unnecessary. Besides, their meetings were always on a professional level. Arborshaw did not apologize for the delay, but explained that he had been supervising the autopsy of an apparent suicide from the night before. Powell had heard about it on the radio driving into the city. A jumper from the top floor of a twelve-story apartment building who landed on solid concrete. Powell didn't relish the coroner the task of having to observe let alone dissect that corpse.

Arborshaw didn't bother to remove his green surgical gown which still displayed smearings of blood and other matter Powell did not care to identify, and instead motioned for Powell to follow him out into the hall. Powell walked alongside Arborshaw down the long corridor toward the morgue.

"Was it?" Powell asked mildly.

"Was it *what*?" Arborshaw said curtly.

"A suicide?"

Arborshaw gave his head a swift nod in reply. "Yes, it was." After a brief pause he added lightly, "Always seeking the homicide angle?"

Powell didn't acknowledge, but he did have to concede that Arborshaw's question (or was it intended more as a remark?) was accurate. After all, he was a cop and an inquiring nature came with the territory, just as it did with Arborshaw's job.

Powell was familiar with the facility, but he still experienced a sick, almost nauseous feeling each time he visited the morgue. The smell alone was offensive. Sometimes it took him a good hour to rid his nostrils of the powerful antiseptic that permeated the air. He couldn't understand how anyone could tolerate being around such a cloying odor. He had to assume that the coroner and his people had simply grown accustomed to it. Powell doubted it was something that he himself would ever be able to get used to.

Arborshaw slid open the heavy metal door that opened to the morgue. Powell followed the coroner inside the large, sterile room and they walked across to the far wall which housed metal drawers reminiscent of office filing cabinets. Arborshaw's assistant, Andrew, nodded to Powell in a perfunctory greeting then rose from behind the desk where he had been concentrating on both a sandwich and some paperwork.

"Well, what can you tell me?" Powell asked the coroner in a deliberately dispassionate tone, intended to keep his emotions in check.

"I won't have the toxicology results for several weeks, but I don't expect that report to yield any significant findings," Arborshaw said. He spoke to the point, a blunt pronouncement. "Cause of death, asphyxiation." His many years as an M.E., clinically-trained and out of necessity detached from the human component of his work, had precluded him from expressing any hint of compassion when presenting his conclusions. Powell could appreciate such an attitude from the coroner. Arborshaw had conducted countless autopsies on bodies subjected to all manner of death, persons ranging in age from infant to centenarian. Powell imagined there was little he hadn't seen—there wasn't much that would disturb him or give rise to any personal feelings.

"They were strangled?" Powell said tonelessly.

Arborshaw gestured for his assistant to open one of the drawers. A small, covered form was pulled out from the compartment on a sliding metal table, and as the white sheet was drawn back over the chalky face Powell knew he had to get a grip on himself, as he found himself instantly on the brink of surrendering his professionalism to his emotions. He struggled against a mixture of grief and intense anger. The thought that some maniac could take the life of a child sickened him to the core. Arborshaw made no comment, but he had taken notice of the tight, fixed look screwed into the chief's features. He wasn't unfamiliar with the expression. He had seen that same look on Chief Powell's face not so very long ago, under equally tragic circumstances.

"No," Arborshaw said in answer to Powell's question. "Neither of the bodies display bruises or constriction marks conducive to manual or ligature strangulation. Nor was there a fracturing of the larynx which such pressure surely would have caused. After all, given their age, we're dealing with delicate tissue."

Powell suppressed a grimace.

"So then, how . . .?" he asked without finishing.

Arborshaw paused before he replied, "My opinion is that they were smothered."

Powell frowned. "Smothered. Like…with a pillow or a bag stuffed over their head?"

Arborshaw gave a firm shake of his head. "I'd say that whoever did this suffocated them by—" He demonstrated in a brief pantomime, taking his hand and clamping it tightly over his mouth.

Powell spoke with a cautious optimism. "By hand? Then the killer could have left prints."

Arborshaw lowered his head and gave it another shake, weaker this time. "Doubtful. We found fibers that suggest whoever was responsible was likely wearing gloves. Naturally those fibers were sent to the police lab for analysis. But frankly, as far as compelling evidence, that's a needle in the haystack."

Powell exhaled a breath. "Yeah, should have guessed as much. No prints at the murder site, either. Whoever did this took every precaution to avoid detection."

The room went quiet for several moments. And without sound no place is as oppressively silent as a morgue.

Powell nibbled at the corner of his bottom lip. "Any idea how long it took for them to die?" he next asked.

"They probably became unconscious within two to three minutes," Arborshaw replied.

"No, how long to *die*?" Powell said with more emphasis.

Arborshaw considered briefly. "Likely four to five minutes."

Powell practically had to force out his next words. "What about any other signs? Indications that they might have been—"

He was grateful he didn't have to finish his sentence as Arborshaw understood and quickly answered the question. "They weren't violated or abused in any way. No bruising or other markings to suggest physical trauma on either of the bodies." He paused, then gestured with a tilt of his head toward the cadaver on the metal table. "If you'd like you can see for yourself."

"I'll—take your word for it," Powell said stiffly.

Arborshaw offered a faint understanding smile.

"Okay Andrew, thanks," the coroner then said to his assistant and the young man dutifully slid the table back into its drawer.

Arborshaw looked at Powell and signaled with his hand toward the door. That was fine with Powell. He was ready to leave. The two men walked from the morgue, down the corridor toward the elevator, their footfalls echoing against the concrete walls.

"What always puzzles me is trying to understand the type of sick brain that could do such a thing," Powell pondered.

Arborshaw said quietly, "I'm afraid I can't offer much help there. Abnormal psychiatry is not my area of expertise."

Powell sighed and nodded emptily.

"But I could put you in touch with Dr. Robbie Forrester," Arborshaw then suggested. "She's a forensic psychologist, someone who likely would be able to provide you with insight into the type of person you're dealing with."

Powell regarded Arborshaw with a curious expression. "*She?*"

"Roberta," Arborshaw clarified. "She's a quite brilliant woman. We attended medical school together."

Powell responded with moderate enthusiasm. "Thanks. I…might take you up on that."

As the men approached the elevator that would take them to the main floor, Arborshaw spoke tentatively. "I understand that you might have a suspect."

There was a *ding* and the overhead indicator light turned green, signaling that the elevator had arrived on their subterranean floor. Powell turned to the coroner and said politely, "Can't say too much, Doc. We're still investigating."

Arborshaw blinked his eyes behind his spectacles and nodded. "Certainly. I understand." He turned to face the elevator doors, waiting for them to open.

Powell, too, focused his attention in that direction.

His brain was swirling with troubled thoughts. Regrettably, he decided the minute he stepped outdoors he was going to light that cigarette. Maybe he wasn't displaying much willpower, but for the time being he needed a crutch. He'd think about quitting once he got a handle on this case.

Soon after he said *adios* to Dr. Arborshaw and was standing outside in the clean, clear air he reached for his pack of Camels and wasted no time lighting one. He felt slightly guilty about breaking the vow he'd made to quit smoking, but he then tried to placate himself by making the decision to move from an unfiltered to filtered brand of cigarette.

For the time being he just needed the comfort of a smoke. And to hell with justifying the reason.

In his four years as police chief he'd encountered more than an average number of child tragedies, and deaths not always attributable to illness or accident. Some were of questionable cause. In his official capacity, Powell had to investigate those incidents and in at least one case his suspicions were raised. That was when eight-year-old Larry Krevrich had apparently fallen down a flight of cellar stairs, landing on hard concrete and suffering a coma and broken neck. When Powell arrived at the house the boy's mother was in hysterics, crying that she had repeatedly warned Larry not to move so fast down those steep stairs.

Powell remembered how convincing she appeared, and perhaps her emotion was genuine, but tripping down a flight of stairs could not account for the numerous bruises and even fresh cigarette burns that marked the young boy's body. Powell sat through the trial with his teeth gritted. He wanted to see Mrs. Ida Krevich, whom he perceived as a vicious and vindictive divorcee, convicted and punished accordingly. But she played on the sympathy of the court and was acquitted. The jury accepted her story that her son was troubled, filled with anger and resentment because his father chose not to have any contact with him since the breakup of the marriage and was prone to inflicting punishment on himself.

Perhaps he saw himself in some way responsible for his father's abandonment, Ida Krevich tearfully suggested, the likelihood of which was further reinforced by the psychiatric expert her lawyer had called in on her behalf. As for his falling down the stairs…Larry was highly-strung and given to bouts of erratic, almost spastic behavior where he might become quick and careless.

Two days following Mrs. Krevich's acquittal Larry died of his injuries. Despite the court's verdict Powell remained committed in his own mind that the woman was guilty. Yet each day he saw her about town, shopping, having coffee in the diner and chatting amiably with her cronies—and apparently displaying no sorrow or remorse over the death of her son.

Equally tragic was the suicide of fifteen-year-old Cameron Makefield. Powell recalled him as a bright kid with an inquisitive mind. His questions, thrown at you as quick as darts, made him well-known around the community. It wasn't unusual for the boy to drop in to virtually any business or agency and begin quizzing the proprietor or person in charge (like Powell himself) about the details and intricacies of their work. Yes, Cameron could—and often *did*—make himself a pest, but because of his genuine interest and enthusiasm most indulgently spared him the time, when they could.

Sadly, it wasn't until the day he was found dead of a gunshot wound to the temple that those who considered him a nuisance came to grasp a little more fully the reason for his afterschool forays into their establishments. Cameron's father owned a barbershop in town. His name was Corsetti, Peter Corsetti, which naturally raised some confusion around the town given his son's Anglo-Saxon surname. In fact, many assumed that the boy was adopted, even though he shared the same swarthy looks as his father.

Peter Corsetti was a good man, a self-made man and a hard worker, but he had precious little time to spend with a son who sought from his father both attention and recognition, given Peter's own limited education and knowledge. And then further information came to light. Cameron had been mercilessly bullied by his classmates who regarded him as a "suck-up," someone who always seemed to be seeking favoritism from his teachers with his classroom enthusiasm and constant questions.

Following Cameron's death some sympathetic fellow students came forward to state that wasn't the case. They said that Cameron truly was interested in gaining all types of scholastic knowledge, but ultimately there was no point in arguing against the overall insecurity of the high school mentality and the fragility of adolescent sensibility. Naturally, within the existing classroom clique, a boy like Cameron would be regarded as an outsider. The rumor even started around the halls that he was "queer."

Perhaps it was partly because Peter Corsetti was a simple man who could not properly relate to his son or his problems. He was a man who believed that a boy's growth should be predicated on how he himself took charge of life's situations, which in his own opinion were often difficult but necessary in establishing one's true character. In short, life is hard so to succeed you must learn to fight your own battles otherwise you will never overcome the adversities sure to come your way. It was not that Cameron was prone to complain to his father or anyone else when it came to the abuse and embarrassment he endured in the school halls or, more frequently, out on the playing field. That was not his nature. When he wanted to speak to his father about something that might be troubling him, he would want just to sit privately with his dad in a father-son chat and allude to the problem in such a manner as to exclude himself personally.

Of course, when Peter would spare those moments to listen he could not grasp that his son was really speaking about himself. *His* difficulties. Cameron likely would have found a more willing ear in speaking with his mother. Unfortunately, while he loved her, hers was not the support Cameron felt he needed to hear. Perhaps it was gleaned from his classmates, but he believed that a boy's best advice came from his father. And ultimately those would not be the words of wisdom that Cameron had hoped for when he would broach those questions and concerns related directly to himself and not the problems of some imaginary friend.

They were simple, blunt solutions, administered to Cameron by his father within the security of his own special sanctum, his barbershop, where advice could be dispensed without fear of challenge or reprisal. Words that the old man issued with good intention, meant to help guide his son through the confusion and hardships of youth into the constructiveness of manhood. But that destination remained vague, far off into the future in the mind of a teenager. It was dealing with the present with all its doubts and insecurities that were important to Cameron. As with most youths, the future was little more than an abstract. And when that time would eventually come, the problems of today would no longer be of importance.

So, in his own subtle, indirect way, Cameron began seeking out other men of prominence in the community—on the surface asking superficial questions, but in truth seeking something more substantial to help pave his way into maturity.

Powell recalled specifically the day he was in his office and saw Cameron pass by the big window, walking slightly hunched over with brisk strides, looking to be sobbing. Normally Powell would have regarded it with only a momentary curiosity before returning to whatever else he had been doing at the time. But instead Powell lifted himself from his chair and walked toward the front door to summon him.

"Cameron. Cameron Makefield," he called just as the boy reached the corner of the street.

Cameron halted. He didn't immediately acknowledge the chief. He was embarrassed because he *had* been crying. His cheeks were streaked with tears. Even from where he was standing Powell could notice the emotion that Cameron was struggling—and failing—to hold back. Powell was unsure of the words to say. And Cameron did not budge. Maybe he was simply waiting for Chief Powell to directly ask him to come into his office. To Powell, the boy's edgy posturing seemed to beg for it.

Maybe it would have been better if Powell had not called him back that day. He could not understand why he'd felt compelled to do so, and then when he'd coaxed Cameron into the office he dismissed him so abruptly. It was as if part of him understood there was a necessity that he have a talk with the boy while another aspect of his personality did not want to be troubled with the problems— such as they were—of an adolescent youth.

They talked, but it was a conversation of little consequence. Cameron himself could see that the police chief was not of a mind or manner to speak with him about his concerns, busying himself as he was with trifling details atop his desk. Powell did not even attempt to stop him when Cameron got up to leave. And it was that very same night that Cameron, overwhelmed by whatever demons possessed him, blew part of his skull away with a single shot from his father's handgun. Powell remembered when the telephone rang. It was as if he'd gotten to know which rings were the ones demanding an immediate response. This was one of them. He was called from his bed to the boy's house. The bedside clock read two-thirty-three a.m. The rest of that night…

Although Powell would never talk of it, the guilt stayed burrowed in his brain that if he'd only taken the time to speak with more compassion to Cameron that afternoon, had he not in his own way hurried him on, would the boy have decided on such a desperate measure to end the hidden turmoil with which he had been living?

The deaths of Larry Krevich and Cameron Makefield were memories Powell had not forgotten. He recalled how the undertaker had done commendable work on both of the boys. No one at Larry Krevich's service could have guessed the abuse he had suffered— the telltale signs of violence that no one outside of Powell acknowledged. Flesh burns and bruises and a broken neck—all neatly concealed by the mortician's skilled handiwork. And the bullet hole that had ended Cameron's life was not even visible, as the partially destroyed skull had been skillfully reconstructed and the bullet hole it had been filled in with mortician's wax and painted cosmetically to the proper skin tone before his body was presented in an open casket.

Those were just two of several incidents that troubled Powell. He often would contemplate similar cases, reviewing circumstances and wondering if there had been anything he could have done to prevent both tragedies. But he knew that it was too late for regrets. Life was for the living, such as it was.

What goes on beneath the peaceful veneer of a small town? he would frequently ponder as he drove his patrol car down the residential side streets, gazing at the rows of houses that reflected on their brick or paint-coated surfaces scenarios which appeared picture perfect, representative of a happy family, offering security and protection…

But what was the truth when the window curtains were drawn and the outside world disappeared? What happened when the masks of convention and morality could at day's end be slipped off? Strip away the facade and lay bare those carefully guarded secrets. Since the deaths of Larry Krevich and Cameron Makefield and even some of those other questionable "accidents" and deaths that had occurred among Clear Vista's youngsters, Powell had been exposed to the hypocrisy and perhaps had become jaded enough to believe that even the most outwardly decent and reputable person could be guilty of aberrant or abusive behavior in his private life and that maybe there was no place where one—especially a child—could be truly safe.

And now two more children of the community had died—though their deaths were a mystery—and it was Powell's duty to somehow sort out and come to the truth.

The irony was he still hadn't sorted out his own truth.

Or come to cope with his own loss.

CHAPTER FOUR

Powell checked his wristwatch. It was almost 4:30. Terry Reynolds should be returning from his afternoon patrol shortly, and then Powell decided he'd call it a day.

Reynolds was a good man, young and eager, but a rookie and still a bit raw. He also was not a native of the community and relatively new to Clear Vista and had yet to really establish roots—or earn total trust among the tight-knit, insular community. Powell didn't want to underplay his worth, but he was honest enough to know that as a novice cop Reynolds would be of little help in the current investigation.

Out of obligation if not necessity, he did allow Reynolds in on the periphery of this work, keeping him abreast of developments and letting him voice opinions and even offer suggestions. Reynolds realized that the chief was keeping him on a short leash and was somewhat resentful that Powell assigned him minor duties while he focused most of his own attention on trying to get a lead on the case. The chief handled all the interviews, seeking clues and following through on reports from other nearby locales—all of which thus far had turned up nothing. But even though Reynolds was dissatisfied with what he privately referred to as his "chores," he never expressed it to the chief. He even attempted to justify these token duties as Powell's way of breaking him in—even though in a town like Clear Vista a whole lot of training didn't seem necessary.

Reynolds accepted without complaint any request handed him, including picking up the occasional lunch order from the diner. Because of his attitude and his efficiency Powell considered Reynolds a reliable sort who had the makings of a good cop.

Although Powell wasn't particularly hungry he stopped by Gregg's Grill, the eatery he most often frequented, to pick up a couple of bacon burgers and side order of onion rings to go, conveniently disregarding the fact that his greasy meal was not beneficial to his troubling skin condition. The waitress, a girl named Donna Murray, was always happy to see Powell and today asked if he might prefer to eat in. The restaurant had a fine meatloaf, vegetables and mashed potato special. Powell gave a polite no. There was a time he enjoyed unwinding at the diner after a hard day, but just lately he felt uncomfortable there—or pretty much anyplace else in town, including another favored after work haunt, the hotel beer parlor.

He felt that the eyes of the townspeople were always on him— not quite condemning, but still issuing a silent demand to know if he was any closer to solving the terrible crime that had corrupted their community. And Powell had no answers to give them, though he wished to God he did. These people were his friends and now in their subtle way they regarded him warily, almost as if he had failed them by not making progress on a case that affected them all.

Powell understood their frustration and impatience, but it was unreasonable to expect a solution so soon given the slim information and resources he had to work with. The state police were in on the hunt and law enforcement in other nearby towns had been put on alert. Powell wanted this psychopath brought to justice as much as anyone, and not just to restore the town's faith in him. If he didn't stop the killer, he feared this maniac would strike again.

Still, he wondered what the people of his town would think if they knew he was observing them, too, and not casually but with a police officer's trained eye. Each citizen was a potential suspect until they found the perpetrator.

He drove the few blocks to his house, up the slight slope of the driveway and slowed to a stop outside the garage. He switched off the ignition and stared unseeing at the garage door. Chewing at his bottom lip, he took a deep breath. He sighed. He never parked his car inside anymore. Fifteen months ago, his kids' bikes had been left lying haphazardly on the cement of the garage floor, blocking his car's entry. After that night, he had never moved them. He just couldn't bring himself to lift and stand them upright against the far wall, where they were supposed to be put. He smiled grimly, recalling all the times he used to scold Ruthie and Randy because in a typical kids' rush they would just drop their bikes like stones onto the ground, eager to get inside for supper.

He stepped out of the car and walked to the front door, removing the house key from his pocket and inserting it into the lock. He heaved a deep, steadying breath before walking inside.

Damn, even after all this time he still couldn't get used to the quiet and stillness that greeted him each day he came home from his shift. He doubted he ever would. Where once his return from work was filled with whoops and hollers and cries of "Daddy's home!" from his two kids and a welcoming kiss from his wife, Cassidy, the perfect cure for any day's troubles, now there was only a framed 8x10 photograph of the three of them, smiling at the camera. It's all he had to remind him that there had ever been such love in this house.

Powell carelessly kicked off his shoes and went directly into the kitchen to pour himself a glass of rye whiskey. He'd heard that alcohol was another source that could aggravate his psoriasis; his condition *had* worsened back when he was drinking more heavily, but he preferred to blame it more on stress and justified this indulgence by convincing himself that alcohol helped him relax. He needed a drink or two after work these days. He knew of no better way to unwind. Or to forget, although it never quite worked out that way.

He left the bag of burgers and onion rings on the counter. He'd deal with his appetite later. He opened the cupboard over the kitchen sink and reached for the bottle of whiskey next to the box of *Treasure Chest* cereal his kids had never finished and Powell couldn't bring himself to throw away. He regarded the cereal only briefly before he took the bottle and gently closed the cupboard door. Then, half-filled tumbler of equally-mixed whiskey and ginger ale in hand, he went into the living room, switched on the television and settled into his recliner. He rubbed his hand affectionately over the Naugahyde upholstered arm of the chair. The recliner was a Christmas gift from Cassidy. A smile flickered across his face as he remembered how excited she was that Christmas morning when he came out of the bedroom sleepy-eyed and still in his pajamas and saw the chair wrapped in a wide red ribbon. He could still hear her voice saying, "A hardworking man should have a comfortable chair to enjoy at the end of the day."

His smile dissolved as fast as it had appeared and he took a quick swallow of his drink. He used the remote to switch through the channels, but found nothing of interest. He rarely did anymore. Where once it had been cartoons with the kids scrunched up on his lap, now he purposely skipped those channels. *To hell with Bugs Bunny*. He would have to wait until six p.m. for the news. Until then, besides sipping his whiskey, he didn't know what to do with himself. He had hoped to relax once he got home, but instead he felt restless. Even slightly agitated. Well, just the one solution for that, he decided, and he downed the remainder of his drink in a swift swallow. He got up from his chair and returned to the kitchen to pour himself another, even stiffer this time. By the time he stepped back over to his recliner he could already feel the mellowing effects of the alcohol.

Finally feeling more relaxed, he muttered aloud, "Damn fine."

But his contentment did not last long. Maybe it was the quick action of the whiskey, or more probably the recollections that were never far from his thoughts when he was inside his too quiet house. Or maybe the deaths of those two little girls evoked today's painful rush of memories.

Memories of that terrible spring night fifteen months ago…

It hadn't been a particularly outstanding day. In fact, typical— the kind of day he experienced on a more or less regular basis before the recent events in town. The highpoint of his shift was being called into Field's Grocery to deal with a teenage shoplifter who had pocketed a couple of packages of AAA batteries. A stern lecture, a promise from the kid to behave, and Powell had earned another day's pay.

Still, he was tired and was looking forward to watching a baseball game on television. Cassidy walked up to him with a beguiling look pasted on her pretty face while he relaxed in his recliner enjoying his beer and she gently reminded him that he had promised to take the children, seven-year-old Ruthie and five-year-old Randy, out for ice cream that night, at the new refreshment stand built along the coast highway. Powell regarded her with an uncomprehending expression. It had completely slipped his mind and his ignorance of this commitment was honest even to the probing eyes of his wife. But then the light bulb switched on and he instantly felt lousy.

"Meathead," he scolded himself.

Cassidy looked about ready to chastise him as well. But instead her features softened and she gave him a playfully critical look and sighed. "Well, don't worry about it. After dinner I can take the kids if my working man desperately needs to relax."

"Owww," Powell responded, as if he'd been kicked in the groin.

Cassidy planted her fists against her hips in a frustrated "What am I going to do with you?" gesture.

"That wasn't the plan," Powell reminded her, though his words weren't brimming with self-reproach.

Cassidy shrugged. "I can take them," she said again with another exhale. "You probably have a ballgame or something you want to watch anyway."

"Actually..." Powell started to say.

"I knew it," Cassidy said with a pursing of her lips.

Powell still regretted his forgetfulness, but he wasn't about to argue if she was okay with taking the kids for their ice cream. He gave her a sheepish look. "Would you mind very much?"

Cassidy sat herself on his lap. She frowned good-naturedly. "Not too much."

She put her arms around her husband and planted a big kiss on his lips. Powell felt instantly stimulated and the can of beer almost dropped from his hand. He hurriedly shuffled his fingers along the end table to deposit his beverage before it actually did slide from his grip.

With both hands now free he wrapped his arms around Cassidy's slim waist and drew her close.

"Uh, what about the kids," he said to her after another long lip-lock.

"What about 'em?" Cassidy replied provocatively.

Powell shook his head briskly. "Hell, like I always suspected. I married a nympho."

Cassidy pulled herself free of her husband's arms. Then she stood up and took a step backward. "No," she said with mock dignity. "Just a tease."

"Do I at least get a meal out of the deal?" Powell asked with a petulant expression.

Cassidy puckered her lips and looked thoughtful. And then she rocked her head. "I suppose that's a fair exchange."

"Exchange, maybe," Powell said. "Fair...definitely not."

Cassidy blew him a kiss and walked into the kitchen. Powell turned his attention from the evening news on television to admire her gently swaying hips and perfectly formed buttocks, particularly fetching in her tight, faded jeans. Sonofabitch, he thought. He was almost breathless. She'd got him good and horny and he would be fresh out of luck until later. Still, he couldn't help himself. He leaped up from his chair and followed her into the kitchen. He came up behind her and wrapped then locked her arms in a loving bear hug.

"My God, there's no stopping you," Cassidy muttered. "I should call the police. Help! I'm being stalked."

"Won't do you much good. Chief of police is officially off duty for the day."

Cassidy spoke with a feigned panic. "But operator, my stalker is the chief of police."

"Well, what are you gonna do?" Powell said in a breathy whisper. "Your cop just happened to make the mistake of marrying a gal he's crazy about."

Cassidy turned around and gazed up at her husband. She wore a puzzled frown. "Mistake?"

"Nope. Never," Powell reassured her softly.

Powell thought he was a lucky man. Cassidy was beautiful in his eyes. A sweet and gorgeous thirty-three-year-old brunette. Maybe not a cover girl, but possessed of a fresh, natural, unaffected loveliness. She had the purest skin with just a faint sprinkling of freckles and wide, long-lashed, sparkling eyes that could express the most genuine love a man—at least this man—could ever hope to receive. A cute button nose and a mouth that widened into an oblong, toothy smile, framed by full, wide luscious lips that never failed to draw his own lips toward her like a magnet.

"What did I ever do in my life to deserve you?" Powell said, his words perhaps romantically corny, but spoken with sincere wonderment.

Cassidy turned her eyes from him, shyly. She appeared to blush just a little.

"Beautiful...and modest, too," Powell said.

She glanced back at her husband. "The total package?" she said with an impish grin.

"Oh yeah," Powell murmured with a swift flicker of his head.

He was just about to plant another kiss on those inviting lips when the door swung open and he heard his children rush inside the house.

"The cavalry," Cassidy joked as she swung her face toward the front door, the movement causing her long hair to spill over her front shoulder. Powell gingerly brushed it back. As soft as cotton, he thought.

"Yeah, now I know how Geronimo felt," he remarked with mock displeasure.

Cassidy called out to the kids, "Wash your hands, you two. Dinner's ready."

Powell stepped over to the stove, opened the door and peered inside. He'd been enjoying the aroma of the meatloaf since he got home and was delighted to see that it looked as tempting as it smelled. Another one of the perks of being married to Cassidy was that she was a hell of a cook. She knew what he liked and how he liked it prepared. Of course he was always careful how he expressed that appreciation. He didn't want her to get the idea he was a chauvinist. Yet, if he were to be totally honest with himself, he did sort of slide in that direction. But if he were even more truthful, he had a suspicion that Cassidy had already guessed that...and was okay with it.

As long as he kept his machismo in check.

...Back in the present Powell smiled unconsciously and took a sip of his whiskey. He remembered it as a special evening meal. Was it really any more memorable than other dinners the family shared, or did it just hold significance because...*because*...

He physically and firmly erased that thought from his mind with a swift and reflexive jerking of his head. He didn't need to torture himself with such reflection.

But his efforts aside, the memories continued to come at him...

He remembered that the kids were at first a little upset that daddy wouldn't be taking them for ice cream. But their excitement over having frosty treats for dessert soon overrode their disappointment. Cassidy sweetened the deal in a way that pleased her husband. Ruthie and Randy had to promise to go to bed without argument once they got home. The kids naturally agreed to mommy's terms. Bedtime was expected in any case; the ice cream was hardly an inducement. With that settled, Cassidy gave Powell a wink. He responded with an approving nod.

"Clever," he complimented her. "It's bribery. But effective."

The kids rushed to give their daddy a big hug and kiss and then just as hurriedly ran out to the car. Cassidy went to get her purse. She opened her billfold and checked her cash.

Powell put up a hand to halt her, with the determination of a traffic cop halting a speeder. "Hell no," he said. "Definitely my treat."

Cassidy eyed him speculatively. "For services rendered?"

Powell gave his head a deliberate shake. "Oh no. Services rendered are reserved for later," he told her.

Cassidy gazed at her husband inquisitively before her lips separated in a smile and she lifted her eyebrows expectantly. She pushed up on her toes to kiss her husband.

"You know I love you," she said.

"Damn well better," Powell said teasingly.

Powell suppressed a shiver. He remembered that kiss. They kissed and held onto each other for such a long while that little Ruthie had to run back inside to impatiently fetch her mommy. Why did they hold that embrace for so long? Powell found himself wondering long afterwards. And…it was her mostly. As if she didn't want to let him go. As if…

No. Powell didn't want to consider that. Sometimes the guilt so overwhelmed him that he felt he was going to lose all reason. The tears welled up. He brushed his eyes dry with an abrupt sweep of the back of his hand.

Dammit!

His last words to her were, "Drive carefully."

She answered him with a smile and another kiss and the assurance, "Won't be long."

Powell was a passionate baseball fan and he tried to keep his concentration on the televised game, but his thoughts kept veering back to Cassidy coming home and the two of them sharing some serious lovemaking. She was an amazing partner and never failed to please him. He hoped he could restrain himself until then. He was getting restless and active in a specific part of his anatomy.

Nine o'clock came. The game was still on—seventh inning or something like that—but by now Powell wasn't paying it any attention. The beers he'd consumed had relaxed him sufficiently so that he briefly drifted off to sleep. When he awoke he glanced at the tableside clock…and less than five minutes later looked at it again. He began to grow concerned. They'd been gone for almost two hours. The way he figured, with the drive there and back along with time to enjoy their ice cream, Cassidy and the kids should have been home a half hour ago.

Cassidy had driven the coast highway many times—and she was a careful driver, especially when she was chauffeuring the children, although there were some lunatics who used that stretch of road as a speedway despite its steep and sharp curves. Both officially and off-duty Powell knew that well. He'd chased down and ticketed many of those would-be Mario Andretti's.

It started to rain. He could hear the steady patter of rainfall outside the front window and while it didn't sound as if the conditions were treacherous, the rains could make the highway slippery.

He again reminded himself that Cassidy would use caution.

Ten o'clock. It was dark outside. The rain was still coming down, a little more heavily now. Without even checking the score of the game he'd watched so inattentively, Powell switched off the television and readied himself to go out and check on what had happened to Cassidy and the kids. He didn't want to acknowledge the tightness in his gut or the pounding that had started to drum beat in his chest. But he could not ignore the feeling that something might be wrong. He went over to the drawer to grab his car keys and stood there only for a moment, trying to steady breathing that had gotten heavy in his lungs.

"Everything's all right. Cassidy…probably just had some car trouble," he muttered as he tried to convince himself that really was the case. Cassidy's Volvo had been giving her some minor problems and was overdue for servicing. He had been after her to take it in to

Mitch Winchell's garage and she finally had promised to have it checked out before the end of the week.

Just as Powell's mood began to ease—

There came a knock at the door. Hard. Rapid. Sounding urgent.

Both the suddenness and determination of the knock almost caused Powell's thumping heart to burst from his rib cage.

Powell knew it wasn't his wife outside. The door was unlocked. And even if it wasn't, Cassidy had her house key.

The knocking continued. Powell swallowed past a large lump in his throat as he slowly approached the door. He wasn't psychic, wasn't seized by any kind of intuition or premonition, but he couldn't erase the apprehension that his worst fears were about to be realized.

And when he peered out through the side window and saw his young patrolman Terry Reynolds standing nervously on the porch, he knew for certain that his dread was soon to be confirmed.

He turned the knob and opened the door…

According to witnesses the Volvo had skidded out of control while attempting to navigate one of the rain-slicked curves. The car slid wildly across the two lanes before hitting another slippery wet patch and careening off the side of the road to collide with the front end of another vehicle, and then slamming into the hard edge of the gradient.

Reynolds was reluctant to inform Powell of the condition of his wife and two children. He really didn't have to—Powell already knew, in his own mind—but the chief insisted he be told.

"Might be better if we just drive out—" Reynolds started to suggest.

"Tell me, dammit!" Powell demanded in a shout.

Reynolds still could not bring himself to say the words. His head lowered and his lips trembled.

"All right," Powell finally muttered. He knew what it was that his patrolman would not—could not—tell him, but that was all right. Maybe he really wasn't ready to hear confirmation. Perhaps it was better just to hold on to the vaguest hope.

He put his hand on Reynolds' shoulder as the two men walked out the door.

They drove the short distance to the crash site in silence. For Reynolds, it seemed a long ride. Even though at times he resented Powell for what he perceived as the chief's lack of confidence in his abilities, he truly respected and admired the man—both professionally and personally. But as the patrol car raced through the dark and the rain, its lights flashing, the man now sitting beside him was like a completely different person. The man of strength and commitment that Reynolds had come to know was nowhere present. Instead Reynolds saw someone who looked as deflated and vulnerable as any scared and repentant young offender who had ever been arrested and brought into police headquarters to answer charges or to be outright booked for an offense.

They could see the lights from the other emergency vehicles at a distance. Ambulances had already arrived from Breckridge. Cars were pulled over to the side of the road. Other vehicles could not be rerouted so they had to turn back and wait until the road was cleared of debris and the investigators were through with their preliminary examination of the scene. Even though it was raining, people were milling about outside their vehicles, though kept at a distance by highway patrol officers.

"Witnesses...or ghouls?" Powell muttered under his breath as Reynolds steered the car over to the right shoulder and slowed to a stop.

Reynolds had heard the comment, but didn't say anything.

He parked near the guardrail on the outer ridge that overlooked a precipitous drop into the dark, choppy waters of the bay. The echoing sound of the waves relentlessly slapping against the rocky shoreline could be heard from where they were standing. The wind whistled mournfully.

The two men exited the patrol car. It was dark and with the rain coming down, visibility was poor, but Powell could still make out the wreck of what once had been his wife's Volvo. A breath hitched in his throat and for a long while he didn't—maybe couldn't—move. He just stood by the door of the patrol car, his eyes glued on the activity across the road. One of the State Highway patrol officers wearing a yellow rain poncho stepped away from the scene and hurried over to Reynolds.

"Reynolds?" he asked.

Reynolds nodded and nudged his head toward his superior.

"That's Chief Powell," he said.

The officer looked at Powell compassionately. The chief didn't acknowledge the man. He seemed oblivious to most everything—except his wife's damaged vehicle.

"I'm Officer Curtis," the officer said as he extended his hand to Reynolds.

"Oh yes," Reynolds said as he accepted the handshake. "Thanks for calling this in." His appreciation was offered grimly as his concern remained focused on Powell.

Curtis tilted his chin toward Powell and said in a gentle tone, "Does he…"

Reynolds looked at Powell. "Chief?" he said in a gentle urging.

Powell slowly turned his head toward the young officer. Reynolds hesitated before he gestured to the two ambulances. Powell nodded vacantly and he followed Reynolds and Officer Curtis across the road.

Reynolds asked Curtis, "How are the occupants of the other car?"

"Shaken, but otherwise seem to be all right. They'll be taken into Breckridge to be checked out."

"Thank God for that, at least," Reynolds said with an exhale.

"Car's a write-off, though."

Reynolds ignored the comment which in light of all else seemed wholly insignificant.

Powell first walked over to the ambulance that held his wife. Her body lay inside a rubber body bag in back of the vehicle. Powell halted as stress lines embedded themselves into his features.

"Oh God," he breathed.

He wanted to see her…yet he didn't. He just could not conceive of his beautiful, loving Cassidy being dead. Just hours earlier they had been in each other's embrace. They'd planned a beautiful night together.

It wasn't fair. It just wasn't possible.

The attendant knelt patiently next to the stretcher, the metal legs of which were now folded underneath. His hand didn't even touch the bag, no gesture or silent suggestion for the police chief to rush. Not until Powell was ready. Finally, after many long moments, Powell gave a nod and the attendant gently slid open the zipper just enough to reveal Cassidy's face. Powell momentarily faltered before he called upon his professionalism and all of his willpower to remain composed.

And yet in a way he was surprised. He had expected to see his wife's features ruined by the crash, but she looked perfect. Not a scratch or bruise marred her face. And her expression…it was peaceful, serene. Outside of the paleness of her skin and slight purple discoloration of her lips his lovely Cassidy appeared as if she were merely asleep. As she looked the many nights Powell had awoken from his own slumber and simply laid on his pillow gazing at her and thinking how blessed he was that such a person had come into his life.

Powell was grateful that his lovely Cassidy had not been disfigured in the crash. At the same time it distressed him, tore deep into his heart, to see her lying there so still—yet looking so natural. He expected her at any moment to flutter open her eyelids and smile at him.

Powell wanted to bend over to kiss her, but he resisted. He had to maintain his professionalism, even in light of a personal tragedy. He finally nodded to the attendant who dutifully re-zippered the bag and Powell stepped from the ambulance. Before he could start toward the second emergency vehicle, which held his two children, Ruthie and Randy, Officer Curtis came up to him.

His voice was strict. "Chief Powell, it—it's only fair to warn you. Your son..."

Powell's troubled eyes suddenly flashed at him. "What are you trying to tell me?"

The officer's words stalled, then came haltingly. "Your son was in the front seat when the accident occurred. He—apparently was wearing a seat belt, but the impact was too strong."

Powell looked intently yet painfully at the officer. His expression conveyed to Curtis that he wanted him to finish what he was trying to avoid saying.

"The seat belt didn't hold," Officer Curtis told him outright.

Powell didn't need to hear any more. He understood what that meant and now he almost wished he hadn't asked. He knew that, unlike his wife, his five-year-old boy, so small, had been horribly mangled in the crash. He suspected what had happened...was certain, in fact since he'd been at the scene of road accidents where *seat belts had not been worn. But this time he did not want to be told the details.*

"Ruthie...my daughter," he then uttered in a barely audible voice.

"She was in the back seat," Curtis said.

Powell gave an empty nod and he exhaled a slow, lengthy breath through his nostrils. He remained oblivious to the rain falling upon him or the wind that whipped about him and this tragic scene. He just kept his eyes steady on the second ambulance. He debated, but finally decided against going over to it.

Instead he said to Officer Curtis, mutedly, "I'll—visit with them later."

Curtis thought that was a peculiar choice of phrasing, but he understood that any reaction under the circumstances might be a little odd and would have to be accepted without one trying to rationalize the intent. He nodded and went to inform the driver that he could start toward Breckridge.

Then came that terrible day of the funerals. The morning had started out sunny, the skies almost a crystal blue—but perhaps appropriately for what was to come, as early afternoon approached, a thick band of clouds rolled in from Buchanan Bay, rapidly turning the skies slate gray and threatening to bring rain.

Three caskets were brought inside the church that Saturday, one standard size and two smaller coffins, each white and all covered with flowers and floral arrangements that were of such quantity that many spilled out onto the carpet, stems and petals extending to the pulpit. Each casket was positioned lengthwise to the altar. Virtually the whole community turned out for the service. The pews were filled to capacity and many of the mourners were made to stand outside on the steps of the church, straining to hear the minister as he spoke words intended to bring comfort to the bereaved. Powell sat in the front pew, hearing what was being said but giving it no value. His wife and children were dead, end of story. The so-called glory of the Resurrection might have helped others cope with what had happened but to Powell such an everlasting "promise" held as much significance as those fairy stories about Jonah and Samson and David and Goliath that he'd listened to as a boy in Sunday School. Even then he thought it was so much hokey. They might as well have been part of his Saturday morning cartoon fare.

Afterward, it was time for the ride to the cemetery. Three hearses chauffeured the caskets out to Resurrection Gardens—two of the vehicles borrowed from a funeral home in Breckridge by the local undertaker, Mr. Borys. While the caskets bearing the bodies of the two children were taken to the section known as Heavenly Angels, the minister delivered his final words beside Cassidy Powell's grave. It was then a short walk to where he would once more speak his words of promised ascension over the children's tiny caskets.

Through it all Powell valiantly restrained his despair. It was difficult. He could barely pull his eyes away from the caskets, both at the church and now at the cemetery. He had to force himself to stay numb, otherwise he feared he would not be able to contain his sorrow—and overwhelmed by grief or not, he was still the town's chief of police and had an image to uphold.

Once the graveside services were over, people finally walked over to Powell to offer hushed but heartfelt condolences. Powell received them all with polite courtesy. A wake was going to be held at the church hall and Powell muttered to the minister that he would be along shortly. He wanted to stay with his children and his wife a little longer. The other cars left the cemetery, but Terry Reynolds stayed and offered to drive Powell back into town. Seeing Powell's anguished face, he stepped away to let his chief have his time alone.

He knew how difficult it had been for Powell to hold up through this ordeal and beyond sharing his chief's grief, Reynolds also felt honored to know such a courageous man.

A splash of rain fell from the sky. Then another. It began to drizzle. Powell stood with his head bowed next to his wife's casket and seemed oblivious to the droplets that pattered against the lid of the coffin and about him and onto the ground. Off to the side Reynolds studied the clouds overhead and thought it peculiar how there had been precious little precipitation for much of the season and yet rain had come twice this week—and by curious coincidence, on the night the chief's family was in that accident and today as their bodies were being laid to rest. The rain was getting heavier and threatened to turn into a downpour. Reynolds was reluctant to interrupt Powell's solitude, but it was a bit of a walk back to the car. As the rain began to fall with even more intensity, Reynolds finally walked over to Powell. He took him gently by the arm and whispered that they had better leave. Powell was silent, but he didn't resist and the two men walked across the lawn to finally allow the cemetery workers to begin the grim task of filling in the graves.

The memories faded. Remembrances that were as clear and familiar to him as if they had happened just yesterday. How he wished the memory would end with that final embrace he'd had with Cassidy. A freeze-frame. But it never was to be. Not tonight…not ever. Cruelly, when his will surrendered and mental imagery replayed the events of that night, it was as if his brain simply would not allow him to forget the tragedy that followed, and as if that weren't painful enough, it always brought back vividly the dreadful anguish that had consumed him in the days that followed—those that continued to haunt him long after the burials.

Was it fifteen months ago? Fifteen years? Fifteen minutes? All he knew was that spring had turned into another summer and now the following autumn was here.

After the funerals he took some time off work, but soon he could no longer bear the loneliness or the ghosts that haunted his house and he convinced himself he was well enough to return to his job. His work became his therapy. It helped to keep the remorse buried in some closet of his psyche—otherwise it would overwhelm him to a point where he could not be sure of what he might be capable…if he gave full vent to it.

Powell's mood settled as his brain cleared. He'd had his visit with the past and it was over—for the time being. The clarity of those memories faded. All the images that had passed through his consciousness seemed to dissipate into a misty vapor. And he could regard that as a bittersweet kindness.

Yet the fact remained that Powell could never bring himself to confide in anyone that he held himself responsible for what happened that night. Whether from shame or the guilt that he always carried with him, the true tragedy of that night, as he saw it, was to remain his secret.

He finished his drink with a determined swallow. He collected himself. It was time to move on with the present.

And that meant dealing with a problem that brought stress of its own. One which Powell feared might have just as unpleasant an outcome.

CHAPTER FIVE

Powell debated his decision over the weekend, but on Monday morning he finally cast aside his doubts and made an appointment to meet with forensic psychologist Dr. Robbie Forrester. He personally put little faith in the opinions of "headshrinkers," regardless of their area of specialization. The fact that Robbie Forrester was a woman also didn't promote confidence in Powell. It was really more out of curiosity that he had arranged this meeting, to try to determine for himself if she could provide any insight into what twisted perversion existed in the brain of a child killer.

Dr. Forrester's morning schedule was open and she agreed to see the police chief at her downtown office at 11:30 a.m. It meant another three-quarter hour drive to Breckridge. Powell only hoped it wouldn't prove a waste of time.

He drove out from town just before noon and made the trip to the city in just over a half hour as the pre-lunch highway traffic was surprisingly light. Dr. Forrester's office was situated on the 18th floor of a modern professional building. Powell parked his vehicle in the carport behind the building and walked 'round to the front of the high rise, entering through the revolving doors. Inside the lobby he approached the directory panel and ran a finger along the tenant listing, stopping at Room 1807. He then stepped over to the bank of elevators, pushed the "up" button and waited for the car to arrive. Once the doors slid open smoothly and soundlessly on their tracks Powell stuffed himself into the compartment along with a crowd of passengers who had suddenly appeared like a flock of gulls while he was watching the slow progression of the floor indicator lights. He was dressed in his police uniform and was not immune to the looks that passed his way from the other passengers. Powell couldn't help feeling like the odd man out, as the saying went. They were all professional types, the men dressed in tailored business suits, the ladies in executive office wear. The air in the elevator compartment very quickly became a cloying blend of perfume and cologne. Powell was sensitive to strong fragrances and he breathed shallowly through his nose. It was a slow ride up, with the elevator making deposits on virtually every floor. By the time the elevator reached his floor he was the last to depart.

Powell stepped from the compartment and looking to see that no one else was around, pulled a tissue from his pocket and blew his nose into it, hoping to clear the residue of the perfume/cologne combo from his nostrils. Then he started down the richly carpeted hallway, checking the numbers on each door until he came to 1807. A gold-trimmed plaque affixed to the door read simply, DR. ROBBIE FORRESTER. Powell regarded the plaque for several seconds before he tapped lightly on the door. A voice from inside invited him to come in.

Dr. Forrester was seated at her desk, but rose as Powell entered. She was a tall woman who walked across the floor of her office with brisk, confident strides. She was wearing a dark, knee-length chestnut-colored dress and jacket made out of some sort of shiny gray or silver material. She extended her hand and Powell met it with his own. She had a remarkably firm grip.

"Chief Powell?"

Powell nodded.

"I'm Dr. Forrester," she said pleasantly if with proper formality.

"Pleased to meet you," Powell returned with a polite if wary smile.

He didn't want to appear obvious, but was frankly surprised by Dr. Forrester. He remembered that Dr. Arborshaw had said they'd attended medical school together, but she looked a good ten years younger than her classmate. A hell of a lot more attractive, too. Long auburn hair that cascaded over her shoulders and down her back, professionally styled and parted softly and not severely in the center; smooth porcelain skin that she didn't powder under mounds of makeup. She obviously took good care of herself. She easily could have passed for being in her mid-thirties.

Appearance aside, what he instantly determined was that Dr. Forrester was a no-nonsense professional who doubtlessly took her job seriously.

Unfortunately, the fragrance she wore was more than detectable to his nasal sensitivity. It seemed to flood the room. That alone assured Powell he would leave this meeting with a throbbing head. He wasn't about to perform the tissue trick in front of her.

Powell allowed himself a moment to glance around the spacious and tastefully furnished office. He noticed the tiered bookshelf next to the doctor's desk that was lined with thick volumes of psychiatric literature. He became momentarily cynical, wondering if Dr. Forrester was really as intellectual as her display of books with their twelve-syllable-word titles seemed to suggest or if she was just trying to impress her clients.

She invited Powell to take a seat across from her desk. He accepted and Dr. Forrester returned to her own high-back tufted leather chair across from him.

She started off by offering a curious observation directed at her visitor. "Can I take it you might be somewhat surprised to find that I'm a woman?"

Powell wrinkled his brow and appeared somewhat taken aback by her comment. He replied in as genuine a manner as he could. "No. Of course not. Dr. Arborshaw already told me—"

Dr. Forrester placed fingers against her chin and smiled wryly as she interjected, "But an unusual line of work for a female, forensic psychologist."

Powell smiled back at her. "You're making a presumption. And an incorrect one."

Dr. Forrester's own smile broadened. She settled back in her chair. "Just like to get that out of the way before we begin," she confessed.

"You find it's a problem?" Powell asked idly.

Dr. Forrester looked momentarily thoughtful. "No, not often," she answered. "But on occasion. Something I've become acute to, either by inference or direct observation."

"I feel like I should be on my guard," Powell said lightly.

Dr. Forrester took a beat before she added, "And usually when I'm dealing with someone who 'serves and protects'."

A bit of a bite there, Powell detected, even though he suspected she meant her remark good-naturedly. *Maybe.*

He failed to suppress a self-conscious clearing of his throat. "Yeah, guess that sometimes can be the attitude."

"Well, let's get down to cases, shall we?" Dr. Forrester said. Her professional formality had returned.

Powell took a moment to collect his thoughts. He then related to her all the relevant details behind the murder of the Loewen girls, deliberately presenting this information in a cool, detached manner, even though at moments during the telling he felt his own emotions start to emerge and he had to fight them back. Dr. Forrester listened attentively, never once interrupting to ask a question or make a comment. She waited until Powell had told her all that he could provide. Afterwards she didn't immediately speak. The look on her face seemed to express that she was evaluating all that she had heard.

The office went quiet for nearly a full minute.

Dr. Forrester finally spoke, and she presented her words thoughtfully, but with conviction. "First off, Chief Powell, this perpetrator is not a pedophile, but a molester."

Powell listened, considered, and then shrugged in an inquiring yet deliberately challenging gesture. "What's the difference?"

"Pedophiles don't need to harass or physically harm children," Dr. Forrester explained. "Molesters, on the other hand, do possess the need to commit a crime against a child. You did mention that these girls were not physically abused or sexually violated?"

"No, not violated. Just murdered," Powell said, betraying his professional demeanor with the tight delivery of his words.

Dr. Forrester's attention flickered across his face, alerting him that she'd noticed his reaction, but she tactfully pretended not to notice. Or at least not acknowledge. She went on. "The reason I bring that up is a molester's motives for his crimes are typically not sexual."

Powell edged forward in his chair. "So, for clarification, in your opinion, we're discussing a molester, not a pedophile."

Dr. Forrester responded with a slight nodding of her head.

"All right. What more can you tell me about this type of deviant from a psychological standpoint?" Powell asked her.

"There are two categories of child molesters, the situational molester and the preferential molester. With what you've described, the person you're seeking is the former, a situational molester. That type does not possess a genuine sexual preference for children. Rather, the motives are criminal in nature."

"Including murder?" Powell questioned darkly.

Dr. Forrester didn't answer directly. Instead she said, "This deviation generally develops in childhood. The situational child molester typically acts out the abuse that he—or she—had suffered earlier in life."

Powell spoke up. "I don't think we're talking about a woman here. The person we suspect—with good cause—is a man."

"Then focusing specifically on that gender, *he* is possessed of low esteem and questionable morals because of the violence in his upbringing and compensates by becoming abusive toward others in his life."

"Like…his family?" Powell asked.

Dr. Forrester studiously rocked her head. "Family, friends, even coworkers. If he's married, his wife may be the recipient of his abuse. She may even be in the know about his fetishes. For her own protection, she may even participate in them."

"Go so far as to cover for him?"

"Possibly."

"Out of fear."

"Or willingly."

"There have been such instances, yes."

Powell's mind flashed back to a case he had not been involved in but was familiar with. A couple in Tucson who were accused of abducting and abusing young girls. When the pair was finally apprehended, the woman involved claimed as her defense that she had partaken of these crimes only because she feared for her life. That had she not participated in these acts her partner assured her that he would kill her. It was a convenient if transparent plea that the jury hastily disregarded.

"And if he has children…?" Powell ventured, swallowing back the bile in his throat.

Dr. Forrester replied straightly. "What is important to understand is that no one in his circle is immune. Often this impulse is triggered when the person is under stress. He may react to a built-up sexual impulse…or a pent-up anger that he releases through this aggression. We can sub-categorize even deeper and I would classify the man you're describing as morally indiscriminate. He's someone who seeks a victim who is vulnerable, one whom he lures through force or manipulation. His crimes against children happen almost circumstantially. He may find his opportunity randomly, rather than actively seeking one out. When he's presented with this opportunity, he seizes it, and surrenders wholly to the urge to inflict pain and violence upon whoever he perceives as helpless."

"But to detect one of these types…just someone you might pass on the street and not even notice? One of the crowd, as it were," Powell wanted to know.

"In many cases, yes, that's so. Could easily be a professional type. Or a blue- collar worker. There's really no distinction. You see there are two types of behavior we're looking at, high and low functioning. The higher functioning ones can be harder to recognize because they are able to cover up their disorder better. On a surface level they are completely average. They hold down responsible jobs and appear to be leading a perfectly normal life. On the other hand, there's the type who might not be so difficult to spot as he's perceived by others as a social misfit or even a psychopathic personality who harbors a deep-rooted resentment and hostility toward society. Again, it really has nothing to do with the person's occupation."

"Wouldn't this type of sicko seek out a job where he would be around children?" Powell questioned. "Working in some capacity at a school or maybe a playground instructor. Something like, say, a little league coach."

"Some do, certainly. But keep in mind that if something should happen to a child in their care, they're usually among the first to be suspected, so they run that risk of discovery."

Powell's expression reflected his disgust. He muttered, "Clever in their compulsion."

"At any rate that doesn't seem to be what you're dealing with," Dr. Forrester was quick to stress. "Unless of course there's something you haven't told me."

"Although it looks pretty certain we have a suspect—a transient who came into Clear Vista just a couple of days before the girls were murdered—I still haven't ruled out anyone from the community," Powell admitted. "But truthfully I can't think of anyone specific I could cast suspicion on. There was one fellow who at first seemed as if he might be a likely candidate, but he didn't match the description given to us by a couple of kids who saw this character." He sighed in frustration. "But…then no one in Clear Vista does."

"There is one characteristic of the situational molester that should be noted," Dr. Forrester said.

Powell gave a tilt of his head.

"Their victims tend to be few," the doctor explained. "They might commit their act once or twice and never do it again."

Powell sat silent for a moment, assimilating and considering. He said ruefully, "Reckon the question to be asked is if that's a good thing or bad? If he disappears into obscurity that lessens the chance he'll ever be caught. Or he might wait 'til everyone's forgotten about him and five, ten years later strike again." He flashed his eyes toward the doctor. "That's a possibility, too," he said, phrasing his words as a statement rather than a question.

Dr. Forrester replied slowly, "When you're dealing with that type of psychopathy, nothing is ever really an absolute."

"So…what do you do with someone like that?" Powell questioned. "What's the remedy?"

Dr. Forrester barely suppressed her amusement at his choice of wording. "*Remedy?* Sounds as if you're looking for a simple drug store solution."

Powell shook his head slowly, determinedly. "Just interested in your professional opinion." He added with an edge, "Which I assume you have."

Dr. Forrester determined there was not much room for compromise with the police chief. The apparent condescension he felt toward her either personally or professionally was not being filtered very well. Their talk had taken on the tone of verbal thrust and parry. But she wasn't about to surrender her own professional integrity to satisfy him. "They must undergo intensive therapy to curb these tendencies," she said straightly.

"Which generally happens *only* after they're caught," Powell retorted.

Dr. Forrester hesitated before she gave a regrettable nod.

"After they've had their kicks," Powell added acidly, eyes narrowed almost accusingly at the psychologist.

The doctor didn't respond either to his expression or the bluntness of the remark.

Powell gave vent to his frustration and spoke even more bluntly. "No offense, Dr. Forrester, but in a situation like that I'd prefer to see the switch pulled on the sonofabitch rather than have him tell his tale of childhood woe relaxing on a contour couch. These twisted types can so fake it they come across as more intelligent than the so-called expert examining them. Blame their behavior on their sorry upbringing or how they were misunderstood and mistreated by society. Play on sympathy that lands them in a psychiatric institution with a bed and three squares a day. No, I say to hell with that therapy mumbo-jumbo and just shoot the current through them."

Dr. Forrester smiled indulgently. "I can understand—from your standpoint. But I'm afraid on that issue we'll have to agree to disagree."

"I'm less interested in a clinical justification than making sure no child will ever be harmed again," Powell said candidly.

Dr. Forrester's face took on a concerned look. "Assuming that the person you're after is this transient you mention, have you considered that he might still be in the vicinity?"

Powell wore a questioning expression. "Is that likely?"

Dr. Forrester elaborated. "There's always the possibility an element of self-loathing comes into the equation. If this man is dealing with an urge he despises yet one that he can't control, he might want to be caught. That may be his dilemma. He wants to stop, knows the only way that will happen is if he's apprehended, yet he won't voluntarily surrender."

Powell digested this before he said, "So he'd just loiter around the town, waiting for another opportunity…yet hoping we'll catch him in the act?"

Dr. Forrester offered more. "Another consideration is that in defense against his low self-esteem he may become effused with delusions of grandeur in which he establishes a challenge, believing he's superior to the law and that he won't be caught. Especially if he got away successfully the first time. It's akin to a gambler on a winning streak who wants to keep trying his luck."

"Yeah, but you can't play against the odds forever," Powell responded sharply. He began scratching at an itch on his scalp, and then he sighed and said, "But I can't buy either of those possibilities. Even though I'm getting conflicting descriptions on what this character looks like, he's made himself too visible around Clear Vista and sooner or later someone is going to spot him and say 'he's the one'. And I just can't grasp that someone like that would be waiting around, wanting—*hoping*—to be recognized. The way I see it, if our man is this fellow who passed through town, he's back on the road already. The traveling psycho."

Powell stood up from the chair and straightened his posture. He looked contemplative.

"And that's odd, isn't it?" he asked. "Those descriptions, I mean. Not one really matches up with the other. We could just as well be talking about several different people."

"Panic, excitement, people trying to cope with what happened," Dr. Forrester proposed. "The type of situation where everyone wants to offer help, no matter how vague or even contradictory that information may be. But that also has to be controlled. Because if results aren't forthcoming, it can develop to where everyone becomes a potential suspect."

"Which is what we're trying to avoid," Powell said grimly. "Neighbor starting to accuse neighbor." He considered and smiled without amusement. "Think I saw something like that in an old *Twilight Zone* episode."

Dr. Forrester nodded sympathetically. "Until this man is caught, you are dealing with a delicate situation."

"I appreciate your time, Dr. Forrester," Powell said before he turned to walk toward the door. "Don't know how much help it's gonna be—and it sure hasn't changed my opinion about the type of man we're dealing with. Hell, sickens me even to refer to this *vermin* as a human being."

Dr. Forrester didn't rise from behind her desk. But she did say, "I hope you find him, Chief Powell. And if I can be of any further service, please don't hesitate to call."

Powell nodded, creased his lips in a smile and left the office.

* * *

When he arrived back in Clear Vista it was almost 2:30 in the afternoon. He'd stopped for a quick lunch at a fast food joint in Breckridge where he took the time to relax and think out all that Dr. Forrester had told him. He had gained some insight into the mind of a child molester, but as he saw it, the only information of value was her saying there was a chance this character had fulfilled his murderous fantasies and might never strike again. A lot of the rest of what she'd said sounded straight from a textbook. His focus was on facts, not theory.

But he had his doubts this was the last anyone would hear from this fiend. The man was a psychopath and it seemed unlikely he would give up his hunt for children now that he'd tasted blood. And even though Powell did not agree with the psychologist that it was possible the killer might still be somewhere in the vicinity of the town, he did harbor a vague hope that could be the case. Because *he* wanted to be the one to apprehend this maniac.

It was something he owed the children.

In a strange way…it was what he owed *his* children.

CHAPTER SIX

When Powell walked into his office later that afternoon he found Terry Reynolds seated at his desk, scribbling on a piece of paper. Reynolds appeared so engrossed in whatever he was doing that he didn't immediately notice the chief as he entered.

Only when Powell was well inside the office did Reynolds look up. He wore a queerly intense expression, as though he were still absorbed in concentration.

"What's up?" Powell asked, gesturing with a jerk of his head to the paper Reynolds was working on.

Reynolds maintained his peculiar look as he took the paper in his hand, stood up from behind the desk and stepped over to Powell. The young officer appeared momentarily hesitant. Powell thought he was about to discard the paper but instead Reynolds thrust it at the chief and pointed past several scribbled and crossed-out words to one written in large block letters, seemingly exaggerated in their penmanship.

HADES.

Powell arched an eyebrow. He didn't say anything.

"You might think it's crazy," Reynolds said as he observed the chief's dubious expression, and his voice was utterly serious. "Or even that *I'm* crazy, but I was intrigued by that name 'Shade'. I know it's an alias and just started to play around and…well, it's also…it could be an anagram. Shade…*Hades*."

Powell regarded Reynolds with a speculative look that suggested that while the young officer might not be crazy he could have had too much time on his hands that afternoon.

"I know, I know," Reynolds said impatiently. "But we both know 'Shade' is not his real name."

Powell was unimpressed. "He chose an alias that a smart boy like you figures out relates somehow to his true character." He smirked and spoke briskly. "Or maybe we are dealing with a Satan worshipper? Or maybe old Beelzebub himself?"

Reynolds was slightly offended by the chief's flippancy. He crumpled up the paper with a tight clenching of his fist and tossed a perfect bounce shot into the wastepaper basket.

Powell smirked. "Next you'll want to be calling in a psychic."

Reynolds regarded Powell with a look that seemed to suggest that might not be such a bad idea.

Powell spoke to placate him—and perhaps to even justify his own frustration. "Don't mean to sound so cynical, Terry. Hell—or Hades, at this point you might be right on the money."

Reynolds nodded, a gesture to show that he pardoned the putdown.

"How did things go with the psychologist?" he then asked.

Powell went behind the desk and seated himself. He stretched out in his chair. "Learned more than I care to about what makes a child molester tick," he said.

"Child molester? But the girls weren't—"

"That was the doc's analysis."

"Anything more to maybe give us a lead?"

Powell's grin was not intended to be humorous. "Oh, he might disappear like a wisp of wind—*she* says. And that I doubt. She also offered a theory that our Mr. Shade might still be in town."

Reynolds scrunched up his face. "Think that's possible?"

"That's what the lady said." Powell smiled wryly. "That he might be waiting to be caught or possibly that he's playing some type of head game with us. Cute thought, huh?"

Reynolds' eyelids lowered and he slowly swung his head from side to side.

"By the way, got visitors again today," he then said as he raised his face back to the chief. "Want to know if we're making any progress."

"And you told them…?"

Reynolds shrugged. "Me? I'm still the new boy in town in their eyes. They don't expect me to say too much." He brandished a finger at Powell. "They want to hear it from you."

Powell combed the fingers of both hands through his hair. His scalp was itching, but he didn't want to appear obvious about it.

"Even with what Dr. Forrester suggests is a possibility, I think we can safely assume he's out of our jurisdiction," he said. "The best we can do is wait for a report to come in."

"And hope that won't take long," Reynolds added.

Powell nodded. He considered pouring himself a cup of coffee but saw that the Pyrex coffee pot was nearly empty and he didn't feel ambitious enough to brew a fresh pot.

"Why don't you go make your rounds?" Powell suggested. "I'll deal with any inquisitive citizens who might pop in."

"And Mr. Stromm?" Reynolds asked as he stepped over to the coat rack and started to slide into his police jacket.

Powell's face took on a look of exasperation. "Has he been around?"

Reynolds shook his head. "No, fortunately. Called, though."

Powell began to rock in his swivel chair. "And how was *his* manner?"

Reynolds gave a weak smile. "Abrupt. The usual."

"Well, much to Mr. Walter Stromm's dissatisfaction, he'll have to wait like everyone else, unless he thinks his influence can pull rabbits out of hats."

"Or child murderers," Reynolds put in.

Powell shot him a strict, disapproving look. Reynolds appeared embarrassed. He realized too late that he shouldn't have said what he had. It was in bad taste.

"Sorry," he apologized meekly.

Powell just held his frown and gave a swift nod.

Before Reynolds reached the door he halted, then turned to Powell.

He said, "But you know, Chief, the way this so-called Mr. Shade's description varies according to those witnesses you spoke to, maybe he *could* still be in town and no one would even know."

Powell looked to be considering what Reynolds was suggesting, but then he dismissed it. He wouldn't accept that possibility. He said sardonically, "Sure. Hiding under a haystack, next to the proverbial needle."

Reynolds lifted a shoulder. "Well, doesn't hurt to keep our eyes open."

"No, it doesn't."

Only minutes after Reynolds left the office the telephone rang. Powell furrowed his brow, thinking that he'd lift the receiver and it would be Walter Stromm again. He let the phone ring a couple more times while he steeled himself for the brusque, intimidating conversation that was sure to come.

Finally he mumbled a reassuring "Okay fella" to himself and he picked up the receiver.

As always, he kept his tone official—even as he suspected who it was on the other end. "Clear Vista Police Department. Chief Powell speaking."

He was surprised when following a brief pause he heard a female voice he could just slightly recognize.

"Chief Powell," the voice said, tentatively.

"Yes. Who is this?" Powell said politely.

Another hesitation. Then, just as timidly, "Donna. Donna Murray." No acknowledgment on the other end and so she clarified, "From Gregg's Grill."

The diner, where Powell ate many of his meals. He spoke amiably, pleased to hear from her. Hell, he would have appreciated hearing from anyone besides Walter Stromm.

"Yes, Donna, of course. How are you? What can I do for you?"

He was admittedly puzzled by the call. Donna Murray would have no reason to phone the office, unless Reynolds had put in a takeout order that was ready for pickup.

Powell had spoken to Donna only a couple of days earlier, when he called her into his office to interview her in connection with the Loewen twins' murder. His primary suspect, the mysterious transient, had been seen at Gregg's Grill—and by no less than himself. But Powell had hoped that perhaps Donna would be able to pinpoint something unique about the man, maybe offer a more solid description since she likely had served him his meal order. Unfortunately, Donna was unable to provide much more than anyone else with whom the chief had spoken. She remembered the stranger, yes—he had ordered only a cup of coffee, nothing from the menu—but, as with everyone else, she could not recall anything specific about him. Strangers frequently came into the diner and to a busy server one patron hardly varied from another.

Donna did have a reason for making today's call. Nothing official. Rather, it was personal. The truth was that Donna Murray, a twenty-eight-year-old divorcee, had long been attracted to Braden Powell, though outside of maybe being a trifle overly solicitous when serving him at the diner, she had kept those feelings to herself. She was always careful when passing him furtive glances on those occasions when he would come into the restaurant and sit at a booth or at the far end of the counter consuming his usual double bacon cheeseburger.

Her attraction to Powell began the day an intoxicated diner began harassing her after she'd made a mistake on his meal order— no gravy on his fries. His playful if suggestive remarks escalated to the point where he got loud, started to talk abusively when Donna began defending herself, and finally the restaurant owner got involved. But, despite his attempts to be diplomatic, he got slugged for his troubles. The man then turned his attention back to Donna, threatening to teach her proper manners. There were only a few other diners in the place at the time but they were clearly too frightened to get involved and it looked as if Donna was on her own. Fortunately, before things could get even uglier, Powell happened to walk into the restaurant. He also tried to reason with the guy, but by that point the man was aggressive beyond rational thinking. He made the mistake of trying to attack the police chief. Powell instantly subdued him with some type of martial arts move (that unbeknownst to Donna he had learned in defense classes during military basic training prior to his deployment overseas) and actually physically took the guy by the collar and escorted him several blocks to police headquarters, much to the man's humiliation but to the cheers of passersby. The way he had handled the situation and come to her rescue—Donna's heart started to flutter. Sure, she recognized she probably had fallen under the spell of a "white knight in shining armor," but that didn't concern her. Maybe she was a romantic, but from that day forward she'd harbored a crush on Braden Powell.

The previous year she had taken a leave of absence from her job and been away from Clear Vista for about six months helping her aunt care for her aged grandmother, and when she returned she had learned about Powell's misfortune. She was as upset as anyone else in town and out of respect never gave any hint of her feelings toward him. But lately she'd heard—and indeed overheard—that Powell seemed such a lonely man and especially now, with many in the town not exactly turning against him, but demanding that he step up his attempts to solve the double murder that had shattered the community, she felt he might appreciate a sympathetic friend. Someone on his side. It presented the opportunity she had been hoping for and Donna became firm in her decision after having her interview in the police chief's office.

Donna Murray was a rarity among the ladies in the community. Most possessed old-fashioned values, but Donna was a progressive gal not afraid to take the initiative when there was something she wanted. It was not always the most comfortable situation to be in, was oftentimes awkward, but many times it was the only way to get things done. As she remembered her father saying, "Never be afraid to take the bull by the horns."

Now that Donna had "taken the bull by the horns," it was time to run with it. She had to say *something*, otherwise she'd feel like a damn fool and probably not be able to face Powell the next time he came into Gregg's Grill.

She kept her voice smooth and confident, which was the most important thing. She was genuine in her intentions and did not want the police chief to misinterpret what she was going to say. In short, it was a balancing act.

"Chief Powell," she began, "I was calling to see if you might be busy this evening."

"Busy?" Powell replied, curious.

"Well, yes," Donna said. "If you happen to be free, I was just wondering if…you might like to see a movie?"

Now it was Powell's turn to fall silent. Donna Murray. Calling him. For what sounded…like a date. He didn't know what to say. He liked the girl. They were always friendly with each other. But he could have been knocked over with a feather. The invitation came totally out of left field.

On the other end of the line Donna waited nervously. She could feel her heart pumping, but tried to remain steady. There, she'd said it. She couldn't take it back now. All she could hope was that if he did turn down her offer he wouldn't think badly of her.

Powell smiled to himself. He decided to have some fun. Be a little mischievous. It had been a long while since he'd taken the opportunity to enjoy himself and partake of a little levity. He made his voice sound official. "Well Donna, I just got back from Breckridge…oh, about a half hour ago."

He mentioned that fact because if they were to take in a show, the nearest theater was over in Breckridge.

He thought he could hear Donna breathe a sigh through the receiver.

"Well," she then said, trying to keep her voice upbeat but not succeeding very well, "it—was just a suggestion. I just thought that you could use a little relaxation, and that it might not be something you'd think of for yourself."

Donna felt slightly proud of herself, believing she'd just cleverly slipped her way out of a potentially humiliating situation.

"That's very kind of you, Donna," Powell said appreciatively.

A moment of awkward silence on Donna's end. Powell waited patiently.

"Well…I don't suppose I should bother you any longer," Donna next said. "I know you've got a lot of things to do."

"Yes, I do," Powell said frankly. Then, after a deliberate pause, "What time should I pick you up?"

Donna sounded unsure. "Are you saying you'd *like* to go out with me?"

She could not see that Powell was grinning broadly on the other end. It had been so long since he'd allowed himself a genuine smile even *he* was unaware of the beaming expression on his face.

"Sure. A night out might be just what the doctor ordered," he told her.

"I can come by your office at six," Donna offered. "After I get off work."

"Sounds fine. You pick the show. And maybe we can grab ourselves a little something to eat in the city."

They said goodbye and Powell hung up the receiver. He leaned back in his chair and clasped his hands behind his neck. He wore a look of subtle bewilderment. He still couldn't quite figure out what had just happened…only that for the first time in a long while he felt he might be permitted to shed some of his professional constraints. In fact, he was feeling pretty damn good.

Then—just for a moment he experienced a pang of guilt. It had been fifteen months since he'd lost Cassidy, but he paused to question if he had done the right thing by accepting Donna Murray's invitation. But then after some deliberation he told himself he was only going out with a friend. He did need some relaxation—and certainly some fresh companionship besides Terry Reynolds, with whom he would occasionally loosen his collar and go bowling. He glanced upward and smiled, using that private moment to connect with his late wife. And he truly believed he could feel her presence, assuring Powell that she loved him and that she approved.

* * *

It didn't take Powell long to realize how much he had missed female companionship. And Donna was favorable company. They'd been acquainted with each other for several years, but until tonight they'd never really *known* each other. Donna was almost ten years younger than Powell and had a youthful, almost collegiate-type disposition, though Powell didn't feel old or ill-at-ease with her. That was because she also possessed a mature independence that she'd demonstrated when she made the call inviting Powell out this evening. In some indistinct way she also reminded Powell of Cassidy, even though there was nothing even remotely similar between them physically or even in personality. But Powell understood that strange comparison would probably come into play to some extent with almost any woman he might go out with.

They caught the 8:30 show at the Breckridge Cinema, munching on a shared tub of buttered popcorn, as they weren't going to grab a meal until after the movie. Donna seemed interested in the romantic comedy she had chosen and succumbed to bouts of laughter throughout the silly proceedings. Powell didn't find the picture particularly humorous, but faked a laugh at many of the scenes that amused Donna and the audience. By picture's end his throat hurt from all the phony laughter.

But he was grateful that for at least two hours he was able to give his brain a rest from police work, particularly trying to piece together the puzzle surrounding the recent murders, as well as his frustrating attempt to solve the mystery behind the suspect that everyone—yet no one—saw.

They had dinner at a small Italian restaurant. Powell had left the choice to Donna, hoping she wasn't given to extravagant tastes, and she said she was in the mood for a cheese and bacon pizza. Exactly what Powell could appreciate, and afford. They'd spotted the restaurant when they drove into Breckridge, located just about a block and a half from the theater. Donna suggested they walk. It was a clear night and the temperature was just right. A comfortable cool. Powell agreed and as they proceeded down the street, Donna hooked her arm around his. Powell felt himself stiffen only for an instant before he let himself relax. He asked her if she minded if he smoked. She said not at all. He offered her a cigarette. She looked tempted, but declined. Powell shook a Camel unfiltered from the pack, matched it, drew a few contented puffs and found himself wondering why he'd even considered giving up the habit.

Venetia Pizza had a dark, intimate, and decidedly romantic ambience. Each table was supplied with a candle in a glass jar centerpiece that emitted a gentle flickering glow. Soft Italian music wafted through the small dining area, which tonight seated only two other couples. If he'd had any doubt, Powell definitely now felt that he was on a date. He got the distinct impression that his companion had already decided that for herself.

Donna ordered a glass of Merlot and Powell asked for a domestic beer. After she studied the dinner menu Donna changed her meal preference and decided on a plate of chicken fettuccine. Powell didn't mind. He stayed with his choice of a medium cheese and bacon pizza. While they waited for their meal they chatted pleasantly. The night was turning out well, Powell thought. He hadn't felt this relaxed…well, he couldn't remember when. He also appreciated that Donna never mentioned or questioned him about his psoriasis. Tonight he was particularly self-conscious about his hairline and forehead lesions. If she did notice, which she would have to be blind not to, she was being tactful.

Powell pulled a long swallow from his beer, and then he said, "You went to college?"

Donna took a more delicate sip from her wine. "Mmmhmm," she answered in a purr. "But I didn't graduate. Got married instead." She sighed. "That didn't work out. Came back here and because I don't have a degree I work shifts at Gregg's Grill."

"You seem to enjoy your work," Powell commented. He grinned at her. "You're always cheerful and pleasant."

"I get paid for being cheerful and pleasant," Donna remarked, responding with a slightly enigmatic smile. "And that can sometimes be a chore."

"Imagine it could, dealing with people all day," Powell said, speaking for himself as well as her. He chose not to comment on that incident with the aggressive diner. He held his beer in both hands and focused on the bubbles as they rose to the surface of the glass. He then asked, "Ever think about going back and getting that degree?"

Donna shrugged. "Think about it. Probably won't ever do it, though. What about you?"

Powell looked amused. "Me?"

Donna nodded. "You go to college?"

Powell appeared to stifle a laugh. "Hardly. High school drifter. Completed the courses without having any idea where I was headed."

"So you became a policeman?"

Powell didn't really want the conversation to segue into that direction. "Not right away," he said.

"No?"

Powell set his beer down and picked up the napkin from the table and began fiddling with it. "No," he said, drawing out a sigh. "Guess you could say I did some globe-trotting first."

Donna cocked her head inquisitively.

"Well, as far as Southeast Asia," Powell clarified.

"Vietnam?" Donna said quietly.

Powell nodded slowly. "Cambodia." His voice sounded distant.

Donna regretted her questioning as she noticed how Powell became quiet and a strange expression appeared on his face. She could understand his reaction and apparent reticence to say anything more. Her mother's younger brother had served in that terrible conflict (he refused to refer to it as a "war"). He had, in fact, been captured by the Viet Cong and subjected to all manner of physical and psychological abuse during his long interment in a POW camp. While he survived, he was never the same man she remembered as a little girl. The playful twinkle was gone from his eye, replaced by a glassy emptiness. He seldom laughed, a forlorn smile seemed to be all he was capable of. Most of all, while she recalled how he would sometimes sit for hours in a strange solitude, as if reliving or trying to come to grips with what he had endured during those years, he would never discuss any of it. Donna came to learn how many veterans of that...*conflict* were reluctant to talk about their experiences and she determined that Powell was also of that mind.

The silence between them had become a little awkward. Unsure of what to say, but realizing she should shift the topic, she practically blurted, "Do you enjoy being a policeman?"

Powell squinted his eyes at her. He was both amused and a mite perturbed. It was kind of a sophomoric question. The type he would expect to be asked by kids in grade school during a career day. Donna probably hadn't paid it much attention, but Powell had left his police issue jacket back at the office and instead had thrown on his khaki overcoat. That was intentional. He didn't want anything to remind him that he was a cop tonight. Tomorrow and whatever professional problems might come along with it would arrive soon enough.

He returned her a slow smile in place of a reply. The waiter broke the silence between them, setting down a basket of breadsticks and asking if either wanted another drink. Donna declined but Powell said he'd like another beer. Once the waiter departed back into the kitchen Powell and Donna looked at each other. Donna's lips were pulled down in a slight frown. She'd gotten the distinct impression that Powell was not any more eager to discuss his job than he was to talk about his time as a soldier.

"Maybe I shouldn't have asked you that," she said apologetically. "Your job."

"Well, that is one subject I'd prefer not to talk about tonight," Powell admitted.

Donna could understand. She smiled a shy apology. She reached for a breadstick, snapped it in half and lathered both broken ends with a generous helping of butter. Powell was intrigued. The girl seemed to have quite an appetite yet still maintained a fine figure. Powell had seen Donna many times over the years, but this was the first time he'd really looked at her. She was attractive in an academic sort of way. Not "soft-pretty," as such, she had the appearance of a girl one might expect to find buried in a book at the library. Her shoulder-length brown hair was meticulously combed and parted to the side, the ends sweeping above the collar of her shirt in a slight curl. Her features, though lively when she smiled or laughed, as she did pretty much throughout that silly movie, could also settle into a more serious expression, as if she were in a contemplative or introspective frame of mind.

Donna appeared to be in that mood as she chewed thoughtfully on her piece of bread. She dabbed around her lips with her napkin and said, "I guess you must have been surprised when I called to ask you out."

Powell emitted an exaggerated exhale and rocked his head solidly. "Yes. I have to say I was."

"My intentions were wholly honorable," Donna joked straight-faced, raising the palm of her hand upright.

Powell lifted his half-empty glass of beer in a salute. "I wouldn't think otherwise."

And then they both became quiet. Over the muted flickering of the candle flame their eyes met and neither looked away from the other, both clearly absorbed with their own thoughts. Perhaps at the moment Donna's feelings were more apparent to Powell than Powell's mood was decipherable to her. Perhaps she should not even expect more. She had to remind herself that it had just been over a year since Powell lost his wife. And Donna knew how close the two had been. If truth be told, she envied and was even a little jealous of the togetherness they had shared. She could still sometimes recognize his melancholy when he came into the diner and sat off by himself. Occasionally she was sure she could even hear his wistful sigh. He might not yet feel ready to enter into another relationship. He might not even feel that *she* was the one he'd want to become involved with. Maybe it was better just to keep things simple for now.

She couldn't deny that she wanted to be with him. But he had to be the one to decide when—and if—the time was right.

CHAPTER SEVEN

One would have a difficult time finding a more dismal or foreboding place than Resurrection Gardens after the sun set and darkness accompanied by the lengthening shadows crept over the still, silent grounds. The atmosphere was so morbidly oppressive that come Halloween teenagers from Clear Vista and even from outside the town would dare each other to wander about what they disrespectfully referred to as "the boneyard," to maneuver 'round the gnarled trees and wretched tombstones in the old cemetery. To anyone's knowledge, no one had ever accepted the challenge, even if fortified with quantities of beer or other substances.

But even before and after late October, people kept their distance from the graveyard after nightfall. It was a blemish on the town's façade. Although many of the community past and present were buried there, it was never really accepted as an extension of Clear Vista. It existed as a separate entity, situated safely on the outskirts of town where no one had to give it much thought…except perhaps as an eventual "practical" consideration.

Yet…there was one man who didn't fear Resurrection Gardens. That was Caspar McGee, a grizzled, rarely sober former handyman employee of the town whose main work had been ensuring that the newer part of the cemetery was maintained, keeping the lawn trimmed, picking up carelessly-discarded trash, and helping with the opening and closing of graves. He did what he could with the old graveyard, but it was as if the property worked against him and, since no one really cared that much anyway, he finally gave up and let it fall deeper into ruin. The old man finally tired of his duties—even though they had been reduced to part time—and on the day he reached his sixty-fifth birthday he handed in his notice. He had earned a small pension and that was enough for him to get by on, living with minimal needs in a rooming house, so retirement was all right with him. For a few months he settled in his small room with his bottles of booze and his black and white portable television.

But he soon grew bored. He found he missed his old "haunt." He enjoyed the outdoors and the contentment that came with serving the dead. He had come to regard many of those residing underground as his "friends," those who wouldn't judge him for his so-called peculiarities, as others of a more critical personality did, and he would stop by familiar plots to talk to the departed. People in the community often stumbled upon this bizarre sight, but most knew old McGee was somewhat tetched in the head anyhow—helped along by his fondness for drink—and, while keeping their distance, they let him ramble on.

Caspar McGee was troubled tonight. Bothered that someone had used his tool shed to murder two young girls. What's worse was that he was considered a suspect and had been hauled in for questioning, as if anyone could think that *he* would harm a child. Why, he was immensely fond, no, he could truthfully say that he adored children. He'd fumed about this and tonight, after some stiff fortification from his cheap whiskey, he decided he was going to head out to the graveyard and see if he might be able to seek out some clues as to the perpetrator's identity. Maybe he'd get even luckier, if the cowardly killer had the audacity to return to the scene of his crime. Hell, he might collect himself a reward if he could give the cops a good lead on the suspect.

Sure, that was the motivation he needed. Why, he'd wait out the whole night if that was what he had to do. He was a-feared of no man.

It was just getting on for 11:30 when he parked his rusted pickup on the gravel side road and unlocked the gate of the old cemetery using his personal key that he'd had cut at his own expense and that he never bothered to turn in to the town with his other "official" set. He then staggered onto the property, gripping the flashlight in his unsteady fingers. Gray clouds scudded across the black tapestry of night, gusts of winds beginning to whip through the barren branches of the trees, howling and whistling, ghostly sounds that would raise a shiver of dread in most people but were familiar to McGee. Once in a while he'd hear the quick scurrying into the bush of some small night creature, searching for food or returning to the protection of its shelter. As occasionally happened when the cool air from Buchanan Bay settled, a faint low-lying mist blanketed the ground. Aged monuments and ruined tombstones were silhouetted in the moonlight.

"Just so's yuh know, I'm here waitin' for yuh," McGee announced in a slurred voice as he settled into the shadows, propping himself up against a tree, bottle in hand, with a view of the tool shed.

He waited for nearly an hour, finishing his bottle and, after shaking out the last few drops onto his tongue, tossing it aside with disgust. Without a drink to keep him company he quickly grew bored and restless. And even a mite forgetful as to why he'd come out here. Finally a bit of common sense penetrated his blurred consciousness and he realized that what he was doing made little sense and was likely a waste of time.

"Ain't no preevert gonna be comin' back here tonight," he grumbled. He struggled to pull himself to his feet and once upright, he staggered away. There were only a few stars out this night and with the moon now shadowed behind drifting cloud cover, the cemetery grounds were nearly pitch dark. The whitish beam from his flashlight that speared into the blackness was starting to fade. And soon the light was extinguished. McGee had forgot to pop in new batteries. But he wasn't concerned. He knew these grounds as well as he knew the shelves of the liquor store and could navigate his way out of the cemetery—drunk or sober. He managed to maintain his balance, barely, and began to sing some forgotten ditty, lowly, under his breath.

He wandered about for a bit until he halted, swayed uncertainly for a moment, glanced around and pulled off his cap to scratch the wisps of hair on his scalp. He was still in the cemetery all right, but, "Sonofagun, I got m'self all turned 'round."

The dark and all the liquor he had consumed had thrown McGee off his bearings. He frowned as his bewhiskered old head lolled. He was absorbing the chill that permeated the night air as well as feeling the slap of the wind, gusting strongly if intermittently, that whipped the fallen dry autumn leaves into a skipping frenzy across the grounds, and he wrapped his ragged old denim jacket tightly around himself.

"Damn well don't wanta sleep out here," he muttered. He walked on a little farther, hoping to find a vantage point he could recognize and follow out of the graveyard. He'd worked at Resurrection Gardens for years, but until now had never been aware of just how large the cemetery was—or at least how large it seemed when one couldn't find his way out. He reached into the breast pocket of his plaid shirt and withdrew the butt of a cigar. He fumbled with a match to light it, then took several hurried puffs. He figured that maybe the glow from the tip of the stogie might give him a little needed light.

The clouds passed by the moon and suddenly it once more shone full and bright, as round and as brilliant as a silver disc, spreading a haunting light that illuminated McGee's path. He quickly glanced about and recognized where he was, in the children's section of the cemetery. Heavenly Angels. The only place in all of Resurrection Gardens where he never felt entirely comfortable. McGee had never married, was never blessed with kids of his own, but even though most children in Clear Vista avoided him (probably because of their parents' influence, he reckoned), his affection for youngsters made him dread each time he had to open and close a plot of earth in Heavenly Angels.

Although his vision was fuzzy and the light in the distance muted, McGee detected what he thought was a movement over by one of the children's graves. He gave his head a shake and strained his eyes to try and get a better, clearer look.

He wasn't mistaken. Sure enough, there was someone on the grounds. Too late for a visitor, he determined. It had to be a trespasser. *Who the hell trespassed into a graveyard after dark?* he asked himself. The answer came to him suddenly. *Why sure, who else could it be?* It had to be that phantom stalker. McGee held himself back, watching. He resisted the brief, passing urge to call out. But all of his earlier bravado had dissipated along with those final drops of whiskey. In fact, he found himself sobering up rather quickly. Maybe he really hadn't believed he would encounter someone at the cemetery tonight. But he had, and he was looking directly at whoever that was.

And he could not make himself believe it was some whiskey-enforced hallucination.

But if he could somehow get a good look, without making himself seen, that might be all he'd need to give to the police and earn himself that reward he believed would be due him. For the first time in a long while he wished that he were just a little less drunk and a bit more sober.

He had to be careful. Very careful. Not move too fast. If he was spotted, that person might panic and run off. He avoided thinking of what else could possibly happen should he be seen.

"Don't know what I was thinkin'," McGee mumbled under his breath. "Shoulda brung my gun."

He scolded himself for his questionable priorities. He'd brought along a bottle of whiskey but had left his .38 in a drawer in his room.

The figure was indistinct, almost wraith-like, but appeared to be dressed all in black. Outside of flashes of gray that McGee distinguished each time a movement caught the moonlight, the shape's vague silhouette blended into the starkness of the nocturnal backdrop.

McGee also saw that the figure appeared to be wearing a long, loose garment that swirled around its tall, lean form each time a strong gust of wind swept across the open ground. The features, though, were obscured both by the night shadows and a long, pointed hood that covered the head.

McGee was puzzled and starting to grow uneasy. The scenario became even more peculiar and disturbing. Of a sudden the cloaked figure had begun a very strange series of movements, as if the hands were performing some strange ritual over one particular grave.

And then...*voices*, children's voices, emanating from somewhere in the distance, yet from no specific source, conversing among one another, the words faint, whispered, oftentimes voiced in a sing-song. Indiscernible, yet eerie and strangely ominous.

It was all too much for the old man. He sensed a sinister presence standing yonder and he did not want to risk being noticed by it. He tossed his cigar to the ground and stamped his foot on the butt, extinguishing the dim glow and scattering tiny embers that quickly sparked out. He took careful steps backward, trying to envelope himself entirely in the protection of the dark—then he turned, stumbled over his own shoe, scrambled back to his feet and half-ran, half-staggered as far away from Heavenly Angels as his feet would take him.

At the gravesite the black-robed figure completed the ritual and held still. Very still. And then the figure began to utter a deep-throated, yet whispery chanting. It got down on its knees and gently placed both chalky white hands atop the grass-sprouting mound of sod covering the grave, splaying the abnormally long and slender, almost skeletal fingers to their widest separation. There was a hissing…and a slight smoldering from where the palms pressed.

A silence.

Stillness.

And presently there came a faint pulsing from within the earth.

CHAPTER EIGHT

Walter Stromm thundered into the kitchen. He thumped his impressive bulk over to the cabinet where the liquor was stored and poured himself a tall, stiff drink of bourbon that he wasted no time tossing back. He'd had another all-out argument with his wife Barbara and he was fed up. The woman just could never see it his way. Certainly he was preoccupied with business matters. If that was not so she wouldn't be living in an exclusive neighborhood in one of the most beautiful bungalows in Clear Vista. But all she did was complain that if he wasn't spending all day at the office he was at home locked in his study conducting business on the telephone. The problem as Stromm saw it was that she didn't have enough to keep her occupied and relied on him to provide her with entertainment. And *that* he could blame on himself. He'd made it too damn easy for her. She didn't have to do housework. The three-times-a-week maid handled that chore. She had no interest in gardening, so a man was hired to come over once a week to help with the maintenance of the sprawling yard. He tried to encourage her to join a woman's club or volunteer with a local charity, but whenever he made the suggestion, that was when she became quiet.

Stromm leaned against the counter and loosened his necktie with a flourish of frustration. Then he poured himself another generous glass of bourbon. A few more swallows and his resentment eased and he started to mellow out. Oh, he knew what the problem was. Barbara had never been the same since their daughter Margaret was killed in that hit and run. Once again, Stromm's features grew taut and his ruddy expression reddened even more as he remembered that day. Damn fool girl, he thought. A huge yard to play in and she chooses to go near the road with her friends and chase out onto the street after a ball. Some crazy punk kid rammed into her and dragged her for half a block before he panicked and sped off. Chief Powell happened to be on patrol that day and managed to chase the kid down before he could disappear onto the coastal highway. One that he owed Powell, Stromm thought impassively.

Stromm was a man who rarely accepted blame and so did not think it wrong when he faulted his daughter more for the accident than the driver of that Camaro. *There simply was no need for her to have left the yard,* he reasoned.

Barbara knew how he felt and this added to the tension between them. Although she never dared to express her feelings at the time, she considered her husband to be hardhearted and uncaring. She could never forget how not once did he shed a tear at the loss of their daughter, or did much to comfort her as she dealt with her grief. And as a mother she also struggled with her own guilt. She should have been paying more attention to Margaret that day. She should not have assumed she was playing in the yard with her little friends.

Should have...*should have*... such useless, hopeless words, but they preyed on her mind incessantly.

She felt alone—and she *hated* being alone—when all of those thoughts would descend upon her and overwhelm her, tightening their grip on her misery. And there was never any compassion or support from her husband. His world was his own and she had come to exist in it only on the most extreme periphery. His routine catered only to himself. He preferred to come home, wolf down a quick dinner and then sequester himself in his office to carry on with his business affairs.

Now tonight she had finally had enough. She told her husband outright that she was leaving him. She didn't care about the fancy house and all the possessions Stromm had given her through the years. The jewelry and costly trinkets were a meaningless gesture from him, and she valued them as little as the thought that went into their purchase. They were merely meant to appease her, keep her quiet and docile, like tossing a milk bone to a disobedient dog.

Stromm hardly even acknowledged her when Barbara told him of her intentions. It was just more drama, at which his wife had become an expert. And when her words finally did penetrate, he simply gave her an amused, patronizing look and turned away. She half-expected him to pat her on the head and tell her to be a good girl. There was a time when she would have succumbed to his condescending attitude, because she had been meek and afraid. She knew her husband had a temper, and he was a big man. But lately she had stood up to him and tonight when Stromm saw that she was serious and not about to back down, the argument erupted.

Very few people dared to stand up to Walter Stromm, not business associates, not the few "true" friends that he had in his circle. Even in the privacy of his home Stromm's pride would not allow him to be challenged. Not by a woman—particularly the wife he supported. Despite his bouncer-like physique, he was not a physical man, but his sheer presence was daunting and his voice intimidating when raised in anger.

The argument ended as it usually did. Stromm's booming shouts drowned out his wife's words and finally, in frustrated defeat, Barbara turned and walked off to another part of the house, her husband's shouting still ringing in her ears.

Stromm watched her go, heard the slam of a door, then he went into the kitchen to pour himself that relaxing glass of bourbon.

As his mood calmed, he allowed himself a self-satisfied smile. He had to wonder if the day would come when Barbara ever would leave him. He was a man who did not have a strong grasp on human psychology. All he could recognize in his dollars-and-cents mentality was that it was unlikely she'd ever walk away from the perks his bank account had provided her.

Threats. All threats, he told himself once again. But his lips tightened and his beady eyes narrowed as he then considered that if these outbursts went on for much longer Barbara wouldn't have to leave. He'd throw her out. He had enough to deal with tending to his business affairs—particularly a big leasing deal he'd been working on that now might be compromised because of what happened to those two girls.

Pathetic little urchins, letting themselves be carted off by some…murderous *transient* who none of the idiots in town even took the trouble to get a decent description of when he was out walking among them.

Stromm finished his drink and glanced at the kitchen wall clock. It was past midnight. Too late to get any more calls done. He might as well go to bed—alone—and get a fresh start in the morning.

CHAPTER NINE

If she did not think it might seem somewhat inappropriate, Donna would have invited Chief Powell to come inside her apartment for a cup of coffee. Her intentions would have been genuine—coffee, nothing more—but she resisted because she wasn't sure how Powell might interpret the offer. She didn't want him to think she was being too forward and might have another motive in mind. She couldn't know for certain how he was coping with his loss and that might still be a sensitive area he wasn't yet ready to have someone encroach upon. He didn't speak much of his wife and children that night—only a couple of brief mentions—but each time he did Donna could detect the shadow of pain in his voice and on his expression.

She understood. And by the time their date was over she came to accept that their relationship might just have to be kept on a friendship basis.

It was after midnight. They were sitting in the car outside of her apartment building preparing to say their goodnights to each other. The breeze that blew in from Buchanan Bay had chilled the night air. Powell kept the windows rolled up and refrained from lighting the cigarette he was craving. For the first time that night he felt a little awkward. They'd had a wonderful evening. After their Italian meal they drove to a little roadhouse just off the highway, equidistance between Breckridge and Clear Vista where they had a couple of beers and listened to the country band Kenny Carlyle and The Stompers. They weren't able to get much talking done as the group played their music full volume.

A little loud for Powell, but Donna got into it, foot-tapping away with the beat. He could tell that she would have welcomed him asking her for a dance, but Powell never could get into cowboy music. Not to mention he could hardly dance a step.

But now their night was over and Powell wasn't sure what was in order, a kiss goodnight…or maybe a polite handshake.

Donna prided herself on her perceptiveness, enhanced no doubt from her years of working with people, and she could read into Powell's predicament. She decided to make it easy for him. She leaned her body sideways and kissed him gently on the cheek.

And then she ventured, "I hope we can do this again sometime."

Powell pivoted his head toward her. He smiled and said gently yet without commitment, "I'd like that."

Donna gave her head a brisk nod and started to exit the car. Powell hesitated, debating whether their "date" should end on that note…or should he risk another potentially awkward moment and offer to see her to the doorstep? Well, he figured, if nothing else no one could accuse him of not being a gentleman. His hand reached for the door latch.

Donna again made it easy for him. "Oh no, don't bother," she said. "Just up the walkway."

"You sure?" Powell asked, quietly grateful that she declined his offer.

Donna rocked her head a couple of times. But maybe a little too briskly.

Powell shut his door. "Okay. But I'll sit here and wait 'til you get inside."

Donna smiled and gave another nod.

She walked with swift steps up the thin stretch of pavement and retrieved her apartment key from her handbag. Before she entered the building, she halted, slowly turned back to the car and gave a wave. Powell waved back at her. But once she was safely inside he didn't immediately drive away. He sat in the car for several minutes, thinking.

To help sort out his thoughts he indulged himself in that cigarette he'd been holding off on since leaving the roadhouse. He needed those first few relaxing drags. Because now that the pleasantness of the evening was over, it was back to reality. And with that came an uncertainty. Only this one took on a different complexion. He wasn't sure if he was ready to move forward into a relationship. It wasn't anything against Donna—in fact, under different circumstances he could see the two of them going on future dates. It wasn't even the memory of Cassidy or combating the guilt that still could haunt him. No, what stalled him was a practical consideration. He had to keep himself focused. He had the responsibility of the murder investigation, a crime that had filled his community with such dread, and perhaps had even stirred a mounting suspicion among his fellow citizens. He'd allowed himself these hours of relaxation tonight. They were necessary, he needed a diversion, but otherwise the investigation had to remain a priority. Unfortunately, he was still at a dead end not only in tracking the murderer, but even in securing a clue as to who he might be. He still hadn't totally abandoned the possibility that the killer could be someone living in the town. He didn't have a suspect in that regard, but that didn't mean that a Clear Vista resident everyone was familiar with wasn't hiding a dark, twisted secret. After all, who would ever have thought that nice Ida Krevich could have done what she'd done to her boy Larry? There wasn't so much as a scratch of doubt in Powell's mind that that "churchgoing, community-spirited lady" had not only gotten away with murder, but likely long periods of abuse beforehand.

Still, as was pointed out to him by members of the town council, to cast any suspicion upon a citizen of Clear Vista was a delicate matter. One that could have serious repercussions to the community—and to himself, if he actively pursued this avenue only to discover that it was a blind alley.

Powell absently studied the orange glow at the tip of his cigarette and pondered until he came to the conclusion that getting involved with someone now would only prove a distraction…and depending on whatever it was that he was up against, might also become dangerous for anyone close to him. Whoever this murderer was, he was a certified psychopath. Powell understood that someone cold-blooded enough to brutally murder two eight-year-old girls would have no hesitation about killing anyone else if he felt threatened, and until he was caught or, preferably, exterminated like the vermin he was, no one was safe.

What concerned Powell was if the killer knew that he was on his trail he might use any tactic to prevent him from pursuing his investigation. Powell could take care of himself, he had no concern there, but it wasn't sensible for him to add to his worries by putting someone else in jeopardy.

And if that was a selfish motive, he couldn't overlook another consideration. He'd suffered a tragic loss in his life, one for which he blamed himself. He could not add to the guilt he already carried by being responsible for another misfortune.

But he could not deny that for one crazy moment he had almost surrendered to another impulse. The urge to rush out of the car and follow Donna into her apartment and fulfill that natural human need which he had not experienced for so long. Since before that night when Cassidy left him. Donna had left the door open, if not literally than certainly figuratively—at least how he interpreted it. He could admit that he'd struggled with holding himself back since both had left the restaurant, the urge intensifying after their stop at the roadhouse. He wanted not only to touch her, but to hold her and he didn't dance with her at the roadhouse not only because he had all the grace of a hayseed, but sharing that time with her in such a sexually-charged setting would only strengthen the desire that he knew had to be kept in restraint.

He released his frustration with a tight, single utterance, "*Damn.*"

Powell finished his cigarette. He'd been so caught up in trying to work out his thoughts that he was hardly aware he'd smoked the cigarette to the filter, close to where he risked burning his fingers. He quickly rolled down the window to toss out the butt and to let some fresh air inside the vehicle. A shimmer of smoke drifted out into the night. He shifted the car into gear and slowly pulled away from the curb, glancing out the passenger window to see if Donna might still be watching him from inside the building.

She wasn't.

CHAPTER TEN

At 2:14 a.m. Stromm awoke with a start, eyes wide and staring up at the heavy beams that crossed the arched ceiling above his head. His immediate awareness was of the breeze that wafted through the screen door that opened onto the shaded patio and the faint, transparent shaft of moonlight that streamed into the bedroom through the window glass. But in the next instant his heavy body strained forward as he sat upright in his bed.

Was that a scream he had heard? A scream—or a shriek—emanating from somewhere in the house that had aroused him from his slumber? He considered with concern. He felt chilled and uneasy. And then he gradually calmed himself. He was a sensible man. A dream. Yes, just a dream—though for the life of him he had no recollection of what dream could have caused him to react with such an immediate sense of panic.

He settled back onto the mattress, turned onto his side—and his brow furrowed. Barbara was not beside him. A moment of uncertainty before he once more relaxed himself with the thought that she was probably still in her pout and had decided once again to sleep on the couch in the den.

Well, fine, he thought as he lifted himself onto an elbow and plumped up his pillow.

Although he tried, he wasn't able to immediately get back to sleep. Instead, and inexplicably, a strange sensation came over him. His ears were alert, abnormally attuned, it seemed, and he listened carefully. The house was very quiet.

Too quiet, it seemed. Even at this late hour.

The silence rang heavy in his ears. And all of a sudden, it sounded…strangely ominous. A quiet that somehow wasn't a quiet.

It was then that he heard the soft padding of footsteps across the hallway floor, moving toward the bedroom. But as he listened more closely he detected that the footfalls sounded peculiar. Not quite a shuffling, but slow, unsteady—almost a step-heavy dragging…yet light against the carpeting. As if it were a small child coming his way.

A groan. A deep, unsettling groan . . .

"Barbara…is that you?" Stromm said in a whisper.

No answer, though the muffled steps were getting nearer to the open door. Suddenly the hall light switched on. Stromm maneuvered his body into a half-sitting position and focused on the open doorway. His eyes lowered as he saw the faint blob of a shadow…an indistinct dark outline against the carpet that started to lengthen. Enlarge.

And that was when the shadow took form.

The "thing" that once had been his daughter, Margaret, hit and killed by a reckless driver eight months ago, stood before him in the doorway, her small body twitching spasmodically. In fingers ripe with decay she limply held onto the dolly, now moist and soiled, that her mother had tenderly placed into the casket with her. The other arm swung listlessly at her side, the fingers hooked into a claw. As she stepped awkwardly into the muted glow of the moon-spilled light, Walter Stromm, to his unimaginable horror, could see her all too clearly. His throat constricted and suddenly he found it difficult to breathe. What breaths he could manage came shallowly.

Her pink burial dress was discolored, mossy and befouled by the damp earth of the grave in which her corpse had lain. As her complexion was now free of the pasty undertaking cosmetics, her flesh was exposed gray and in the process of rapid decomposition, patchy and peeling from the strands of fat and muscle fiber underneath. The soft curls of her ashen hair that had been perfectly styled for her funeral were loose, stringy and hanging at the sides of her head in a lifeless tangle. Her head lolled lazily on a stem of a neck. The stench of putrefaction accompanied her presence, wafting heavily into the bedroom and assailing Stromm's nostrils.

The expression on her face was dull, vapid, her eyes sunken into their sockets, glazed and dim, as if she had just come awake from a long, deep, exaggerated slumber. Soon, slowly, the lips moved, the thin wire embalming clamps that held the mouth closed snapped open with a soft, dry *ping* and as the lower jaw went slack a yellow fluid spattered out with the effort. It trickled thickly down her chin. She gurgled and then emitted a slow, unearthly groan that seemed to echo from deep within her throat.

"Da..."

And the words that she struggled to speak finally came, emanating as if she were speaking through a mouthful of grit.

"Daddy...where...were...you...and Mommy..." the dead girl said plaintively. Stromm could almost recognize the voice as belonging to his daughter, though the cadence was distant and mournful.

"...when I woke up?"

Stromm was too numb even to attempt to speak. His chest tightened as if a sudden weight had been placed upon it. His breathing became even more labored. With effort, he drew himself higher in the bed, not believing that any of this could be real.

Yet he was fully awake. It *was* real. All too real.

The dead girl's mouth twisted downward in an exaggerated grimace, then her lips lifted as she (*it*) struggled to speak more. Her words were preceded by another deep, guttural groan.

"It was dark...and cold...and you...and Mommy...weren't there."

Stromm could only mouth the word, "Mommy?"

"Why did you . . . leave me alone . . . in that bad place?"

Stromm's heart began to pump so fast and desperately that he could feel it reverberate like a physical echo.

"I...was scared."

Again, that terrible moan that ripped into Stromm's soul.

"Mommy...got scared too...I...wanted...to hug her."

She twisted her body with a stiff sudden jolt, her head now swaying uncertainly on her neck.

"She got...so scared."

Stromm shook his head, stiffly. His fingers skittered across his chest.

"She got...so scared. Only wanted . . . to hug her."

And the dead girl began to shamble toward the bed where Stromm lay cringing, petrified with fear, his face and torso soaked with sweat and his pajamas wet with urine that bled from a bladder he could no longer control.

Her tottering corpse, clots of dirt falling from her dress, once more dissolving into a shadow in the shaft of blackness.

Stromm's beady eyes grew into saucers. The shadowy form was getting nearer to his side of the bed.

"Isn't...that funny...Daddy?" she said dully. *"I...scared mommy."*

Closer...

"Hug me...Daddy."

She let the dolly fall from the grip of her upturned hand and she slowly raised both of her arms, each quavering, as if afflicted with a palsy, seeking an embrace.

Stromm couldn't bear to look at her. The next time she came into the light she would be standing right in front of his face, and whatever "horror" this was—this ghastly night visitor—he would not accept that it could be his daughter. Some apparition. Some unholy thing. Maybe even some madness that had taken hold of his mind.

But not his little girl!

His hands trembling, he started to draw the sheets up over his head, to put himself in a place where he tried to convince himself he would be protected and spared this living nightmare.

"Daddy…aren't you glad…to…see me?"

As he lay cowering under the sheets Walter Stromm's mouth widened and he wanted to scream.

"Why won't you…hug me?"

But as Stromm felt her cold, dead presence next to him, his throat locked even tighter and no sound—not even a whimper—escaped his lips. As his heart prepared to thump out its final beats he no longer possessed the strength to resist.

"Hug me…Daddy!"

Determined gnarled fingers gripped at the material and began to pull the sheets down from his face…

CHAPTER ELEVEN

Walter Stromm followed a strict routine. Six days a week he arrived at his office promptly at 8 o'clock a.m. He was a man who thrived on work and didn't allow a single minute to be wasted. He might on some days come in earlier, but never later, unless he had a meeting to attend or needed to be out at a site. Therefore when 8:30 rolled around, then nine o'clock, and her boss still hadn't arrived, his secretary, Norma Cullington, dialed the number to his house. She silently hoped that if he were still at home that he would be the one to pick up the receiver. Norma always detected a coolness whenever she had to speak with his wife. Barbara Stromm was an odd woman, and had gotten more so following the death of their little girl. Norma got the distinct impression that Barbara suspected there might be a little hanky-panky going on between her and her boss, probably because they spent so much time together and Stromm was known to frequently put in late nights at the office.

Barbara's concern could not have been more wrong. Norma and Walter Stromm shared only a strictly professional relationship. She could say in all truthfulness that her boss had never once so much as suggested an office or after-hours tryst. His sole interest was in expanding his portfolio. And Norma was glad for that. Physically, Walter Stromm held no appeal to her; in fact, if she were to be completely honest, she found him crude and rather repulsive. In addition, Norma had at least a good five years on the man.

Norma sat with the receiver pressed against her ear and listened to eight rings. No answer. She tried several more times, and by the time 9:30 came she decided something was not right and, while hoping that she wasn't acting in haste, she put in a call to the police.

But she was concerned, and perhaps with reason. Barbara's possible suspicions about the two of them aside, she knew of the other troubles her boss had been having with his wife. Norma was the only person in town whom Stromm would confide in concerning such matters. She had been with Stromm's firm since the day he went into business for himself and began putting together his own real estate and development deals, and Stromm had come to trust her more than anyone else—and that included his wife.

In her position with the company there was no way Norma could not be in the know about some of her boss's questionable business practices and she frequently felt a tug of conscience when she saw the oft-times tricky maneuvers Stromm employed in his various dealings. *She knew where the bodies were buried*, as it were. But overriding any pangs of guilt was the fact that Walter Stromm had given her a well-paying job at a time when she was in a desperate situation. Her husband had been killed in a freak construction mishap in Breckridge, leaving no insurance outside of a meager company accident payout, and three young children for Norma to raise by herself—and to this day she felt she owed Stromm a debt of loyalty. Stromm knew it, too, which was why he felt he could confide in her. Under any other circumstance he would never give of his trust so freely.

It was Terry Reynolds who answered the telephone at police headquarters. Norma kept her voice calm, as was her nature, but Reynolds noted a hint of subdued apprehension in her tone. He assured her that he would check it out. He then dialed Chief Powell's home number. Powell had just dried off from the shower and was getting into his uniform when he picked up the receiver from the phone in his bedroom. When Reynolds told him of Norma Cullington's call, Powell was not particularly concerned. If there was one person who could take care of himself it was Walter

Stromm. By the same token, if there was one person he could care less if he took care of himself it was Walter Stromm.

"Well, she did say it's not like her boss," Reynolds mentioned to the chief. "Says he's a man who adheres to a strict pattern. Precisely timetables even his lunch hours."

Powell did not have to be told that. He drew a breath that came through loud and clear on the other end of the line.

"All right," he said. "Why don't you go check it out, Terry?"

Reynolds sounded mildly hesitant. "And if there's nothing's wrong…" The truth was he was no different from a lot of the people in town and was a little timid of direct contact with Stromm, and was not particularly eager to deal with the man if it turned out there was no reason for concern.

"Handle it," Powell said shortly. He hung up, smiled to himself, and finished getting dressed.

By the time Powell got to the office the phone was ringing relentlessly. Powell frowned. *Yeah, this day's getting off to a great start*, he thought with self-justified sarcasm. Not even the chance to brew some coffee.

Powell picked up the receiver. Before he could get out "Clear Vista Police—" he heard Reynolds's voice on the other end.

"Better get over here right away, Chief," the officer said, sounding urgent, and even a little frantic.

Powell had never heard that tone in Reynolds. He was concerned but responded evenly. "What's up?"

"Just—get over here," Reynolds repeated.

"Okay, calm down," Powell said. "Just tell me what—"

"They're—dead, both of them," Reynolds stammered.

There were a few seconds of quiet on the other end before Reynolds heard Powell utter, *"Dead?"*

"Stromm…and his wife."

"I'll be right there," Powell told him before slamming down the receiver.

The next hours passed by as if in a surrealistic blur. When Powell arrived at the country-style bungalow on Kensington Road he found Terry Reynolds pacing outside on the doorstep. As Powell walked toward him he noticed that the young patrolman also seemed to be trembling. Whatever he'd come upon inside the house had affected him so badly that he couldn't seem to get a grip on himself. Reynolds wasn't what Powell would call a seasoned police officer, but he was trained in dealing with all types of situations and Powell expressed disapproval at what he perceived as the man's unprofessional conduct.

Reynolds was apologetic. "I—I'm sorry, Chief. I hadda come outside. I—just can't look at them."

Powell nodded vacantly. "I put in a call to Breckridge," he said. "The medical examiner should be out in about an hour." He gave Reynolds a steely stare. "You gonna be all right to come back inside?"

No, he was *not* going to be all right. But Reynolds couldn't admit that truth. His behavior had apparently already disappointed the police chief.

"Take a minute first, if you need," Powell told him, and not too delicately. This was a police matter and he didn't need a cop falling apart on him. "Where are they?"

Reynolds took a rattled breath. He was making a gallant effort to steady himself. "Woman's in the kitchen. He…he's…in the bedroom."

Powell turned to the door.

"Chief," Reynolds then said. "When I got here…both front and patio doors were locked. No sign of any forced entry."

Powell cocked an eyebrow. "How'd you get in?"

"Only way I could. Through the patio. Had to cut a hole in the screen to open the latch. That's when I walked into the bedroom and saw—"

Powell halted him. "Okay. Just come inside when you're ready. But don't take too long."

"And Chief…there's one more thing," Reynolds added. He spoke uneasily. "I found something on the floor in the bedroom. I didn't touch it, it's still there. Thing is…I can't make sense of it."

Powell shot him an impatient look. "Well, what is it?"

Reynolds hesitated for just a moment. "A doll."

"A doll?" Powell echoed.

Reynolds rocked his head in a nod. "A child's doll."

Powell considered momentarily before he lifted his shoulder in a "So what?" gesture. Nothing particularly unusual about that. Walter and Barbara did have a daughter. Naturally they might have kept some of her toys after her death.

Reynolds elucidated. "It's just that…what's strange is that there's this…mud spread throughout the house."

Powell gave an inquisitive look.

"Not topsoil," Reynolds explained. "It's moist and has a claylike texture, as if pulled or dug up from under the ground. What's more, the doll is also soiled with it."

Powell regarded Reynolds with a mildly interested expression before he opened the front door that Reynolds had unlocked when he'd exited the house in a hurry, and went inside. Of a sudden he was a little wary himself. Reynolds's attitude had unnerved him sufficiently to put him on his guard. He didn't know what exactly he was walking into. Or what precisely he could expect to find.

He glanced about the large living room. He'd never been invited to Stromm's house and had no idea that the inside was so large and spacious and expensively furnished. He suppressed his momentary envy when he remembered it was strongly suspected that most of Stromm's wealth had been earned through devious business practices and outright bribery and corruption.

Powell stepped out of the main room into the kitchen, where he halted abruptly as he glanced down at the floor. He puffed out a slow, heavy breath.

Barbara Stromm was dead all right. She lay as a corpse in the sun-bright kitchen. But that wasn't the worst of it. What Powell found disturbing was the look of horror that distorted her features, the odd rigor mortis that had frozen her arms in what looked like a reaching grasp, fingers curled into clutching claws. A most curious and unnatural death pose. As if in those final moments of her life she'd been clutching or trying to grab at something.

Once Powell recovered from this initial shock he lowered to his haunches and took a quick study of the body, seeking any obvious signs of violence—none of which he could detect. No blood. There appeared to be no physical trauma—outside of that twisted expression on her face. If Powell had to hazard a guess based on the condition of the body, he would say—as farfetched as it seemed—that Barbara Stromm looked to have been frightened to death. Once more he steadied himself. There was still Walter Stromm to check out. Powell walked out of the kitchen, through the living room and down the long hallway. He became aware that he was walking with slow, heavy, almost tentative steps and with embarrassment he realized that while he had been quick to criticize Reynolds, at this moment he was not faring much better himself.

He finally reached the bedroom. He hesitated for a moment…and then he turned into the room.

He froze just inside the doorway. What he saw inside the room was even more shocking than the scene in the kitchen. A terrifying tableau. Stromm was lying as still as a stone in his bed, his corpse rigid. His head was peeking out from under the covers which he clutched with stiff, bloodless fingers. His face was also unnaturally contorted, the eyes, though glazed and sightless, were wide and bulging and looked as stricken with fright as did his wife's.

"Jesus Christ…" Powell muttered under his breath. He stood unmoving for several moments.

A hand fell upon Powell's shoulder and he reacted with a start. He spun around to face Reynolds.

"*Jesus Christ*!" he said again, this time as an exclamation.

"Sorry, Chief," Reynolds apologized quickly.

Powell patted the young man's shoulder as he regained his breath and damn near his equilibrium.

"What the hell happened here?" Powell asked rhetorically, his words a near-whisper.

Reynolds pointed a finger over to the far side of the bed, where the mud-smudged doll lay. Powell walked over to the toy while Reynolds held back, hesitant to step back inside the room to get another look at Walter Stromm's hideous corpse. Powell took a moment to take a brief, closer study of the body before he turned away from it, trying to conceal his own unease. He then removed a cloth from his pocket and carefully picked up the doll by one of its dangling arms. He stepped back outside the room to Reynolds.

"Pretty rough condition," he commented as he examined the toy, turning it over slowly in his hand and scraping off with a fingernail some of the mud clinging to it. He wore a perplexed expression but presented a simple observation. "Looks like it's been left outside for a while."

"Think it means anything?" Reynolds asked.

"The dirt or the doll?"

Reynolds gave a vague lift of his shoulder.

Powell didn't have an answer other than, "Bag it and we'll send it over to the crime lab in Breckridge. Maybe they can tell us something."

"Fingerprints?"

"Maybe," Powell said with a shrug.

"You don't sound too hopeful."

Powell responded with a blank look. He frankly didn't know where to begin and where this investigation would lead him.

They searched the house thoroughly, but all that seemed out of the ordinary was the doll and scattered patches of damp, sticky mud that were found in the kitchen, the hallway, and in the bedroom. Not much to go on, but indications that at some point during the night someone else had been in the house besides the Stromms. The question was…had this person been familiar to the couple and been invited inside? At the moment that seemed the likely scenario since that would account for the locked doors and no sign of forced entry. A visitor known to both who had come with a sinister agenda. But *what*…and *how*?

A dusting for fingerprints would later turn up no other prints than those belonging to Stromm and his wife. Hardly an overwhelming surprise to Chief Powell.

The coroner, Dr. Rice Arborshaw, came out of the bedroom where he'd done a preliminary examination on Walter Stromm's body before it was prepared to be sent along with his wife's corpse to the hospital in Breckridge where the autopsies would be performed. He met with Powell in the living room.

Powell noticed how as Arborshaw walked toward him his features betrayed no emotion at witnessing the gruesome conditions of the bodies. But, interestingly, he did detect a slight paleness to his complexion.

"I'm asking myself if there might be some connection between what happened here and the murder of the Loewen girls," Powell mused aloud.

Arborshaw eyed him directly and spoke in a straightforward manner. "This doesn't appear to be a murder." And then he drew his lips down in a frown. "At least not the way we would define it."

"Meaning?" Powell queried with a creasing of his brow.

"No outward sign of injuries on either of the bodies," Arborshaw replied. "Of course my examination was only of a preliminary nature. An autopsy should tell us more."

"Then what went on here?" Powell questioned in a low, puzzled voice.

Arborshaw said, "At the moment that's anyone's guess." He eyed Powell speculatively. "But you saw what I did."

Powell shook a cigarette from his pack, tapped it against the back of his hand and slid it between his lips. He patted his jacket pocket for his matches, and then he hesitated. "The looks on their faces. In my experiences, both on the job and when I was overseas, I've seen plenty of expressions on corpses and they're rarely pleasant, but I can say I've never come across anything that ghastly. And the way it looks as if Stromm was… cowering in his bed, as if whatever he saw terrified him so much." He said with bewildered emphasis, "But Walter Stromm? A man like him. For something to be that horrifying…"

"Reckon your only witness is that doll," Arborshaw remarked, and his words were not intended to be humorous.

"Yeah," Powell said tautly. "Sent it on to the crime lab. Might be able to get some prints off it. Doubtful, though." His face then took on a contemplative look. "Thing is, there's something familiar about that doll. Strange. I can't quite put my finger on it."

"Well, I wish you luck," Arborshaw said dismissively. "I still have my work to do."

Powell drew a hefty breath and his mouth twisted in a sarcastic smile. "Luck? Could use it."

Just as the bodies were being removed from the house Mayor Edward Warrington hurried up the walkway, helped along by valiant strokes from his cane. He stood aside looking almost squeamish as the two occupied gurneys rolled past him.

"His Honor," Powell said out the corner of his mouth to Arborshaw.

Warrington's complexion was pallid. He looked agitated, in a state of disbelief. He maneuvered his cane to quickly step over to Powell, offering just a hasty nod to Dr. Arborshaw.

"Braden," Warrington said to the chief. It was peremptory, not a greeting.

"Not much to tell you at present," Powell said, answering in anticipation of the mayor's question.

Warrington swallowed. When he first spoke his voice was weak, as though his throat was parched. Powell half expected the mayor to ask him to go fetch him a glass of water.

"Both of them? Walter *and Barbara?*" he said.

Powell nodded. He finally matched his cigarette and drew a long, deep drag.

Warrington found a chair that he slumped himself into. He held his cane securely in both hands, as if for support. "This isn't good," he said, his voice only a little stronger now. "Two more murders, and Walter Stromm, of all people."

Powell spoke abruptly. "Dr. Arborshaw and I aren't convinced they're murders. At least not directly."

Warrington gave him a fretful look. "What's that supposed to mean?" he demanded.

"Take a gander at the bodies," Powell suggested flatly as his eyes searched about the room for an ashtray.

It was evident by the mayor's expression that he would disregard that suggestion. He didn't respond, just cleared his throat in an obvious gesture. He lifted his head and looked directly at the coroner. "Then what is the cause of death?"

Arborshaw answered, "Appears to be heart failure."

For only a moment Warrington felt a flush of relief. Although unfortunate, he and especially the town could handle a death from natural causes. But then he frowned and asked quizzically, "Heart failure? Both of them?"

Arborshaw nodded. "Pending an autopsy that's how it looks."

Warrington appeared skeptical. "I can't speak for Barbara, but Walter never gave any indication of having heart problems." He put up both hands in a flustered gesture. "So…how do we explain this?"

Arborshaw turned to Powell. The police chief said, "No definite verdict."

Warrington was impatient. "That's not good enough."

Once more the coroner and police chief exchanged a glance.

"You both obviously have a theory," Warrington said.

It was Powell who answered. "It appears as if they were frightened to death."

The mayor went silent. His face seemed to sag.

"I know," Powell said, sympathetic to the mayor's skepticism. "But you'd have to have seen the bodies."

"Yes, well, maybe, I'm glad I didn't," Warrington admitted unashamedly.

Arborshaw concluded with, "I'll get back to you with my findings. I'll see myself out."

Powell nodded his thanks to the doctor, who returned the nod and left the house.

Mayor Warrington stayed seated in his chair, his features strained. He finally spoke in a quiet, contemplative voice. "What's going on in this town? What do we say to the people…with *this* happening so soon after those girls… How do we make sense of it?"

He gazed up at Powell with troubled eyes, as if hoping that the police chief could provide an answer. Some suggestion of how to resolve the mystery that had thrown a shadow over their community. Powell couldn't offer anything. He knew the mayor was not a strong man. Maybe he was a man of character once, but since he'd allowed himself to be bought off by the town bigwigs he had come to depend on others, particularly Walter Stromm, to advise him in his decisions concerning the affairs of Clear Vista. Now, at this moment, Warrington looked about as defeated a man as Powell had ever seen. Hardly the community leader to inspire confidence and assurance to the people he represented at this crucial time.

Warrington thrust his gaze on Powell. "If there's any truth to what you're saying, we have to keep this under wraps. I'm going to talk with Birdlong. He's ambitious, has ideals, but I think I can make him understand that this is a sensitive matter. I don't want anything out of the ordinary printed about this in the paper."

"That's still going to be tricky," Powell put in. "It's Walter Stromm we're talking about here. Not Sam the garage mechanic."

Warrington gave his head a vigorous nod. "I know. I—don't see how we can explain what happened here. To offer a rational, acceptable explanation for how both of the Stromms died on the same night. But I do not want the people of this town to start letting their imaginations go wild and think there's some *gargoyle* loose among us." He lowered his gaze to the floor and muttered tensely,

"Children being murdered, people being frightened to death. How does one make sense of any of this?"

Powell withdrew another cigarette from his package. He lit it and pulled a long inhale, his expression taut yet contemplative.

As he blew out a fine stream of smoke that trailed up toward the ceiling in a slow, dissipating spiral he half-seriously considered that maybe a "gargoyle" was not too far beyond the realm of possibility.

CHAPTER TWELVE

At 3 p.m. Powell was in his office, where he had kept himself throughout most of the day, ever since returning from the Stromm home. He was waiting for the call from the coroner with the results of the autopsies. Dr. Arborshaw was thorough in his post-mortem examinations, but Powell doubted he would find anything outside of the obvious, that Walter Stromm and his wife had died from heart failure—possibly stemming from extreme fright. But what could have been so terrifying to shock them both into sudden death?

The tattered doll and soggy mud that had been tracked throughout the house provided intriguing evidence, yet what did they point to? The report from the Breckridge crime lab concluded that no fingerprints or other potentially telltale markings were found on the doll, just as the police chief had anticipated and responded to with a frustrated smile. Still, Powell knew he had to find some significance in these clues, no matter how slight. The only sources of dirt around the Stromm house were within the two strategically placed flowerbeds that decorated the front lawn. But not only were these flowerbeds set at a distance from the house on the expansive property, each was examined and there was no sign of any disturbance to the ground.

The topsoil was smooth and fresh and the flowers untouched. In addition, there were no traces of dirt found anywhere along the front walkway or so much as a smearing of soil discovered around the sparkling clean back patio, which was of concrete construction and covered the whole of the backyard, a length stretching from the high outer fence that protected the swimming pool to the east wall and the patio door. And what remained most baffling was that there seemed to be no obvious point of entry. The front door and the patio door were latched and locked and no window had been opened, each having been sealed from the inside. Yet somehow someone had gotten inside the house, leaving traces of mud which marked a path, or so it appeared, from the bedroom all the way into the kitchen. From where? From whom?

It remained Powell's theory that whoever that person was he had to have been invited inside. Which meant that he—or she—was likely known to the Stromms. But what was the purpose behind leaving tracks of mud . . . and that doll?

Powell had spoken with the thrice-weekly maid who worked for the Stromms. His questions were kept general—nothing to alarm her but, as he explained, part of official procedure. He was careful not to say anything that might give rise to suspicion, even as he realized that to any rational human being the so-called "coincidence" of a double death occurring on the same night in the same house was unusual enough. He mentioned nothing about the conditions of the bodies or gave any hint that what he was asking her was more than routine. The maid was cooperative, but couldn't provide anything of value. She told Powell that she had finished her work yesterday at six p.m. and then went home. Outside of Mrs. Stromm seeming a trifle stressed, as she had appeared to be as of late, she hadn't notice anything out of the ordinary. Powell had also hoped to speak with the gardener, Raymundo, but he was quickly crossed off the list when it was learned he'd been away on a two-week vacation visiting family in Puerto Rico.

The one fact he could not overlook was that Walter Stromm, despite his self-proclaimed and strategically cultivated position of importance, had a lot of enemies. He was clever in his business maneuverings, operating just inside the confines of the law, but there were still a few people smart enough to discover they had been taken in by his various machinations. Unfortunately, this was usually after the damage had been done. Powell personally knew of only one of these dupes. But he was now residing in a Breckridge retirement facility, apparently in the progressive stages of dementia. It was a sad story. The fellow had thought he was entering into a profitable partnership with Stromm, had foolishly signed papers without first having a lawyer go over the documents, and soon found himself involved in a convoluted legal entanglement that, once the affairs were sorted out, left the poor sucker ruined financially with Walter Stromm taking control of his assets.

Powell was certain that was just one of many situations where Stromm had taken advantage of a person's trust or gullibility to increase his own profits. Because of that, Powell would have to search through all of Stromm's records in an attempt to track these people down: a time-consuming process that Powell doubted would amount to anything. No, Powell was convinced there had to be something more insidious behind his death. But who could be so embittered to devise such a diabolical scheme? A plan so effective it gave a fatal fright not only to Stromm but also his wife? It wasn't as simple as threatening them with a gun, which was how Powell believed one of Stromm's dupes would have handled the matter. And besides, Stromm would stand up to such a threat, even if it killed him. With a bullet to the heart.

Questions. But no answers.

Powell hadn't had much time to consider the various possibilities. Throughout the day the phone rang almost incessantly. The news about the Stromms spread throughout the town with an urgency similar to the panic that followed the discovery of the bodies of the Loewen twins. It was difficult to cover up such news in a small town. Powell answered every call and assured each of the callers that there was nothing suspicious about either of the deaths.

Odd yes, but just a coincidence that they both happened to die on the same night. Some folks were accepting, others apparently not as convinced. Powell did his best to allay any of their doubts or suspicions, but it wasn't an easy task. It would have been difficult under normal circumstances. But with the recent abduction and murders still fresh in everyone's mind, this proved a particularly difficult responsibility for the police chief.

Powell finally received the call from Dr. Arborshaw. The coroner was direct and to the point and what he said came as no surprise to the police chief. Both Walter Stromm and his wife had died of sudden heart failure. What was the probable cause? Only what both Powell and Arborshaw suspected, based on the disturbing conditions of the bodies, they most likely had been exposed to some stimulus that had literally frightened them to death.

Once again Powell presented the most crucial question, "What the hell can be so terrifying it scares a man like Walter Stromm into having a heart attack?"

"I certainly can't suggest the catalyst," Arborshaw replied. "But I can offer you the probable physiological reason."

"Shoot," Powell told him.

"Ventricular fibrillation," Arborshaw said, adding, "which can result from a massive release of epinephrine—"

Powell cut in. "Epine-*what*?"

"Epinephrine," Arborshaw repeated. "A hormone that stimulates the heart that can lead to acute myocardial infarction. Or in layman's terms an excessive secretion of adrenalin causing heart failure. The trigger can be extreme excitement…or intense terror."

Powell spoke wearily into the receiver. "Guess I was picking at crumbs."

"Crumbs?"

"Hoping you might find that million-to-one coincidence that could give a more natural explanation for Stromm and his wife dying together," Powell said.

Arborshaw asserted, "For what it's worth I can tell you that Mrs. Stromm was deceased before her husband. I'd say she died at least two hours before him."

"Are you sure?" Powell wanted to know.

"I based my finding on the degree of rigor mortis present in both bodies," Arborshaw explained patiently.

"And that's an accurate finding?" Powell pressed.

"If determined early enough. Rigor mortis can continue for up to fifteen hours. The muscle rigidity in Walter Stromm was less than what we found in his wife. There was still a certain amount of limb manipulation which was not the case with Mrs. Stromm."

"Then what you're saying is that someone just hung around the house during those two hours before walking in on Stromm to do whatever it was that hit him with his coronary?" Powell said, the irritation evident in his tone.

"I'm not suggesting anything," Arborshaw replied abruptly. "I'm just reporting what I found during my examination."

Powell relaxed his tone. "I know," he admitted.

"How are you planning to handle it?" Arborshaw asked him.

Powell considered his answer. "Death by fright seems an abstract, not an absolute, regardless of what we saw and what we consider might be the reason—whatever the hell that was. Naturally Warrington wants to downplay it. He's spoken to our man at the newspaper. He's hoping—guess we both are—that the citizens will accept that million-to-one coincidence."

"Well," Arborshaw drawled. "If it's any consolation, such a thing isn't entirely outside the realm of possibility."

"How do you mean?"

"I recall hearing of a couple upstate some years back. Both went to bed, neither woke up. Only in that instance the couple was quite elderly. Walter Stromm was a relatively young man and from what my examination could reveal, in all other ways seemed to be as fit as a bear."

"Yeah. That's what makes this 'death by fright' thing so damn hard to comprehend."

Powell hung up the phone without thanking Arborshaw for his discouraging report. He leaned back in his chair, his brain a muddle of thoughts. Up until a week ago Clear Vista had been a comparatively uneventful town. Oh, of course he knew about some of the town's dark secrets but there was no "mystery" behind any of those situations. Even the tragedies that had befallen some of the town's children could be explained—if not always made sense of. Until what happened to the Loewen twins. And that was why Powell pondered whether there might be some connection between the two occurrences. Both incidents happening so close to each another.

But if that were so, it led to troubling and frightening speculation.

He needed to get out for a while. He felt as if he were beginning to suffocate from being cooped up inside the office answering phone calls and lying through his teeth each time he picked up the receiver. He considered taking a walk over to the diner for a cup of coffee and a pastry, only he knew that whoever he met there would likely bombard him with more questions. And he'd answered all the queries he cared to for one day.

Powell checked the time. Reynolds should be back from his patrol soon. Maybe he would take advantage of a couple of hours and indulge himself to a drive along the coast. The fresh, salty sea air might help to clear his head.

And then just as he started to contemplate some relaxation the door to the office swung open. It was Caspar McGee, looking haggard and dirty—and damn near wild-eyed, who entered.

"Gotta speak with yuh, Chief," he said in an excited voice.

Powell squinted his eyes and regarded the old man critically. "Been drinking, Caspar?"

McGee shook his head "no" with three determined wags. His aquiline features looked more hawk-like than usual. He stepped over to the front of the desk. He planted his hands firmly on the worn surface and leaned his body forward. Powell noticed an unpleasant odor wafting off his person, but he equated that to Caspar not having bathed for a while. He didn't detect the smell of any rotgut.

"Why don't you take a seat?" Powell proffered, pointing to the chair next to where McGee was standing, far enough from the desk so Powell's sensitive sense of smell would not be offended by the old man's pungency.

"Think I will sit," McGee mumbled. He plopped himself onto the hard-backed chair. He glanced about the office before refocusing his attention on Powell.

"What I gotta be tellin' yuh, Chief," he said, drumming a finger against his knee. "Well, it ain't normal."

With all that had been happening in town Powell couldn't help but think, *not normal? What else is new?* Still, he was willing to let the old codger have his say.

McGee took a moment to try and gather his thoughts, then he shifted forward in his chair.

But his words came in a whisper, as if he didn't want to risk having anyone else hear what he had to say. Not that there was anyone other than himself and Powell in the office.

"I seen somethin' last night," he began. "Somethin' out of the ordinary that scared me near to dumpin' in my drawers."

Powell looked unimpressed, but he thought how McGee's choice of wording seemed appropriate given the wicked stench emanating off the old man. He gave his head a meager nudge to encourage him to go on.

McGee's eyes shifted nervously around the office.

"There's nobody here but us," Powell assured him.

"Maybe I ain't worried none 'bout that," McGee said abruptly. "Maybe it's…them other eyes that you and me cain't see."

Powell knitted his brow. It had been a long day, his scalp was beginning to itch, and he wasn't in the mood for any more riddles. He wanted the old man just to speak to the point.

"Caspar, I've got a lot of work to do," he said, straining to keep his voice level.

"I'm gettin' to it, Chief," McGee told him with a swift lift of his hand. "Only…it ain't so easy for me to say. 'Cause what I seen, well, I know I seen it but I just cain't make no sense of it."

"Just tell me, Caspar. Get it off your chest. Tell it to me slow and calmly."

McGee again looked to steady himself. He settled back in his chair before he once more restlessly pushed himself forward.

"I'll tell yuh, Chief," he said, and as lucidly as he could he recounted to Powell his midnight visit of the night before to Resurrection Gardens—and his strange encounter.

When he was finished he waited for Powell's reaction. He couldn't tell by the blank look on the chief's face whether he believed him or not. When Powell finally spoke, his only words were a blunt, "Were you drinking last night?"

McGee was just as forthright in his answer. "Sure I was." He lifted a tobacco-stained finger straight up as if brandishing a pencil and waved it. "But I can tell yuh, I sobered up faster than a priest once I seen what I seen. All dressed in black. Wearin' that black hood and, reckon it was some sort of a cape, swirlin' and twistin' 'round him in the wind. I remember well, Chief 'cause no way I can forget what I seen. Don't figger I ever will."

The more Powell listened to the old man the less he felt that Caspar was engaging him in some crazy, possibly alcohol-induced delusion. McGee apparently was sober right now and dead-set serious in what he was telling him.

But it sounded so unreal, something that a rational person would have a difficult time wrapping his brain around. Except for one intriguing and startling claim. McGee further said he'd gone back to the cemetery that morning, to try and pinpoint exactly where he saw that black-garbed figure do that strange ritual with his hands. And McGee told Powell he had located the spot.

It was Margaret Stromm's grave.

* * *

"Grave don't seem like it's been disturbed none," McGee went on, cocking an eye and rubbing the palm of his hand along the bristle that peppered his bony cheeks and narrow jaw. "But I did see somethin' odd. When I did some inspectin' this mornin', saw what looks like handprints on the mound of sod. Like someone was pushin' on it. Now that ground's hard. Damn well purty solid-like. Someone hadda be pushin' down on it mighty hard, usin' a lotta strength, and even usin' that kinda muscle I don't see how one coulda pushed in them handprints to make 'em as clear as they is."

Powell looked both thoughtful and doubtful at what McGee was telling him. Reflexively, his body began to gently rock in the swivel chair. Of a sudden the old man's words stimulated a vague memory. A specific memory, and what was beginning to take shape in his brain disturbed him. At the mention of Margaret Stromm's grave he reflected back to the day of her funeral, which he had attended. The little cream-colored casket had been open for a viewing both before and after the service. Powell remembered as he filed by the coffin along with the other mourners that the little girl had been holding a doll that had been tucked inside the crook of her arm by her mother. Powell couldn't remember anything about the doll, only that…

He now tried to remember if it had been buried with the girl. He never watched the closing of the casket, nor did he ride out with the procession to the cemetery. Had Barbara Stromm possibly taken the doll from the casket before the lid was shut for the final time?

If she hadn't and the doll had been interred with little Margaret…

He stopped himself. It was a crazy, absurd thought. What that possibly suggested was ghoulish, something straight out of an Edgar Allen Poe story. But he then considered that so much in town had taken on a dark, unexplainable edge that perhaps nothing was beyond the realm of possibility.

Powell returned to rational thinking by reminding himself that McGee did say the grave didn't look to have been tampered with. No ghouls had been out there with their shovels, to take a doll from a coffin.

Still, Powell figured the old man's claim was worth at least looking into. He decided to drive out to Heavenly Angels and inspect the grave himself. He got up from behind his desk and escorted McGee from the office, thanking him for taking the time to come by. Before seeing him out the door Powell instructed him, sternly, to keep what he'd just told him strictly to himself. He even added a subtle warning for insurance. If people in town got wind that McGee was paying visits to the cemetery, especially after dark, it might set their suspicions afire, and the old man had already had one experience with many of the citizens casting doubt his way after what happened to the Loewen twins. McGee looked to take the advice seriously. He lifted his hand as if in a pledge and assured Powell that he wouldn't say anything to anyone.

Luckily Terry Reynolds showed up just a few minutes later. The long afternoon ride evidently had done him some good; he looked sufficiently recovered from his

morning ordeal. Powell didn't explain to Reynolds his intent. He wasn't in the mood to answer any more questions, even from one of his own patrolmen. He merely said that he had to run out for a bit and to keep watch on the office. The phone had been ringing for most of the day but should be quiet now. But if any more calls did come in just to keep up the facade that there was nothing specifically suspicious about the deaths of the Stromms outside of the odds-against likelihood of them dying within hours of each other.

"Well, that sounds suspicious enough," Reynolds remarked.

"I know," Powell said with exasperation. He took his head in his hands and massaged his fingers alongside his temples. "Been dealing with it for most of the day. Hopefully once the story gets printed in the *Chronicle* we can stop fielding questions and get down to some real work."

"Are most of those callers accepting of what you've been telling them?" Reynolds wanted to know.

"Appears that way." Powell sucked a tooth then exhaled. "But who knows?"

Reynolds wore a slanted smile and spoke in a reflective cadence. "When I graduated from the police academy I chose a small community because I thought…well, that it would be nice, quiet work."

Powell allowed himself a weak grin. "Rude awakening to the realities of being a cop."

"Suppose so," Reynolds said with a sigh.

It wasn't a long drive to the cemetery but it was a trip Powell didn't relish taking, and for obvious personal reasons. Heavenly Angels was where his own two children were buried and he'd only been out to visit their graves on a couple of occasions, and each time briefly. He still could not bring himself to visit his wife's burial plot in the cemetery proper. Perhaps it was strange, but to stand by that plot of land and see Cassidy's name and date of her life span engraved on a bronze plaque would serve as a blunt acknowledgement that she truly was dead, and in an odd way he still embraced those fleeting moments where his memory spared him a reprieve and he could imagine her alive and waiting for him to come home.

But like it or not, he had a duty to perform. If something out of the ordinary was going on at the cemetery, if some intruder was performing weird ceremonies or was defiling the graves, he needed to find out.

He drove his car along the gravel road and turned through the main gate into the cemetery. He noticed that the grounds were empty. He stepped from the vehicle and suppressed a quick shiver— one he attempted to attribute to the chilly air that drifted across the open landscape. Even if Resurrection Gardens didn't upset him for his own reasons, the graveyard still had a disquieting atmosphere that permeated the property even in the comfort of daylight. And today the skies were dreary and overcast. It was as if an intangible shadow was cast over the grounds, reflecting the sorrow and tragedy that lay beneath the turf. When the stillness was uninterrupted the cemetery became so quiet that if spirits lingered after death a visitor might imagine he could hear their hollow whispers…that is, if one dared to listen closely enough.

Powell walked along the narrow stone pathway that cut neatly through the lolling grass and then forked off, one branch leading toward the children's section and the other continuing on to the main cemetery. He followed the path into Heavenly Angels.

He tried to avert his eyes from where his own children were buried, barely suppressing the shame he felt for doing so. But to acknowledge those graves meant he once more had to burden himself with the guilt that he was responsible for what happened to them—and their mother. That ever-present thought that he should have been the one to take his kids out for ice cream that night. The remorse would never completely leave him. Powell understood and could even accept that. But he also could not permit that interference any more than he could allow himself any other intrusion. He had work to do—difficult, challenging work, but a job he was also oddly grateful for, as it kept his brain occupied and mostly free from troubling memories.

He knew where Margaret Stromm's grave was located; at a distance from where his kids, Randy and Ruthie, lay interred. He walked with care across the grass between the graves, not wanting to step onto any of the plots. It wasn't that he was superstitious, just respectful. Yet it deeply troubled him to be among these graves. Not only his own kids but other children resting there had died tragically…like Larry Krevich, whose grave Powell did pause to look at. As he neared Margaret Stromm's plot he considered how unfair life could often be. And not just because of those children whose lives were cut short through violent and preventable ends. But even for youngsters who fell victim to terrible diseases. Brought into this world to achieve a future…only to have whatever that opportunity may have been so cruelly snatched from them. Never reaching their potential or fulfilling their promise. Never experiencing the pleasures and the pains of life. Could there truly be a greater tragedy? Powell mused. He was never what one might call a religious man, but he often pondered that if God did exist, why did

He allow such terrible things to happen to children? The eternal question for which there seemed to be no answer. In moments of extreme frustration he found himself asking who the true perpetrator of these atrocities was, man or what he believed was his God?

The question came to him again as he viewed the two mounds of earth covered with Astro Turf next to the open plots that would accept the coffins of Heidi and Holly Loewen the following day.

He gave his head a shake to free himself from this troubling contemplation and to concentrate on the business at hand. He took the final steps toward Margaret Stromm's grave. He hunkered down next to it and inspected the small rise that was settling into the earth. And much to his surprise he could just make out what looked to be a pair of handprints with unusually long, slender, and widely separated fingers embedded in the hardened turf. Curious, Powell tried to imprint his own hand into the earth, but old Caspar McGee had been right. The ground was so hard and firm that even using all of his strength he could not make even a slight impression in the sod.

He stood up and scratched at the nape of his neck. Someone had definitely been out to the cemetery, but other than those weird handprint markings there was nothing about the grave to suggest that it had been tampered with. So, what was the point? He tried to think sensibly because he remained particularly troubled by one aspect of this mystery, the doll. And gradually he arrived at a possible explanation. Whoever it was that had frightened Walter Stromm and his wife to death somehow had used their dead daughter as part of their plan. How, specifically, Powell could only speculate. But the doll was important. The way Powell figured, the person behind this scheme likely found a doll similar to the one that had been buried with little Margaret, mussed it up so that it looked as if it had been taken straight from the grave, and brought it along with clumps of mud possibly dug up and taken from the cemetery into the Stromm house. Creating the impression that Margaret Stromm had come back from the grave. It sounded not only extreme, but absurd, even Powell recognized that. Yet he could not come up with another explanation that made more sense.

What was certain was that whatever ghoulish methods this individual had used to carry out this scheme, by killing Stromm and his wife he had succeeded too well.

CHAPTER THIRTEEN

"What you're saying is absurd! Outrageous!" Mayor Warrington exclaimed as he swept his fingertips across his brow in a flustered gesture. "Utterly fantastic."

Powell was careful to maintain his composure. He knew how outlandish his theory sounded but he had to present it in as calm and convincing a manner as possible. After all, he was the chief of police and was treading on shaky ground with what he was suggesting.

"Don't you think I feel the same?" he responded with a deliberate neutral emphasis. "But what if we consider that someone with a personal hatred toward Walter Stromm came up with this macabre idea as a way to get back at him for, I dunno, whatever reason that might be? Maybe intended just to humiliate him. Maybe puncture his bullying arrogance by throwing him a hell of a scare, but the plan backfired because both Stromm and Barbara had the misfortune to die."

Mayor Warrington sat back in the chair behind his desk. His forehead was lined with deep furrows, giving him an aged look, though gradually his troubled expression eased as he allowed his emotions to relax and he gave serious consideration to what Powell was suggesting.

"Maybe there is some truth to what you're saying," he conceded softly, though it was clear to Powell that he was still in conflict with trying to determine a more logical explanation. In that regard both men shared a common bond. They were pragmatists. No matter how extreme the incident, there must be a practical resolution.

Warrington slotted his fingers together and drew his hands up to his mouth. "After all, nothing else makes sense about this, you're right there." He lowered his hands and scrunched up his face. "But this stretches credibility. For someone to go to such an extreme. Why, we're not dealing with a sane mind." He paused again, then added, "And of course, if that is the case, then it's unlikely it has any connection with what happened to the Loewen girls."

"I know," Powell agreed. He added softly, "And I'll be frank with you, I don't know if I find that a relief or not."

"Then you realize you're now dealing with two separate incidents," Warrington said. "If what you're suggesting is so."

Powell gave a weary nod of his head.

Warrington focused his eyes directly at Powell and spoke officially. "Well Chief, so tell me, how does your department handle this?"

Powell frowned both from consternation and trying not to acknowledge the sudden itch flare-up on his scalp. He carefully thought out his answer. "Whoever put this together planned it carefully. Planting clues that aren't clues. And knowing there's a suspect list that could take weeks to pore over, and we still might come up empty because there's really nothing to suggest that's a direction we should be pursuing." He paused to take a breath. "Never mind timing this the way he did. With attention focused on trying to get a lead on the murder of those girls." He pondered. "Intending to lump these together or maybe hoping to have the killings of the Loewen children act as camouflage."

"Funerals were scheduled for tomorrow," Warrington said softly, speaking respectfully. "The Loewen family asked that the services be held off for an extra day. Apparently they received word that other family members will be attending from out of state."

"Postponing the inevitable," Powell said, his lips drawn in a thin line.

"That's a rather insensitive way of putting it," Warrington said in response to what he perceived as a cynical comment.

Powell smirked. "Callous? Maybe that's the way I've become."

"I would hope not, Braden," Warrington said, critical at the chief's remark.

Powell stood up from his chair. "I'm trying to fit together two separate puzzles and they're both missing key pieces, and those pieces might as well be at the bottom of Buchanan Bay."

Powell's words weren't intended to display total hopelessness on his part. He did have one vital clue that he intentionally did not mention to the mayor since he first wanted to source it out himself.

And that clue, such as it was, was the mysterious figure Caspar McGee spoke of who had appeared at the cemetery the night before. It might just be an odd coincidence, but Powell didn't think so. What was this person doing leaving handprints on Margaret Stromm's grave? What was the reason? It made little sense unless it was another morbid ingredient to add to the plot against Walter Stromm. Perhaps if Walter Stromm hadn't died so suddenly, maybe the next step of the plan was to slowly drive him mad.

It was still just the most primitive of guesswork. What Powell decided to do next was a long shot. He was going to have a man out at Resurrection Gardens for the next several nights, taking a chance that the "mystery figure" would return.

CHAPTER FOURTEEN

Pietro (Peter) Corsetti was proud of his heritage even though he had endured hurtful incidents of prejudice along with his parents and siblings when the family first arrived in America from Italy on the big ocean liner. They were taunted and called names from those who resented their heritage—and so in a naive but well-meaning spirit, hoping to spare his own son the embarrassment of having a pronounced ethnic name that many unfairly passed judgment upon, he convinced the woman he had chosen as his wife, a pure American girl, that their boy Cameron take on her maiden name, Makefield. A simple solution to a problem that likely never would have developed. Such racial prejudice simply did not exist in Clear Vista, which was where the family eventually settled to escape the brutal eastern winters that had begun to affect the fragile health of Peter's wife. The difficulties that Cameron encountered had nothing to do with his name or nationality. He just happened to be a boy of a deeply sensitive nature.

Peter Corsetti was not so much upset as he was ashamed that his son, his only child, had taken his own life. Such an act was beyond his comprehension. He did not know that his son had been so troubled. He could not have guessed that his boy could be so weak. Death by suicide was not something his traditional mindset could accept and so he resisted expressing the emotion that any parent would display at the loss of a child. His wife had only a little more understanding into the situation. While Cameron had refused to confide in her, she saw in those days prior to his death that he was behaving differently. He had become quiet, withdrawn. He would come home from school and head directly to his room, where he would sit for hours. Just sit on the edge of his bed, and brood. And while she was not able to reach out to her son, she pleaded with her husband to be there for the boy, to listen to whatever was weighing so heavily on his mind and offer whatever advice he could provide to help their son deal with his troubles. Yet that was not in Peter's nature. He remained firm in his conviction that a boy must stick up for himself if he ever was to become a man.

"Life lessons," he said firmly. This phrase had been spoken shortly before Cameron had died and when tensions were strong between him and his wife, and on this night not long after the boy's suicide his wife was quick to take issue with him.

"Life lessons, you said?" she sneered. "Yet you were the one who insisted that the boy take my name instead of yours. Proud of your heritage, yet ashamed of your name."

Peter Corsetti's eyes narrowed and his tone darkened. He gazed into the tumbler filled with red wine sitting before him on the kitchen table. "Never ashamed. No. But to give him an advantage. So that he could become a man of pride without being tagged a guinea, wop, or a dago."

"As were you?"

"Yes, as was I—and worse, as was my father, right up until the day he died," Peter said emphatically. His subtle Mediterranean accent became pronounced in his anger.

"And yet without him ever having that problem here in Clear Vista, our son was troubled. And were *you* there to comfort him?" his wife said in an indignant tone.

"I did all that I could," Peter said abruptly, defensively, punctuating his statement with a sweeping flourish of his hands.

"As your parents taught you?" his wife said in challenge. "Did they never support you?"

"I fought my own battles growing up. I expected Cameron to do the same. But, he was weak, spineless, God forgive me."

His wife was resentful. "Don't speak of forgiveness from God. Our son needed a father's guidance."

Perhaps that was true. In any case, Peter did not have an adequate response to her accusations. And what did it really matter anyhow? Cameron was dead. He died in a manner that was a blatant insult to the belief and religious customs his father had grown up with and learned to respect. There was no courage or honor in taking a pistol and pulling the trigger. He saw it only as cowardice.

"I cannot discuss this anymore," Peter said with a frustrated finality. He grabbed his tumbler of wine and took back a long swallow, pounding the glass onto the table.

"You'll have to live with it, as will I," his wife said to him.

Peter sighed heavily and he fixed his eyes on his wife. He was slow in responding. "Perhaps. But I think that maybe it might be best if neither of us has the reminder of the other right now."

His wife surprised him as she responded with an accepting look. "You need to be away?"

Peter's tone was gentle, though still tinged with frustration. "For now. Until I can sort this out for myself."

"You feel that's necessary?"

Peter's silence and hard, fixated stare answered her question.

His wife responded after a lengthy pause. "Yes," she said. "I think that might be the right thing for you to do."

Peter rose from his chair and for just a moment looked prepared to show affection to his wife. But that was not his intention. He gazed at her for several moments before he stepped over to the pegboard and removed the car keys.

He turned to her. "Maybe you would like if I blamed myself, Dora. Not you. Not even the boy for what he did to *you*. His mother. You forget that, eh?"

And with those words, spoken in a voice without any sense of compassion, Peter started for the back door of the house, toward the garage. Perhaps his wife might have spoken up to offer words of comfort, to help him accept or at least adjust to the guilt that he appeared to be denying himself. But at the moment there was nothing more he wanted to hear her say. What he needed most was just to be by himself.

Peter knew that despite what he'd intended he would return home later that night. Perhaps if he'd had another option that would not have been his decision. But he had nowhere else to go. He simply needed time alone to work out the thoughts that neither he nor his wife could make sense of, for themselves—or each other.

Before he walked out the door his wife asked him, "Are you coming back tonight?"

Peter halted and started to half turn toward her. Only he didn't answer her question. He would be back, but didn't want her to know it. Maybe her uncertainty might get her to regard him less critically. He merely sighed and then stepped from the house, the screen door swinging on its hinges behind him.

A fog had rolled in from the bay. A natural occurrence. Not heavy, but he would have to drive with caution, especially along the coast highway. He remembered that was where Chief Powell's family was killed and there had been a number of other accidents caused by excessive speed and careless driving. That aside, the ride and the solitude and the clean, crisp sea air would do him good tonight. Help refresh him and his mood.

For only the briefest moment his attitude shifted and he did start to feel better. Unfortunately, this good feeling passed quickly. His thoughts returned to a familiar direction and he realized that he hadn't really come to terms with Cameron's death. He had been focusing so much on *how* he died—the shame that suicide brought to him as a father—that he'd given precious little thought to how the boy's passing would affect him personally. He could admit that he had never been as close to his son as a father should. He was never really a "dad." But that was how Peter himself was raised and it was a situation that he never questioned. The father's primary duty to his family was to put bread on the table. Once again Peter felt himself beginning to grow resentful. Compared to himself, his son had many more advantages. Peter had put up with abuses and insults throughout his childhood and he could proudly say that it was his own strength of character that helped him to overcome these cruelties—through which he had made something out of himself. Maybe he was not a rich man, but he was his *own* man, the proprietor of his own business. His son, too, could have succeeded, but he was weak and unable to cope.

Perhaps Peter was striving to protect his emotions, but he was determined not to permit himself any sympathy for what his son did to him. It was a cruel, selfish act. His wife, on the other hand, she was a woman. A mother. It was in her nature to let emotion overtake her. Fine. But Peter would not succumb to that. Neither would he permit her to force guilt on him for being unresponsive to his son's needs. He felt no regret for placing his priorities on being a good provider.

When he drove off from the house he did not notice that his wife was gazing at him from the kitchen window. As she watched her husband go she wondered not only if he would come back tonight, but more importantly, if things would ever be the same between them if he did. He'd persistently avoided talking about Cameron in virtually any regard. She knew the type of man Peter was and that he would never forgive Cameron for taking his own life. To him, it would almost be as if their son never existed. She sat herself back at the table and tried to figure out in her own mind what she would do.

Peter had been driving for about twenty minutes when he noticed through the damp fog a lone figure walking off to the side of the road. He observed that the gait was slow and somewhat unsteady and to Peter it looked as if that person might have been drinking or perhaps was ill and it was dangerous to be wobbling along that narrow shoulder with cars veering past at high speeds.

Normally Peter would not have given in to such concern and simply would have silently wished the individual well and driven on past. Tonight, though, he felt an odd distress for this person, and, impulsively, he steered his car over to the side of the road, clicking on his hazard lights, and waited for who he now determined was a teenage boy or maybe a young man to approach the vehicle.

Whoever he was, he didn't appear to be in a hurry even though Peter's gesture made it clear that he was prepared to offer him a ride. Peter slid over to unlock the passenger door and then he straightened in his seat and kept his eyes focused on the rear-view mirror, but the fog misting heavily around the figure prevented him from discerning much about the person, other than he appeared to be well-dressed in a dark, though apparently disheveled suit. He was unable to make out his features as he staggered forward with his head bowed and bobbing.

As the figure came up beside the passenger side of the car Peter got a sudden, uneasy feeling. He turned his head to the side, tentatively, and saw the person halt as a wobbly hand reached for the door handle. The ground fog was swirling around him, which was curious—and unnatural. Peter fought back the impulse to snap down the locks and just drive away, pull off from the shoulder onto the highway and spit gravel. But the door had already started to open. The stranger was standing upright, though with his shoulders slightly stooped, and Peter still could not see his face.

But by now he had definitely determined that the guy was drunk or maybe strung-out on some other substance. There was an offensive odor coming off his body and he seemed to have difficulty maneuvering himself into the vehicle. Once more Peter held back the urge to slam his foot down on the accelerator pedal and let this character fend for himself.

He still might have made the decision, but then the individual leaned back in the seat and slowly, awkwardly, turned to face him. The features were dark and etched in shadow—but not unrecognizable to the driver.

Peter was staring into the gray-complected, empty-eyed countenance of his son, Cameron.

Peter shrieked and in an abrupt, reflexive move he threw the car into gear and squealed off the shoulder back onto the road. Hoping desperately to escape, but to where? There was nowhere for him to run.

His son had reclaimed him.

The corpse of Cameron simply regarded his father with a vacant, soulless look before whatever had possessed his lifeless shell awakened itself and growled out a moan.

"They…left the bullet…in my brain, Dad," the voice emanating from his dead throat said hoarsely.

Cameron's tremulous fingers reached up toward his right temple, a digit pointing to the cosmetically-concealed wound before digging industriously into the flesh, prying through the shattered bone and finally pulling free the bullet that had lodged there. And the crease of a smile came to Cameron's purple lips as he displayed the gore-dripping bullet to his father.

"See…Dad. See!"

There was a long scream that nobody heard, sealed as it was within the confines of the car. The vehicle, as if of its own power and purpose, rode on along the curving expanse of cliff-side pavement, its destination unknown.

Just a father and his dead yet supernaturally resurrected son traveling a pathway into oblivion.

CHAPTER FIFTEEN

As strange as it might sound, Ida Krevich missed her son. Larry had been dead for over two years, but she could still feel his presence around the house. He'd never really been a bad boy—just cheeky and on occasion disobedient. No different from other youngsters. But Larry never understood what it was like for a single parent trying to raise a child. He was only six when his father walked out of the house and out of his son's life. What was most painful was that he'd never offered an explanation. One day he simply packed up his belongings and left. Larry stood numbly in the front doorway, watching his father stride briskly down the walkway toward his car, never once glancing back to see the look of uncomprehending distress on his son's face.

Just like that—as swiftly as a snap of a finger—nine years of being a husband and six years of being a father was over.

And when the car drove off Ida was left alone with the boy, a task she was neither prepared for nor one that she particularly wanted. Cliff had been the nurturing parent. He spent most of the time with Larry, taking him to ballgames and other outings, which made the suddenness of his leaving all the more cruel.

Naturally Larry's behavior was affected by his father abandoning him. Day after day he would implore his mother, "When's Daddy coming home?" At night she would hear him cry in his bed, saying over and over, "Why did you leave, Daddy? Why did you leave me?" At first Ida tried to be patient, offering her son assurances that she knew were untrue, only hoping that soon the questioning would cease and that in time he would come to accept their situation.

But Ida continued to wrestle with her own unanswered questions. Had there been another woman? Had Cliff been deceiving her all that time, leading her to believe they had a solid marriage? As she mulled this possibility over in her head she gradually began to accept it as truth, and slowly she started to lose a grip on her reality.

She found it difficult to cope. Despite her certainty over Cliff's betrayal, Ida tried to find herself a safe place of denial, but her kid was a constant reminder of this life she had been forced into, one she stubbornly refused to accept. Cliff must have been involved with someone else. What other reason was strong enough to make him walk away from his son? And that meant she had been living a falsehood. Their picture-perfect marriage had been an illusion, and her "loving" husband had played her for a fool.

Perhaps inevitably, a bitter anger grew in her. It festered, intensified. If she had talked it out with friends, the burden she carried might have been eased. But she was too ashamed. She felt like a failure. She believed that if she confessed her feelings people might say this tense attitude was the reason her husband walked out on her and their son. It was easier to create a false impression—present a bold, self-assured front so that people would look at her with respect, compliment her on how bravely she was holding up.

And that was how she composed herself when she was at work as a sales clerk at the Dominion Merchants thrift store. She would not accept any expression of sympathy from any of her coworkers or customers. Curtly, confidently, she would respond to such expressions of concern that she, and her son, were doing fine, thank you very much. She displayed the same attitude when she got together with friends for an after-work drink at Bailey's Lounge.

To all outward appearances, Ida Krevich was coping admirably.

But behind the closed door of her modest Kent Road house it was a different matter. It got so that Ida could not tolerate the sight of her son. While she put on the facade of loving, protective parent in public, she was cold and uncaring toward Larry in the privacy of their home. As Ida struggled to overcome her own anguish Larry served as a daily reminder of a man she now wanted to forget, a man she grew to despise in her solitude. But each time she looked at her son she saw the face of Cliff, and it taunted her. And finally, one day after Larry began whining for his dad again, Ida snapped. She struck her boy a hard blow across the face. She immediately felt contrite, but the regret of that moment soon passed. She had long felt the urge to hit her son, but had always managed to restrain herself. Now that she had finally succumbed to the temptation the slaps began occurring more frequently. And when that didn't suffice, there came other forms of abuse.

Through it all Larry never told a soul about what was going on at his home. He shrugged aside the questions from classmates prompted by the occasional bruises that would accompany him to school. Even teachers accepted his stories about falling in the playground after classes or some such fabrication. He was not an athletic or particularly well-coordinated boy—as was obvious when the kids played soccer or softball at recess and Larry, inevitably, would be the last to be chosen for a team. And sure, he was a quiet and withdrawn boy given to occasional bouts of explosive temperament, but this was attributed to him dealing with the absence of a father. Everything about the boy's injuries or behavior could be explained away logically.

If compassion was offered, it was always directed toward Larry's mother. She must have been having a difficult time raising a young, moody boy on her own while holding down a menial job and struggling to maintain a home. And through it all, bless her, she never complained or sought pity. She was respected and regarded as a strong and admirable woman.

Ida Krevich didn't know what made her snap that night. Or maybe she did, but it was just easier not to accept it. She had put in a full day at the store, had come home to a house badly in need of cleaning and, to top it off, Larry was in a demanding mood. She had just sat down to indulge in a cigarette when he came tearing out of his room screaming at his mom that she had lied to him. His father would not be coming home. As he told her, some of the older boys at school had decided to pick on Larry and they taunted him cruelly that no father who walked out on his family ever came back. Larry carried on so much that Ida didn't try to explain or even attempt to control her temper. Every resentment that she had been harboring let loose in an unrestrained rage. She leaped up from her chair and grabbed Larry by the arm and, ignoring his pleas, jammed the lit end of her cigarette into his forearm. And then she began hitting him, wildly out of control. And finally, just wanting him out of her sight, she yanked him by the arm into the kitchen and toward the door to the cellar, intending just to lock him down there until he could calm down. But Larry struggled ferociously and tugged his arm free of her grip, losing his balance in the process, and tumbling down the steep set of stairs, landing in a crumpled heap on the concrete floor. He moaned, but otherwise lay still.

Ida panicked. Her fear was not for her boy, but for *herself*. What would happen to her now?

That was her only concern. In a strange, sick way she was almost glad that her son lay motionless at the bottom of the stairs. God forgive her, she didn't want him around anymore. Not the questions. Not the attitude. Not his presence.

And soon he wasn't. He died of his injuries. And the court had been kind. The sympathy of the town poured in for the bereaved mother.

Once again she was admired for her strength and fortitude. She had endured two misfortunes, but she had prevailed and continued to carry herself with dignity.

*   *   *

The saying goes that time heals all wounds, but perhaps that also works in reverse. It took a while, but the prolonged loneliness finally began to weigh on Ida. Her health started to fail and prompted frequent bouts of melancholia. She came home from work, ate a quiet dinner, and then retired to the den, where she would sit in silence and solitude for hours until she was ready for bed. And during that time alone all she thought about was her son. The terrible thing that had happened to him. Of course it was an accident. By now she'd made herself believe that his death was simply a mishap. It was a psychological defense. To further protect herself from the guilt that threatened her sanity she concentrated solely on the good times she and Larry had shared. She put such emphasis on those memories that over time all the other "bad" thoughts faded as if they had never existed. She became the bereaved mother she had pretended to be at the time of her son's death.

Tonight, as the autumn darkness settled on the room, she sat in her rocker, tears glistening in her eyes, and gazed at a framed photograph of six-year-old Larry that rested in her lap.

"I miss you, my son," she murmured.

CHAPTER SIXTEEN

Although put forward as a request rather than an outright favor (which, in truth, it was), Powell appreciated that Terry Reynolds agreed to what he was asking with only a few questions. When he got back to the office after his visit to the cemetery he had asked Reynolds if he might put in some overtime and sit out a watch at Resurrection Gardens. Reynolds' first reaction was to regard his chief with a look of perplexity. Why on earth did he want someone to spend the night patrolling a graveyard? Powell understood the young officer's bewilderment and explained the reason to him, relating what Caspar McGee had told him.

Reynolds immediately protested that the chief shouldn't accept the word of an old drunk who was likely prone to booze-fueled hallucinations. Powell countered with the fact that McGee was stone cold sober when he recounted his experience, and then he mentioned the strange handprints that he himself had found at Margaret Stromm's gravesite. *Now* the reason for Powell asking him for that special duty made some sense to the young officer.

But still, *graveyard duty*? It was a cringe-worthy proposition.

Noticing Reynolds's reluctance Powell said it was unlikely that anyone would be foolhardy to show up at the cemetery again. But, he added, if someone did turn up it might provide the break they were seeking, insofar as getting a handle on the Stromm mystery.

Reynolds was prepared to display a little impudence and ask why he—Chief Powell himself—couldn't take the watch. But in the next instant he stopped himself. He believed he understood the reason. The cemetery and what it represented to him personally was a painful place for Powell. Reynolds sympathized that it could be difficult for him to be out there alone—with his memories.

At least that was the way he tried to justify what his chief was asking of him.

Still, the prospect of such an undertaking (poor choice of wording, he realized) held little appeal for Reynolds. He'd experienced enough morbid sights for one day. He knew that his discovery of Walter Stromm and his wife that morning, the macabre expressions sealed on their faces, would long be etched into his consciousness. To now close out his day in a forlorn graveyard did seem to be asking a lot. But then, he reasoned, he had been hoping that the chief would start to give him more responsibility than handling mundane office duties and doing his daily mobile patrol. Guarding a cemetery at midnight was not exactly the kind of opportunity he had been hoping for, but maybe it was a start.

"I'll have the two-way beside me all night," Powell told Reynolds. "Anything at all suspicious turns up, radio me immediately."

"And you'll come runnin'?" Reynolds said with a slight smile, trying to make light of the uneasiness he was already starting to feel.

"You'll be all right," Powell assured him.

"Yeah. Guess my main concern will be not to react too fast at every gust of wind," Reynolds half-joked.

Powell placed a hand on the younger man's shoulder. "You—do know why I'm asking you to do this? I mean, rather than myself…"

Reynolds nodded gently.

Powell walked over to his desk. "I can't stand being out there, Terry," he admitted unashamedly. "Even after all this time. Well over a year."

Reynolds spoke compassionately. "I know, Chief."

Powell continued, feeling that in fairness to what he was asking of Reynolds he should speak honestly. "It's just hard for me to reconcile that Cassidy and the kids, that they're out there. Out there, yet—I can't see them. God knows if I'll ever come to grips with that."

Powell's voice was pained, and the fact that he had even expressed these words caught Reynolds by surprise. Powell was confessing to a weakness, and that was not in his character. The only other time Reynolds had seen vulnerability in his chief was the night of the accident. Even at the funeral Powell had held himself stoically. And when it came to talking about his wife and kids, Powell had become a taciturn man. Never one to say much about memories or the pain that he might be feeling.

"Don't know if I ever told you, but I haven't visited Cassidy since the funeral," Powell said with a faint glistening in his eyes. "Know that's probably wrong of me. Haven't even gone out there to bring her flowers."

Reynolds appreciated Chief Powell speaking openly to him. He felt that maybe now he could speak just as candidly. "You know, Chief, maybe it's none of my affair. But…" and then he halted.

"No, go on," Powell encouraged him.

Reynolds hesitated, and then spoke what was on his mind. "Well, like I say, it's none of my business, and you can tell me to butt out if you want, but it's no secret that you and that girl from the diner, Donna, went out together." He went no further, waiting for Powell to tell him it was a personal affair and that he should indeed butt out.

Only that never happened. Powell didn't say anything and even looked intrigued to hear Reynolds finish what he'd started.

"What I'm getting at, Chief, is there's nothing wrong with you going out and enjoying yourself once in a while."

Powell stayed quiet for the next several moments and Reynolds had no clue as to what was going through his head.

Powell finally said, "Now's just not the time."

Reynolds cleared his throat and dared to venture a little further. "I—was at the diner today. Donna told me about last night. She, well, she said she enjoyed herself and that she hoped you'd give her a call."

Powell turned his head away and gazed out the window. Reynolds got the impression that maybe he had said enough and should let the matter drop.

In a quiet, barely audible voice, Powell said, "I'll think about it."

Reynolds understood that it wasn't an easy decision for Powell. What's more, he could empathize with the man. That was because he had his own painful past. He lived with a guilt of his own, though it was something that Reynolds kept strictly to himself. Not even the chief knew about his "secret." Years ago, before he became a cop, Reynolds sat talking to his sister Rhonda on a long-distance call and listened without compassion while she threatened to commit suicide, despondent over a breakup with her fiancé, a fellow that her brother knew was a bad sort and that she would be better without. Only he didn't know how deeply in love his sister was. Throughout the conversation Reynolds did not believe Rhonda was serious and—only in jest, partly because he was high on some potent weed—told her that if she did plan on doing herself in just not to leave a mess for their mom to have to clean up. He didn't realize until later, after the suicide note was found next to her body hanging from the bathroom shower curtain rod that she'd needed someone to talk to that night. She was serious in her intent and was desperately hoping to hear some words of comfort from her big brother…and he was not there for her. After he'd hung up the phone he and his pottoking buddies spent the next hour getting themselves further stoned and laughing about Rhonda's silly and dramatic "desperation."

It was a memory that continued to haunt Terry Reynolds. And it was one of the reasons he'd decided to join the police force. He'd shown irresponsibility that night, and he made a solemn promise that he would never be so selfish and thoughtless again.

Powell told Reynolds to go out and get himself some dinner before heading out to Resurrection Gardens. He needed him to be there before nightfall, for if the intruder were to make an appearance, it certainly would be after dark.

And then Powell sat by the telephone, staring at it, considering. Reynolds' words actually made some sense to him. He was tempted, in fact, if only because speaking to Donna might help restore a semblance of normalcy to what was a decidedly untypical situation. But as much as part of him wanted to, he couldn't bring himself to lift the receiver and dial her number. Not her home number, for he had never asked her for that. He would have to call her at the diner. But he didn't. He possessed a stubborn streak and once he made a commitment to himself he almost always held firm on that decision. Maybe when, *if* these mysteries got resolved, he would ask her out, but that would have to wait.

Suddenly he was hungry. He realized that he hadn't eaten since breakfast, and even that was meager, consisting of an overripe banana and half a bowl of corn flakes. He got up and walked to the far end of the office where a little table held paper cups, along with plastic spoons, knives and forks of varying sizes. His food choice was a quarter loaf of bread and near-empty jar of peanut butter. Powell had a peculiar way of eating a peanut butter sandwich, something he started doing as a kid and for whatever reason the habit never left him. He took a spoon, dug it deep into the jar, scooped out a generous portion, and then shoved it into his mouth. He chewed the goop a bit and then he took a piece of bread from its package, folded it in half and started biting off small pieces, combining the mixture in his mouth. He knew it was a weird way to eat a sandwich and so the only time he indulged himself was when no one was around to give him an odd look. In any case, it satisfied him.

A short time later the door to the office swung open and Mayor Warrington hurried inside. That in itself was unusual. Even though the mayor's office was next door, the usual procedure when His Honor wanted to speak to his police chief was for him to call Powell over to *his* office.

Warrington was waving a sheet of what looked like pre-print news copy like it was a victory flag. Wordlessly he walked over to the desk and thrust the paper at Powell. The chief looked curiously both at the mayor and the copy.

LEADING CITIZEN DIES

Walter Stromm, prominent real estate developer and businessman, was found dead at his home early yesterday morning, the victim of an apparent heart attack. In a tragic turn, Stromm's wife Barbara was also discovered deceased in the couple's Kensington Road house. The preliminary investigation concludes that Mrs. Stromm herself suffered a fatal heart attack resulting from the shock of discovering her husband's lifeless body. According to her physician, Mrs. Stromm had been in ill health for some time.

Powell lifted his eyes from the paper. "That true?" he asked, pointing specifically to that last sentence.

"Obtained the news directly from Barbara's GP in Breckridge, a Dr. Henry Ridges. Confirmed by the specialist she'd been seeing," Warrington answered. He inhaled. "So, what do you think?"

"Suppose it couldn't be handled any other way," Powell said ambivalently.

Warrington appeared satisfied. "Precisely. A little tweaking, but otherwise ready for the *Chronicle*." He paused as he then furrowed his brow. "And that takes care of one problem."

Although he didn't voice it, Powell thought, *at least one*.

* * *

The setting sun cast a haze over the lonely graveyard. Dusk was gathering and soon the darkness would be complete. Terry Reynolds was honest enough to admit that he wished he were anyplace else other than Resurrection Gardens. He'd never been out to the cemetery when the sun was setting and he quickly discovered that even at dusk it was as if the gloomy atmosphere were creeping under his skin. The feeling of disquiet only intensified once he made his way over to Heavenly Angels and examined the handprints embedded in the mound settling over little Margaret Stromm's grave. It was definitely puzzling and didn't do much to ease his discomfort about sitting out the night in such a foreboding environment. Even though he was wearing extra clothing to protect him against the night chill, he was shivering—and he knew it had less to do with the autumn weather than his own apprehensions. Powell had wanted him positioned somewhere in the proximity of the children's section, but to keep out of sight so as not to frighten off their mystery man should he show up tonight. Reynolds could think of half a dozen places where he would prefer to keep watch— such as sitting in a warm patrol car outside the gates of the cemetery. But he didn't have to look far before he found a spot that would provide him with adequate cover. As he walked toward it he decided to test the two-way to make sure Powell was able to receive him.

"Radio One calling Chief Powell. Come in, Chief. Over."

A crackle of static, then, "Powell. Read you, Radio One. Over."

"Just doing a communications check, Chief. So far quiet. Everything appears normal. Getting myself into position across the way. I'd say about thirty yards. Next to a…*Jesus*, can't believe I'm saying this, a mausoleum."

"Just keep a sharp watch, Terry. Over."

"Yeah, over." Reynolds smirked to himself and muttered under his breath, "You sonofabitch." He was only partly serious, but still took a quick check to be sure the transmission was closed between them.

He settled himself next to the Morris family crypt, a cross-crowned marble structure with a rusted iron front gate. Then he began his wait. He took out his thermos that he'd filled with hot coffee to warm himself. Strong and black, not the way he preferred his java, but he was drinking for the warmth and the jolt, not the taste. If it turned out to be the long night he dreaded, he needed to keep alert. Not that he thought he'd have any problem keeping awake. *Even a vampire would have a difficult time sleeping out here,* he thought to himself.

It didn't take long for Reynolds to become sensitive to the cemetery silence, hanging so heavily over the grounds that any slight disturbance resonated with him like the report of a pistol. Sudden flurries of wind rustling through the bushes and the barren branches of the trees which were plentiful in the old graveyard; the chirruping or scurrying of an unseen night creature. Each noise was amplified and took on a frightening quality in his imagination, which was acute, a high-tuned frequency. Sounds rose unexpectedly and from unidentifiable locations. It was only as the night progressed that he gradually settled into his surroundings and could recognize the periodic disruptions for what they actually were.

He didn't know how long he had been out there. An undetermined length of time had passed, though he was sure the actual period was much shorter than it seemed to him. He was reluctant to flash his penlight against his wristwatch for fear he'd discover that maybe only a couple of hours had gone by. Now that he had relaxed his unease to some extent, boredom started to set in. Just sitting. Waiting. He understood that stakeouts were part of police work, but if this was going to become a regular routine until this supposed "trespasser" was caught Reynolds half-considered that he might do well to seek out another career option.

He had to get up several times to stretch his legs, walk around—but not too far, he had no desire to go traipsing off into the depths of the cemetery—to get the circulation flowing and to keep himself warm. He gazed up at the skies. The night was clear, stars were twinkling and the moon shone full and bright over Buchanan Bay. He entertained himself with the thought that if he were not on duty tonight he might like to take a drive along the coast, maybe stop in at the roadhouse for a couple of beers and listen to some c/w music. Instead, here he was in a graveyard, sipping on lousy coffee, listening to sounds that would have seemed appropriate in a horror movie.

He finally couldn't hold off any longer. He retrieved the small penlight fastened to his keychain and flashed its beam on the crystal of his watch. 11:34. Later than he expected, but still a long way to go until daybreak. Yet he considered that if midnight came and went and no one showed up, it was unlikely that anyone would. He debated waiting until maybe 1 a.m. and then if things were still quiet, just packing it in. The chief would never know. It was doubtful he'd be driving out to the cemetery to check on him. Yeah, Reynolds decided he just might do that. There was no way he could see himself sitting this out 'til the sun came up.

And then a hand clamped down on his shoulder.

CHAPTER SEVENTEEN

Ida Krevich tilted her head to glance at the clock with the gently swaying and ticking pendulum that adorned the far wall. It was 12:15 a.m. She was startled by the hour. She didn't think she had been up so long. She sighed reflectively as she took a last, lingering look at the photograph of her son. She placed the palm of her hand tenderly upon the glass and then she lifted herself from the rocker and carried the picture over to the end table, carefully placing it back where it belonged and adjusting it to just the correct angle.

She switched off the living room light and went into the kitchen to warm herself some milk. She hadn't been sleeping too well and had to be up by nine to get to her job at the store by 10:30. She had been contemplating asking her manager if she could cut her hours to part-time, or maybe have a lessened work week, three days instead of five. Lately she just seemed to be lacking the stamina to put in a full six-hour day, most spent on her feet and dealing with customers. Mainly demands and complaints, and they were starting to grate on her, straining nerves that had never been that supple to begin with.

While the milk heated in a pot on the stove she considered whether Mr. Gracefeld would agree to such a request. She'd been a good and loyal employee for the past four years and he had been particularly kind to her when she'd lost her son. Yes, the more she thought about it the more she felt certain he would allow her to slow down a bit.

Before the milk could reach a boil she carefully poured it into a mug, then carried it over to the kitchen table. As she sipped on her beverage she looked across to the wall calendar. A pained expression crossed her face as she noticed that in less than a week it would be October 31st, Halloween. A night that the children came out. Always a bittersweet time for her. She enjoyed seeing the youngsters, but at the same time she experienced sadness that her boy Larry would not be among them. Ida didn't know that there likely would be no trick-or-treating this year. Precious few houses in town were decorated for the occasion. Parents in the community wanted their children close to home. Many did not even let their kids walk to school alone. Ida naturally had heard that something "unfortunate" had happened to a couple of the children, but her brain could not properly process the details. It was as if the wall of resistance she had established in dealing with her own son's tragedy had extended even to the misfortune of other young ones. She maintained what little grip she still retained on her reason by convincing herself that everything was all right with the world.

She sat in silence, listening to the gentle, soothing ticking from the clock in the next room. The only sound to interfere with the late hour quiet that pervaded the small house.

. . . Until an unrecognizable sound erupted from down in the cellar, sounding like a dull crash of some sort. Ida started, shaken from whatever thoughts she had been pondering. She held herself steady and still, and waited to hear if there might be another noise.

All was quiet.

Ida relaxed. Probably another stray cat. The latch on the cellar window was broken and a small animal could push its way into the house. It had happened before—and on more than one occasion. Cats could be a particular problem, especially at this time of year when the nights got colder. That's likely what it was, Ida told herself. A stray had crawled inside and probably knocked over an old can of paint or some such thing. She was tired and would tend to that in the morning.

Ida finished her milk and pushed the mug aside. She felt ready for sleep. But just as she began to rise from the table a different sort of noise came from the cellar. It sounded like…

Creeeaaak.

Reflexively, Ida sat herself back down in her chair. She listened attentively. The stairs, she suddenly realized. It was the stairs that were creaking.

Ida began to feel an apprehensiveness creep over her. But she sat perfectly still. The creaking stopped—only for a moment, before it started again, this time getting more pronounced. Indicating that something was coming…very slowly…up the stairs.

Her rheumy eyes veered toward the closed door to the cellar.

The footfalls were louder. Heavier. Clumsier. Whatever was climbing those stairs was no cat or any other small animal. Didn't sound like an animal at all. More like…*human* feet.

Ida tried to lift herself from the chair, but her body felt numb, her muscles weak. She did manage to stammer, "Who—who's there?"

No response, but whatever was on the other side of the door had reached the top step. Ida watched with popping eyes as the outer handle slowly began to turn.

"Whoever you are, just—just go away," she whimpered.

The cellar door started to push open. Ida still couldn't see what—or who—was on the other side. But before the door could open fully she heard a prolonged, terrible moan and then a hoarse, haggard voice. Yet a voice she distinctly knew belonged to a child.

Her child.

"Mommy…"

"Go away!" Ida repeated. Her words were spoken in haste, impulsively. A denial that she did not necessarily intend.

The dull roar of a groan burst forth from the throat.

"Mommy…why did…you…hurt me?"

And the door opened completely and the festering corpse of her son, Larry, who died at the age of eight, shambled into view.

What greeted Ida was little more than an ambulatory skeleton, the burial suit rotted and tattered, exposing bones that protruded through patches of discolored flesh. The neck was twisted at an unnatural angle so that the lifeless, deep-socketed eyes could not meet Ida's too-alive and terrified gaze. What remained of the face was ravaged with decay. There were no lips, the flesh having fallen away, leaving only stringy strands of skin, the mouth drawn back in a hideous gaping maw, the corner of that cavity pulled upward in just the suggestion of a sneer, revealing teeth bare against bone, and through which mournful words were uttered.

"Why, Mommy…why?"

The dead thing just barely recognizable as Ida's boy swayed as it stepped slowly toward her, the arms rising to reveal hands that were just skeletal claws.

"You—stay away from me!" Ida shrieked, her voice high and shrill. All the color had drained from her face until she looked as pale as the milk she had been drinking.

"You hurt me…Mommy…hurt me…bad."

Ida finally managed to pull herself free from her chair, but her legs still felt weak and unsteady. She gripped onto the edge of the kitchen table for support while she struggled to get the strength back into her body.

The walking corpse started to circle the table, the gait awkward and wavering, arms still outstretched as if seeking an obscene embrace. The foul stench that accompanied this horror was overpowering and Ida felt her stomach heave. Mustering every ounce of her willpower she broke free from her paralysis and started to back away. The Larry-thing kept coming toward her, the skeletal jaws moving with a barely perceptible clattering sound, but with no other words being uttered.

"I loved you, Larry," Ida said in a tremulous voice. "I don't deserve this."

"Mommy…"

And in a panic Ida spun around, not realizing that by stepping back she had positioned herself next to the open cellar door. The heel of her foot caught on the top step and she staggered. Her fingers clawed desperately at the air and she released a frantic scream, but in the next instant her body toppled over backward, falling heavily and violently down the same steep stairs that had claimed the life of her son over two years earlier.

Her body lay sprawled at the foot of the stairs, her features wrenched in a grimace…her head turned completely around.

CHAPTER EIGHTEEN

"Sonofabitch," Terry Reynolds blurted as he turned and flashed the narrow beam of his penlight into the ancient face of Caspar McGee, his wrinkled countenance reflecting in the glow like a mummy fresh from the tomb.

"Didn't mean to put no fright into yuh, Officer—*uh*, Reynolds," McGee said quickly as he took a step or two backward, raising both hands in a submissive gesture.

"How'd you think I'd react, sneaking up on me in this godawful place!" Reynolds shot back at the man as he steadied himself. "And just what in hell are you doing out here anyway!"

"Know I shouldn't be," McGee said contritely. Then he spoke with a little more intent. "Only I spent a lotta years lookin' after this place, and just 'cause I put myself out to pasture don't mean I ain't still got a responsibility."

Reynolds gave his head a slow, firm shake. "I don't think so. Your work here was done the day you put in for your pension. Whatever's going on in this cemetery, it's police work."

McGee spat out a short, contemptuous laugh. "You ask me, what I saw out here last night is somethin' maybe even the police ain't prepared to handle."

"What are you talking about?" Reynolds asked, mildly impatient.

McGee edged his head in a little closer to the young officer. His voice took on a deliberately ominous intonation. "What I seen, it weren't anything human."

Reynolds was skeptical. "From what the chief told me, you didn't see much."

"Seen enough," McGee replied in haste. "And it wasn't in no way normal."

"Well, I think you can be assured we don't have any ghouls running around the cemetery," Reynolds said confidently, his eyes scanning the grounds. "Just some wacko."

But Reynolds could not deny the fact that if something out of the ordinary did exist, Resurrection Gardens would have been a perfect setting for its nocturnal prowling.

"Can tell yuh certain, wouldn't be comin' out here tonight alone," McGee said. "But I got a feelin' the chief would have someone out here watchin' after what I told him." He scratched at his thinning scalp. "Only reckoned it might be the chief hisself, though."

"Yeah, well," Reynolds muttered blankly, not explaining the reason for Powell's not being there.

"I got me another feelin'. A suspicion, yuh might call it," McGee went on. He pointed a wobbly finger at Reynold's pen light and said with gruff annoyance, "Y'got with yuh somethin' better than that toy?"

"Sure I do."

"Well, so do I," McGee said huskily and with that he hoisted a battery-powered lantern with three different beam settings and switched it on, casting a wide bright light over the area. "Let's take us a walk," he then said.

Reynolds was doubtful. But he decided to humor the old man. If nothing else it would help to kill some time. He also wasn't worried about the strong glow from the lantern light alerting any trespasser who might be lurking about the cemetery because he was damn positive there would be no unwelcome visitor this night.

As the two crossed the cemetery lawn, the lantern light fanned across the ground.

"He knowed you was gonna be out here tonight," the old man said, his tone distant. "And I figger he already come, but you didn't see him. I just stumbled upon him last night. Don't think he woulda showed hisself otherwise. But he knowed you was comin' so naturally he wouldn't show hisself."

His words were slightly ambiguous, but disquieting all the same. Reynolds didn't acknowledge. He decided it would be smart just to keep his guard up and maintain a close watch on "Fibber" McGee here.

"Gotta be checkin' each of these graves," McGee went on. He slowly turned to Reynolds. "Then you'll know what I'm talkin' 'bout."

Ghosts. Phantoms. Reynolds was starting to feel creeped out. Not by the prospect of the supernatural, but by the old guy himself.

They halted just before the grounds of Heavenly Angels.

McGee suddenly looked grim. "Mighty sad place," he remarked.

Reynolds gave a somber nod in response.

McGee stepped forward, stopped again and surveyed the area. "Not many fresh ones," he observed. "Ceptin' the one I seen with them handprints." He half-turned to Reynolds. "You take a look-see at it?"

"I saw it," the officer replied blankly.

"And them other two that'll be filled tomorrow," McGee added, indicating the open plots for the Loewen twins.

McGee lifted his lantern and shifted it to his other hand, then he began to walk among the graves, lowering the light as he inspected each plot. Reynolds stood back. All that went through his brain was that he'd found himself in a scenario he never could have imagined when he started work that day. Staking out a cemetery at midnight with a strange old man convinced there was some spirit or otherworldly presence roaming about.

After several minutes of careful searching McGee halted and fixed his gaze on one particular grave. He crouched, then slowly pulled himself upright and, without uttering a word, signaled for Reynolds to join him.

The grass had long since settled on the grave, as smooth and level as carpeting. No imprints were visible upon the lawn. But McGee called the young officer's attention to the brass marker. There was a strange discoloration on its surface, just under the name LAWRENCE KREVICH and the dates: 1976 - 1984. Reynolds bent in for a closer inspection. What he saw took him aback. A set of handprints. Imprinted like a dark gray shadow, as if the palms and the long, pencil-thin fingers of both hands had been rubbed solid with a charcoal-like substance before being laid firmly against the brass. Reynolds lightly touched one of the prints with his finger. Then he gave it a gentle rub. A little harder. There was no smudging. It appeared as if the prints had somehow been permanently pressed onto the surface.

Old Caspar McGee couldn't resist expelling a chuckle. "I told yuh."

At first Reynolds didn't know what to make of this discovery. He couldn't figure out how this *manifestation* could have happened during the time he had been there. He hadn't moved from his vantage point until old McGee showed up and if anyone had entered the children's section of the cemetery, he certainly would have seen the individual. There was no chance that he could have missed him—or her—or...*it*. Yet, despite what the old man was saying Reynolds was still not about to accept a paranormal explanation. No, he had to make sense of this his own way, and his explanation was that most likely someone had come out to the cemetery earlier, before Reynolds had arrived, and made those handprints. Some prank or pre-Halloween joke, intended to set the town on edge more than it already was.

McGee sidled over to Reynolds. "I'd be thinkin' it might be smart if you call the chief and have him take a ride out to Ida Krevich's place."

Reynolds looked sharply at the old man. "What'd be the point in that?"

"The markings," McGee said with his eyes wide. "Last time those handprints was found, on that little girl's grave, that was the night somethin' bad happened to the Stromm couple."

"No," Reynolds said adamantly. "You're talking like there's some sort of black magic going on here."

McGee cocked an eye. "Ain't there?"

The old man regarded Reynolds with a set and serious expression. He didn't have to say anything more. The look on his face told it all. In his own mind he was convinced something dark and malicious was at work not only at Resurrection Gardens but in Clear Vista itself.

After a long silence he said, "If only you'da seen what I seen last night." He nodded his head very slowly. "Then you'd know."

Reynolds prided himself on being a rational man. He didn't believe in ghosts or spirits, witches or werewolves. He even questioned the existence of God, a nice, comforting concept, but hardly a belief that could explain or transcend the pain and suffering that people experienced daily. Like the parents of the children buried here. And his doubt in that regard meant that he put little value on devils or demons, though in a strange way they were closer to his own understanding with the world being what it was. But there was something about McGee's attitude that—while it might not have convinced him to ease his skepticism on such matters—got him to thinking it might not be a bad idea to take a ride over to the Krevich place.

"I'll drive you back into town," he offered McGee.

The old man declined with a wave of his hand. "No need," he said. "Got my pickup parked down the road a bit. Surprised you didn't see it comin' in. But I like to keep it outta view."

"Yeah," Reynolds said curtly.

As the old man started to walk away Reynolds radioed Chief Powell, told him of their discovery and said that he was heading out to Ida Krevich's house and asked for the chief to meet him there.

* * *

It was almost 1:00 a.m. when Reynolds saw the chief's cruiser pull up behind him outside the house on Kent Road. It wasn't much of a distance to the Krevich house from where Powell lived and so Reynolds hadn't had to sit out his wait for long. He exited the car and moved briskly to the cruiser, opening the door for Powell in a rather hurried manner. The street itself was autumn quiet but for a faint breeze that rustled the branches of the trees that bordered the boulevard. Powell stepped out and studied the house. The inside lights were turned off, indicating that the woman had gone to bed.

Powell didn't care to be here. He had never lost the resentment he felt toward Ida Krevich. It remained his opinion that she was a murderer who had escaped justice. Whenever he saw her around town he made it a point to steer clear of her, otherwise he couldn't be sure he would be able to restrain himself and might just spew out his accusation. Which wouldn't bode well with his professional standing and with public sentiment still sympathizing with her.

Reynolds didn't know much behind the situation. The Ida Krevich incident had happened before he joined the Clear Vista police department and Powell had never confided in him the reason for his animosity toward her. But he had noticed Powell's cold avoidance of the woman whenever their paths crossed and also detected the tension that seemed to rise up in the chief whenever her name was brought up.

His personal feelings aside, Powell had an official duty to perform. Even if he really wasn't sure why he had been brought out to her house tonight. Reynolds had only mentioned handprints he'd found on the plaque marking Larry Krevich's grave. But that was enough, Powell reckoned, for him to be summoned. He didn't know what was going on with those mysterious cemetery markings. And he was especially bewildered how another defacement could have happened tonight when Reynolds insisted he'd never caught so much as a shadow intruding upon the grounds of Heavenly Angels. Unless he wanted to step wholly into an episode of *The Twilight Zone* he had to accept Reynolds's theory that the grave must have been visited earlier that day and another sick prank had been pulled.

Before they proceeded up the walkway Reynolds said to Powell, "Old Caspar McGee seems convinced something beyond rational explanation is at work here."

"Just too much time on his hands," Powell said dismissively.

Reynolds looked at the chief with a quizzical expression. He spoke a little impudently. "It's because of him that you had me sit out there tonight. And something did go on, with that marker."

Powell nodded. "Sure. Something's going on, but I'm not ready to start pulling out cloves of garlic and wooden stakes." Yet even though his words were frivolous, with each new peculiar development he was becoming less inclined to completely discount *any* possibility.

Powell and Reynolds stepped up onto the porch. Reynolds moved over to the big front window and peered inside, squinting as he tried to penetrate the thin fabric of the curtains. "Can't tell for sure," he said. "But looks like there might be a light on in back."

Powell pulled open the screen and started hammering on the main door. His fist was thumping hard enough for the wood to shudder under the impact, hard enough for Reynolds to cast him a questioning look. He couldn't see the need for such force. Powell ignored his stare. They waited for about a minute and then Powell gave another loud series of knocks.

"Maybe she's not home," Reynolds suggested. He was feeling a mite agitated at the chief's pronounced persistence.

Powell was quick to dismiss that possibility. "At this time of night? Ida Krevich? Outside of her job the woman's damn near become a recluse. She's home."

Reynolds wore a concerned look. "Maybe—"

Powell looked sharply at him. He read into what the young officer was thinking.

"Go 'round back and see if there's any way we can get in," he instructed Reynolds. "Otherwise I'm going to have to use a commando tactic on this door."

"Chief, don't you think that's—" Reynolds started to say.

Powell cut in abruptly. "She's inside and she's not answering. And I don't intend to wait around 'til morning to call a locksmith."

Reynolds gave an unenthusiastic nod. Then he started toward the side of the house, passing through the unlocked iron gate that creaked noisily on its rusted hinges. He noticed that it was the kitchen light that he'd seen through the front window. He glanced through the small square kitchen window, but couldn't see Mrs. Krevich or anything that looked out of place. He then tried to open the back door. He twisted the knob. It turned only partway. Locked. He couldn't see any other way to get inside so he went back around to the front of the house and the waiting Chief Powell.

"Kitchen light is on," he reported. "Back door is secured. Maybe you should try knocking again."

Powell couldn't be sure if Reynolds was serious or being sarcastic. He regarded Reynolds with a sardonic expression of his own. "Probably woke up half the neighborhood already. If that didn't get her up, she's not gonna answer."

Reynolds knew what that meant and even though he was standing far enough away, he moved himself back even farther. Powell positioned himself several feet from the door, then he flung his body full force into it, bursting the door from its hinges. Reynolds cringed, then rushed up the steps to check if the chief was all right. Powell looked intact as he pulled himself upright from the floor, except that he was massaging his shoulder and grimacing slightly. It had to be more than mere discomfort, though the chief naturally wouldn't let on.

As they walked through the living room toward the kitchen the first thing both men noticed was a repulsive, pungent odor—indefinable but suggestive of something left to rot over a period of time. Reynolds felt his stomach grow queasy and he hurriedly clapped a hand over his nose and mouth to prevent himself from gagging. Even though Powell was more sensitive to smells than Reynolds, he didn't seem quite so bothered by the stench. His face was screwed into a mildly unpleasant expression, but that simply could have been either a look of intensity or a reaction to the pain in his shoulder that he courageously attempted to ignore.

Suddenly Reynolds halted Powell and gestured with a nudge of his head down to the floor. Both sets of eyes fell upon something disturbing. Disturbing yet familiar, because both men had seen it before.

Slight scatterings of damp, claylike earth.

Powell knelt down and picked up some of the mud and rubbed its stickiness between his fingers. Then he slowly rose and his eyes instinctively went toward the cellar door that he noticed was ajar.

He looked askance at Reynolds before he started over to it. Reynolds stayed put, still breathing shallowly through his hand. But in the next moment the chief's expression became twisted and fixed and Reynolds knew that Powell had discovered something that he was not eager to see for himself.

Powell turned to Reynolds and gestured him over. Reynolds stepped toward the door. He followed the chief's gaze down into the cellar, and at seeing the head of Ida Krevich twisted at a completely unnatural angle, he spun around and let loose what he had been trying to hold in and vomited.

Powell was hardly aware of the young officer's violent retching. He himself was staggered. He hadn't expected to come across Ida Krevich lying dead on the cold of the cellar floor.

At the same time a strange yet compelling thought took root in his brain:

Poetic justice…

* * *

Another dead body and more of what appeared to be graveyard dirt scattered about the kitchen floor, tracking even down into the cellar. Or had it been tracking *up* from the basement? And this time the deceased was not known to have vengeful or vindictive enemies, unlike Walter Stromm. The only person who had an outright dislike for the woman was the police chief and he could hardly be considered a suspect.

Preliminary indications pointed to Ida Krevich having died as the result of an accident. It was surmised that she'd lost her footing and tripped down the stairs. Ironically it appeared she died in the exact same manner as her son. Even to her having her neck broken in the fall. A coincidence, but not altogether likely the way Powell perceived it. His suspicions were focused in another direction. That she might have been pushed down those stairs. Because an "accident" could not account for those droppings of mud spread throughout the kitchen.

But if it was a homicide, for what reason? Ida Krevich was not a wealthy woman, and no money or other items had been taken from the house. If she had been murdered, it appeared it was for an entirely different, as yet undetermined, motive.

CHAPTER NINETEEN

Powell spoke on the telephone with the Breckridge medical examiner to obtain the results of the autopsy performed on Ida Krevich.

Dr. Arborshaw stated the cause of death was a cervical fracture.

"Precisely the way her boy died," Powell said to the coroner. "Only her death was instantaneous." He took a moment to organize his thoughts. "Pieces of a puzzle that I can't seem to fit together, yet I'm certain there is a solution. A connection, something maybe even tied into the killing of those girls. That seemed to be the beginning of these unexplained occurrences. Two murders, two people apparently scared to death, and now what appears to be a freak accident. And that tracking of cemetery dirt in two of the homes we investigated. How do you make sense of it?"

It was a rhetorical question and Powell didn't expect an answer, and Dr. Arborshaw couldn't provide him with one. Not an answer or even an educated guess that a man of scientific reasoning would offer—or that a logical mind could conceivably accept.

Though the coroner did say, "You seem convinced that the earth you found comes from a cemetery."

"Well, no way to prove for certain," Powell said. "And even if analysis could confirm its source…so what? It's just that *I'm* sure it all points to something more."

Arborshaw humphed through the receiver.

"But that's not all," Powell continued. He rubbed a jagged thumbnail against the itch scabbing under his hairline. "There have been strange things going on at Resurrection Gardens. According to the old man who used to maintain the grounds, he spotted some…figure the other night, in the children's section. Said he saw someone dressed in a black robe or some such getup doing peculiar activities around one of the graves, a grave that turned out to belong to the Stromm girl, Margaret. Checked it out myself and looks as if something did go on there. Found handprints pressed into the hard soil of the grave. First off, hard to think those handprints belonged to anything that we might regard as human. Never seen fingers that long and narrow, or separated so wide. That aside, I tried to duplicate those handprints and couldn't do it. Ground was like, like solid clay. Couldn't make an imprint, no matter how hard I pressed. Had my man Reynolds sit watch last night. He found handprints, too. Same odd shape, with the pencil-like fingers and all. This time on the grave marker of Ida Krevich's son, who died about two years ago. And here's the topper . . ." He inhaled a deep breath. "Went out this morning with a fellow from the lab unit to see if we could lift fingerprints from the marker, or at least try to determine what caused them."

Powell related what happened earlier that day…

"Odd," the pigment-challenged, orange-haired lab worker, Dave Forant, had said as he examined Larry Krevich's grave marker, where two well-defined yet oddly-shaped handprints were clearly visible on the brass. "There doesn't appear to be any residue or other substance that I could scrape off with my instrument to get a sample for analysis. It's like it's a part of the marker itself. Almost a defect, a discoloration in the brass."

"That's *not* the way the plaque was purchased," Powell said with a frown. "Of course, that can always be checked out with the manufacturer. But I can't see any point."

Dave Forant gave an empty nod. It appeared that he, too, couldn't make sense of this anomaly.

"Might have better luck with the other set of prints," Powell suggested.

They stepped over to Margaret Stromm's grave. Powell's eyes did a search across the settling earth mound, then he turned to Dave Forant with a perplexed and troubled expression.

The handprints that he had seen so clearly embedded in the sod the other day, that Officer Reynolds had noticed as well the night before, *had totally vanished.*

"Odd indeed," Arborshaw remarked as Powell concluded his story.

CHAPTER TWENTY

As fear and anxiety over the recent unsolved murders and curious deaths began to take a tighter grip on the community, long-held secrets started to inexplicably resurface among the people of Clear Vista. Despite the outward placidity of the town, everyone had a skeleton in their closet. Most chose to keep their darker secrets cloaked in shadow, buried in some deep recess of the brain, holding back the memory by maintaining focus on the mundane realities of everyday life. Or, when their mind did become susceptible to the intrusion of their conscience, through the use of alcohol or other intoxicants intended to suppress or lessen the recollection that if fully released might have a painful or even traumatic consequence.

It was after the sun set and darkness descended when one was at risk of becoming vulnerable. Night was when one's resistance was weak and an unpleasant memory kept safely in check during the daylight hours could stealthily creep up in one's consciousness. That was when the delicate balance between reason and irrationality could be compromised.

Yet the most fearful threat was to fall victim to one's dreams, *nightmares*, when the defenses surrender wholly and there is no protection from the demons of the mind.

Secrets could be hidden. Protected. They might never be known to others. But if malevolent memories are released without warning or provocation they unfurl only to enfold like the cold wrapping of a burial shroud.

* * *

Mayor Edward Warrington was having just such a nocturnal visit as he lay asleep in his bed. For he, too, was a man plagued by a troubling secret. One with a consequence that he did his best to keep from the people he represented as their elected official. For if that secret were ever to be exposed, made public, it would cast a damning light on his credibility both as a politician and as a man.

Only one other person knew of his secret, and that was his late friend Walter Stromm. Stromm, who had used his own considerable influence to help conceal the shameful scar in Warrington's past. Which came at a price of course. The two men shared a strange association. Stromm needed someone pliable and indebted to him to occupy the mayor's chair. A man who would appeal to the people, but whose true purpose was to work for Stromm's interests.

It was a position that Stromm himself could never hold. He would never be the voter's choice due to questions concerning his business tactics, which many suspected were underhanded if not downright ruthless. And while he could craftily circumvent the parameters of the law in most of his dealings, he could not as easily get around one's moral obligation to his fellow man. But that was barely a consideration where he was concerned. He freely took advantage of those who could benefit him and used people at his own discretion, subtly pulling strings like a skilled puppeteer.

He was intelligent enough to know that despite his very public philanthropic endeavors he could put a positive spin on his image for only so long before people began to get wise both to the man and his practices. As a public official he would be much more prone to scrutiny and that could conceivably lead to the eventual collapse of his various business enterprises. It was simpler to keep himself behind the scenes and manipulate the administration as needed.

And that was why Edward Warrington became a very useful tool to Walter Stromm. Stromm was only too glad to help bury Warrington's shameful secret. Because as payment Warrington was expected to oblige Stromm, even though that often proved an unsavory procedure. Warringtom didn't know everything that went on with Stromm's affairs. In fact, he knew less about the man and his dealings than Stromm's devoted secretary, Norma Cullington—but he still knew enough. Enough so that if Stromm dared to bring his own past to light, Warrington could have brought down both Stromm and his sandcastle empire. But that was never a consideration—Stromm's power far exceeded that of the mayor's and Warrington knew that if he were ever to be so foolish, a time would come when he would simply disappear. And the waters of Buchanan Bay rarely gave up their secrets.

But now Walter Stromm was dead. The secret that Warrington had shared with him would soon be buried with the man, consigned to the cold ground at Resurrection Gardens. The only other person who knew about this disgrace from his past was safely ensconced in a mental hospital—and *not* the best that money could afford—on the East Coast. And there she sat in her own private world, rocking an imaginary baby, continually humming the tune from her favorite childhood movie *Dumbo*, "Baby Mine."

She hummed to the child she could have had, had her husband not demanded that the fetus be aborted. She resisted. She argued that she was a religious woman and would not so much as consider such a blasphemous act. Warrington was basically a meek man but as the tension between him and his wife Susan escalated and an accusation was finally made—one that she did not deny—Warrington, in a rage, lashed out and struck her again and again, and through this violent if uncharacteristic action he aborted the fetus himself. As Susan watched the blood and the unborn life spill from her uterus, her brain snapped and like the extinguishing of a light bulb, the filament of her sanity was gone.

It could have gone badly for Warrington. Not only would his political career have been ruined, but almost certainly he would have been faced with serious prison time. In a panic, before any of that could happen, he called the only man he could think of who could help him. And without question or hesitation Walter Stromm came to his rescue. Stromm discreetly covered up all the evidence that could have implicated Warrington, all the while assuring the shaken man that he had nothing to worry about. Absolutely nothing. No muss. No fuss. Since Susan Warrington's mind was shattered by the brutality of the attack, the terrible truth of that night safely locked away inside a brain that was no longer lucid, it was unlikely she would ever be able to contradict her husband's words.

Stromm concocted the story that she had been assaulted by an intruder who had broken into their house. Yes, she had been in the early stages of pregnancy, but the intruder had abused her so viciously that she had miscarried right where she had fallen. As disturbing as it might appear to the authorities once they arrived, Stromm deliberately left the bloody and malformed fetus, barely recognizable as something human, lying bare on the carpet. It was something that Warrington himself could not cast his eyes upon.

Chief Braden Powell was the lead officer on the scene. He always maintained a vague suspicion about what really happened that night, even after a suspect had been apprehended and charged with the crime. The accused went to trial, pleaded guilty and basically threw himself on the mercy of the court. His crafty lawyer (one Powell found curious that the punk could afford) had employed fancy legal maneuverings and got him off with a three-to-five-year sentence. Token jail time was how Powell regarded it, certain that some generous cash disbursements had been spread around to the right people. Including, most likely, a promised pension to the accused himself.

And so thanks to Walter Stromm's intervention and his wife's descent into the professional prognosis of a permanent catatonic repression, Mayor Warrington's personal life was untainted and his public life remained unblemished.

He didn't often think about what had happened that night. He wasn't particularly haunted by the memory. For a man of his moderate temperament that might be considered odd. While he could put on the appearance of confidence when in his official capacity, there was another side to Edward Warrington that only a very few people were exposed to. The real man "behind the mask" was possessed of a deep insecurity. Walter Stromm, of course, knew and was quick to take advantage of that weakness in his character.

Chief Powell was another who suspected the truth behind the image. He'd always known Warrington operated under a façade, but how transparent that "front" was had been made evident to him over these past days when he had an obligation to stand up to the demands of his office but instead relied on subterfuge tactics. Powell was caught in the same dilemma, of course, but at least he didn't fool himself it was for the public good.

Warrington felt little remorse over what he did to his wife. He certainly experienced no guilt over halting Susan's pregnancy. And that was because he never believed the child was his. The man was virtually impotent and sexual relations between him and his wife were practically nonexistent. He suspected Susan was seeing someone on the side, and her announcement that she was pregnant all but confirmed his suspicions. He'd reacted with what he convinced himself was a justified rage, as any man discovering such blatant unfaithfulness would likely be inclined to do. And in this matter he again had Walter Stromm's support. In fact, Stromm informed Warrington after the incident that he'd known about Susan's infidelities for quite some time, but kept the information from the mayor for fear of hurting him.

After the entire sordid mess was cleaned up and Warrington could move on with his life and his political responsibilities (most which were now even more severely dictated by Stromm), he had lived with only one fear. The worry that somehow, someday, his secret might be exposed.

He actually felt a sense of relief now that Stromm was dead. He'd always carried the dread that if he were ever to do anything to upset or displease Stromm the man would have no compunction about reminding him that he was the only other person who knew the truth about that night and that it would be wise to tread softly with him. Even without Stromm having to hold a direct threat over his head Warrington understood he lived each day under the shadow of blackmail.

Now that was no longer a concern. And perhaps with that burden off his mind he could regain the confidence that he'd surrendered to Walter Stromm's control and effectively deal with trying to pull his community together in the wake of these recent—as he would underplay it—*misfortunes*.

He went to bed that night convinced that all could be well.

Only he hadn't counted on an unexpected encroachment upon his subconscious, and his succumbing to the most terrifying nightmare he could ever remember having.

What made it especially disturbing was that it was a dream that closely intersected with reality. The environment was precisely as it should be. His bedroom. His bed. The firmness of his mattress and comfort of his sheets and bedcover. Each of these visions was familiar and the sensations tangible.

Yet gradually what could be perceived as "normal" seemed to shift. The pervading ambiance became indistinctly surreal. It subtly took on a shadowy setting. The atmosphere not merely unsettling, but of a sudden filled with an escalating dread. And—

inexplicably—memories of Walter Stromm surfaced, his unseen but overwhelming presence presenting itself almost as a dark omen. Warrington became embraced by apprehension expanding into true terror.

Then came the sound.

That awful, ill-defined sound, squishing, slithering—slowly—as if something wet and nasty was sloshing its way across the hardwood floor of his bedroom.

Yes, slithering, and now approaching the side of his bed.

He lay in fearful uncertainty, hesitant to look, for he knew that whatever was to meet his eyes would be something so horrible he would become petrified. Even as he might descend into total fright—perhaps even madness—he doubted he would be able to look away.

The slithering ceased and the room fell into quiet. But before Warrington could calm himself there came a different kind of sound. A…*gurgle*. A sound that an animal might make in the throes of pain or even death. It emanated directly from the side of the bed next to where his head lay deep in his pillow. The gurgling increased, intensified, as if it were trying to utter a specific sound, but was unable because something was clogged within its throat. To Warrington it was as if whatever this "thing" was, it was trying to…*call him*. Get his attention.

"No," Warrington mumbled. "If I don't look it will go away."

But it wasn't going away. As the gurgling grew louder the thing on the floor sounded almost…angry.

He felt a sharp tug on the bed sheets. Then another. It was as though the thing was either trying to pull the sheets off…or lift itself up onto the bed.

Warrington was unable to resist. He had to see what it was that lurked at the side of the bed. He had to see for himself before whatever it was climbed up *to him*. He slowly lifted himself on an elbow and lowered his face over the bedside until he could see the floor.

Once his gaze fell upon the thing, barely discernible in the dark, and he connected with the opaque yellow eyes of the tiny abomination still trying to pull itself onto the bed, he heard it. The single broken word issued forth in a violent, liquefied expectoration . . .

"Daa—da..."

Warrington sputtered a scream. He could see the thing more clearly now and in his frenzied brain he recognized it and even had a vague understanding of why it was there.

The bloody and tissue-coated fetus that his violent action had aborted from his wife!

But no—it wasn't his. More than the horror at what he was seeing, his mind wouldn't accept that he had *killed his own child*!

It struggled up toward him, a terrible grin stretched across its distended, discolored features.

"Daa..."

It was Warrington's own piercing scream that awoke him. His chest was pounding like a jackhammer. He was nearly hyperventilating.

He'd escaped the grip of a nightmare. A dreadful, disturbing nightmare...

As the return to awareness gradually made inroads, he attempted to settle himself with some slow, steady breathing. The drum-thumping in his chest lessened. What he had experienced existed only in his overactive imagination. And as he looked about, he saw that the bedroom was awash with the reassurance of bright morning sunlight that filtered through the sheer fabric of the curtains. Everything was in its proper place. He had nothing to fear. His first thought was that he never wanted to suffer through another night like that again. And then to ease himself he attempted to make sense of his nightmare, tried to dissect it rationally. But that swiftly proved to be a mistake.

What he determined gave him little comfort and instead added to his anxiety. He was forced to conclude that despite all of his efforts at pushing the memory down, he was affected by that action he had committed two years ago. He'd lost his temper and attacked his wife in a fury. He could try to justify it all he wanted, but the truth that existed within his conscience told another story. His conscience or soul or sense of right and wrong—whatever it was— knew and had imprisoned the secret, but finally had unleashed it in the form of a stark, vivid nightmare.

What upset him most was the "thing" struggling to call him what sounded like "Dada." He knew with an almost absolute certainty that the baby was not his. He'd killed another man's child, and he still remained unrepentant that he had done so. He would never accept someone else's *spawn* as his own.

Warrington tried to shift his thoughts away from the dream, but the effort seemed futile. The terrible truth had surfaced and would stay with him, there was no way he would ever be able to erase it. It was like a scar that might fade over time but would never entirely heal. He'd managed to keep the memory submerged, until now. What was the catalyst? He needed to know. Did it have something to do with Walter Stromm's death? Now that the door had been opened, would that memory become a frequent and tormenting night caller?

All at once these contemplations started to plague Warrington. He couldn't seem to focus his thoughts. But he knew that the longer he stayed in bed trying to sort out and make cohesive sense of these abstracts the more intense this mental malignancy would become.

He hastily scrambled out from under the covers and stood up just a little too quickly.

Before he could reach for his cane to support his balance he was only momentarily aware of the soles of his bare feet coming in contact with something wet and sticky staining the hardwood. In the next instant he felt himself slide backward on the slippery substance. As he fell, the back of his skull crashed against the corner of the end table with bone-shattering impact. Mayor Edward Warrington was dead before he hit the floor. His body lay in the thin, smeared trail of blood and bits of tissue and membrane that circled around the side of the bed.

CHAPTER TWENTY-ONE

Day by day the shadow had been expanding, insinuating itself throughout the town like the coastal fog that, when the climate conditions were right, would subtly creep inland from Buchanan Bay and blanket the community with an eerie, shifting mist that hardly anyone would notice until morning came and the streets were all but consumed by the haze.

But *that* was a natural phenomenon. What seemed to be occurring in Clear Vista could not be explained so logically. An atmosphere of gloom and even paranoia had descended over the town. People went about their business in an abrupt, almost perfunctory manner, rarely stopping to chat with neighbors or familiar passersby. Perhaps a quick greeting before each was on his or her way, but now most seemed to avoid polite conversation. Even the merchants and store owners conducted business in a swift, impersonal manner, no longer stepping back from the counter or cash register long enough to inquire with genuine interest about how one or one's family was doing.

Much of the friendliness that had been an inherent quality of Clear Vista seemed to have diminished as people became increasingly insular, afraid to express themselves to those who at one time they would have spoken openly.

Chief Powell observed and absorbed this change in the attitudes of the townspeople and it disturbed him. A pragmatic man, he understood that the citizens were still dealing with the tragedies that had befallen the town and as a result had perhaps developed distrust among themselves. There were those with whom an almost conspiratorial attitude had taken hold, leading them to suspect that there was more afoot than what was being spoon-fed through the police.

He tried to deal with what seemed to be occurring in a rational manner, but Powell could not completely dismiss the possibility that there could be something happening beyond the norm. Some abnormality of which the citizens themselves were not cognizant. Nothing of a supernatural nature, certainly, but perhaps the community had become sensitive to an indefinable negative energy that was affecting dispositions and behavior on a subconscious level. Even Powell wasn't totally immune to it, though for himself he could explain his mood logically. He was a cop investigating uncommon occurrences in Clear Vista and so he understood he would be much more susceptible to a certain degree of paranoia, attuned to doubt and suspicion.

Even prone to mistrust.

Powell woke up, glanced in the bathroom cabinet mirror in preparation of his daily shave, and was distressed to notice that his damned psoriasis looked to be spreading, taking root in other areas of his face. Another unwelcome scaly patch of red had sprouted next to the bridge of his nose. "Oh yeah," he muttered through tightly clenched teeth, "Shoulda known you bastards would pick now to show up."

Had that been the low point of his day Powell would have gotten off easy. But shortly after Powell arrived at the office he took a call from Terry Reynolds. Mayor Warrington had not shown up at a women's breakfast meeting where he was to deliver a speech on specific town developments that seemed irrelevant yet somehow necessary in the wake of recent happenings, to boost community confidence and restore at least a semblance of normalcy to the town.

At one time the call would not have been taken with any degree of concern by Powell. Warrington was not a man of strict routine as was Walter Stromm. In fact, Warrington was known to often show up fashionably late at various events. He liked to "make an appearance," as it were. But since the discoveries of the Stromm couple and now with the "suspicious" death of Ida Krevich, no such irregularity could be dismissed so easily. Powell had to be on top of it.

As he was readying to leave the office to drive out to the Warrington house Donna Murray suddenly appeared in the doorway, carrying a towel-covered tray.

"Donna," Powell said, barely suppressing his surprise at her unexpected visit.

Donna responded with a meek smile and started toward his desk. "I thought you could use some breakfast," she said.

Powell accepted the tray and placed it on the desk. He found himself in an awkward moment. Her thoughtful gesture had caught him totally unprepared—especially under the circumstances, with him about to go out on a call.

"I—uh…" he started to stammer.

Donna looked equally uncertain. Perhaps a little crestfallen that he wasn't responding with more enthusiasm to her "surprise." Or *her*.

"No, no," Powell quickly said with emphasis. "It's not that I don't appreciate, it's just that I have to respond to a call."

"Oh? No, I—I understand," she said.

"Nothing urgent," Powell explained. "Just routine."

Damn, why did she have to do this? he thought to himself. *And why now?*

"Just coffee and some Danish," Donna said, gesturing toward the tray. She then added: "I could keep the coffee warm for you."

"Might not be back for a while," Powell told her.

And at that moment another interruption occurred when Keith Birdlong came into the office. The look on his face and purpose in his step told Powell that he had something important to tell him. It could wait. Powell gave Birdlong a stern look to indicate that he first had another matter to attend to.

Donna saw that her timing was inopportune and that she should leave. "I suppose I'll take this back to the diner," she said, retrieving the breakfast tray. "Maybe you can stop in after you get back."

Powell gave her a smile to let her know that he would drop by if he could.

Birdlong watched as Donna left the office. Once she was gone he swiveled his head toward Powell and said with barely restrained fervor, "Just had an interesting visit from that old gravedigger."

Powell tilted his head. "Caspar?"

"Yeah. Seems you've been holding back," Birdlong said in a firm, but not quite accusatory tone.

Powell responded decisively. "Oh no. Let's get one thing straight. Your paper doesn't start publishing any of *that*."

"Weird figures moseying about in the cemetery at night, mysterious handprints stamped on graves and grave markers," Birdlong recited.

And then Powell's features grew taut. "You say McGee came to you?"

Birdlong maintained a newsman's privilege and neither confirmed nor denied who had come to whom.

But Powell was already wise to him—and to the possible wiliness of Caspar McGee. "Figured as much," he determined. "That old bastard's playing this both ways. So tell me, how much are you paying him?"

"Me?" Birdlong asked, sounding almost indignant at what the chief was presuming.

"Your *paper*?" Powell clarified.

"Who said anything about payment?"

"Don't dig yourself in a hole that you can't get yourself out of, Birdlong," Powell cautioned, expressing himself as a cop but then questioning his peculiar choice of wording under the circumstances. "Don't know how it comes together, but I've had a suspicion McGee's somehow on the inside of all that's been happening." That wasn't necessarily true—McGee was just a nosy old coot with too much time on his hands—but Powell hoped that by saying this it might prompt Birdlong to reveal why McGee had gone against his word not to say anything about those occurrences at Resurrection Gardens.

"No. McGee just has a story he wants to tell," was all Birdlong would offer.

"That he wants to *sell*," Powell said, his tone sardonic.

"He told me that *you* took him seriously enough," Birdlong challenged.

Powell tried not to sound too self-righteous. "That's my duty, *amigo*. And I felt his claim did have some merit."

"And did it?" Birdlong asked.

Powell merely responded with the semblance of a smile.

"I can always drive out there and check for myself," Birdlong said.

"And you can bring Caspar along as your tour guide," Powell wisecracked.

"He seems pretty sincere it's for the benefit of the town," Birdlong remarked, ignoring the chief's sarcasm. "And that the people have a right to know."

"Well, his concern for the town's welfare might be debatable," Powell returned. He impatiently reached for his pack of cigarettes and withdrew a smoke which he waved before Birdlong before lighting. "But he starts spreading this around and he's either going to come across as a crackpot, or as I warned him, people are going to start looking at him with renewed suspicion."

"He's given me a lead on a story," Birdlong said. "And how many more of these incidents do we keep under wraps?"

Powell struck a match to his cigarette and refrained from saying anything more until he inhaled several deep puffs.

"I thought it was agreed that until we get a handle on what's going on we weren't going to release anything that might add to the anxiety of the public," he reminded strongly. He took another drag from his cigarette and his tone lightened. "And by the way, I thought you were on my side."

"Maybe we've been holding off too long," Birdlong countered. His defiant attitude likewise mellowed. "And Chief, believe it or not, I am on your side. But, well, let's face it, you haven't gotten a *handle* on anything yet."

Birdlong wasn't being critical, just presenting a frank observation. And, unfortunately, a correct one. Powell understood and he didn't take offense at Birdlong's words.

"Look," Birdlong said straightly. "I was willing to back off a bit with the murder of those two girls. Also with this, whatever the hell it was with the Stromm couple. But now this woman, Mrs. Krevich, is found at the bottom of the basement stairs with her neck broken and from what I can determine her death also looks mighty suspicious."

"The woman took a tumble down the stairs," Powell responded. "The coroner confirms that it was an accident."

"Uh-huh," Birdlong said, sounding not altogether convinced, reflecting a newspaperman's skepticism. "And coincidentally, just the way it happened to her son."

"You want to put a darker spin on this?" Powell questioned.

Birdlong blinked. "Let's just say I'm not a strong believer in coincidences."

Powell jabbed a finger at himself. "You asking *me* to provide an explanation?" he asked sharply.

"No," Birdlong replied, exhaling a sigh. "No more than I can expect that old cemetery caretaker to satisfy my curiosity." He paused before resuming. "But he has got me to thinking."

Powell determined that he could find himself up against a tough adversary with Keith Birdlong. He realized it could be more to his advantage to have the newspaperman on his side, and the way to achieve that was by expressing himself truthfully.

He took a long, final pull from his cigarette and mashed it in the butt-filled ashtray on his desk. Then he said, "Birdlong, I'm a practical man. Yet I'm of a mind to start opening myself to explanations that may be, well, let's say beyond the realm of rational possibilities. That's why I'm asking you—for now—just to go along with me until we can determine the true facts."

Birdlong looked long and hard at the chief. He understood the man's dilemma. And his own, as well. Any wild reporting before the actual truth was known could damage both his and his newspaper's credibility. He also recognized the benefit of working alongside Powell—to be on the inside and see for himself, with Chief Powell's support, whatever it was that was going on in Clear Vista. He gave his head a steady nod in acknowledgement.

"All right then," Powell said, satisfied. "If I know I can depend on you, trust you, I might as well tell you that we could have ourselves another situation. That's where I'm headed now."

Birdlong's interest was immediately piqued. He waited for Powell to volunteer more information, but the police chief refrained. Instead he gestured for Birdlong to follow him out the door of the office.

* * *

"*Holy Jesus*," Birdlong gasped in reflexive response to what greeted his eyes when Powell finally allowed him into the room after he first had surveyed the situation.

No one could have guessed what Powell and Officer Reynolds would come upon when they responded to the call that Mayor Warrington had not turned up to deliver his talk at the women's breakfast meeting. The three men had met outside the mayor's house on Plymouth Drive. Reynolds had yet to enter the premises.

His greeting to Powell was formal, respectful. His manner was intentional. He was determined to maintain his professional conduct and not compromise it, as he'd done to his embarrassment that morning outside Walter Stromm's house when the chief found him stumbling and trembling.

But Reynolds was curious why Birdlong had come along with the chief. Although he never voiced it, he always felt there was something unsavory about the man. Part of his dislike was that he suspected Birdlong was an opportunist. The kind of cheap journalist who would betray his own mother for a good story. Which was why he couldn't figure out the reason Powell had permitted him to check out this situation.

They had made their way into the house, through the front door which was unlocked for whatever reason, and headed directly into the bedroom where they had made their discovery. Mayor Warringtom was dead. His body was sprawled on the floor in a prone position, a gaping gash at the back of his skull where a great quantity of blood had congealed. But what they also found was something that could not so easily be explained. A separate smearing of blood and fluid mixed with other undetermined matter that seemed to have no precise point of origin, but semi-circled the bed, next to where Edward Warrington's body lay, giving the impression that something had been dragged through the gore. Or an even more disturbing possibility, something had dragged itself through it. Examining closer, Powell noticed that there were tiny markings of the gross substance marking the edges of the bed sheets.

Reynolds struggled to hold onto his composure. The sight and the stench emanating from that slimy, bloody smear was stomach-turning and he didn't want to stand too close to it. Neither did Birdlong, though he seemed to regard the substance with an expression of odd interest. Powell simply tried to ignore its offensiveness and concentrate on the work at hand. And what he found peculiar after a quick check of Warrington's body was that the man looked to have been dead for several hours, yet the blood and fluid that smeared the hardwood next to him had not yet congealed and actually still appeared to be fresh.

Following Birdlong's semi-mute utterance Powell turned to him and gave him a stern reminder, delivered both through his expression and in his words. "Don't forget, we made an agreement."

Birdlong acknowledged with a slow nod.

"What do you figure? Murder?" he then asked the police chief.

Powell didn't answer. He pretended not to hear the question. It was still too early to form any kind of conclusion and he wasn't about to commit himself until a thorough investigation could be completed. Yet the chief's hypothesis was that Warrington might simply have fallen while getting out of bed and smashed his head into the sharp corner of the end table.

But that didn't explain the putrid, bloody spillage next to his body.

"Want to speculate what that is, where it came from?" Powell asked both men, though not really expecting an answer.

Birdlong said sotto voce, "If I told you, I don't think even *I'd* believe it."

"Well, I think we can safely surmise it's not from Warrington's head wound," Powell said. He turned to Reynolds and instructed, "Better put in a call to Dr. Arborshaw, then to the crime lab unit in Breckridge. Whatever it is, the lab boys should be able to identify it."

Birdlong had a curious look to him, as though he had an opinion but wasn't sure if he should volunteer it.

And then he blurted, "I can tell you what it is."

Reynolds halted in the doorway before he could make his calls while Powell gave the newspaperman a look of interest.

"Well, go ahead. I'm open to any opinion," the chief said.

Birdlong's eyes shifted from Powell to Reynolds. Instead of answering directly, Birdlong recounted a story and it was evident from the tone of his voice that the memory still haunted him.

"After I graduated from journalism school, before I started working on a city newspaper, I was assigned to a small community in the Midwest, to get my feet wet. One of the first stories I worked on had to do with the police raid on a clinic that was performing these 'surgical procedures' illegally, operating under a phony corporate front. This *clinic*, if you want to call it that—could better be described as a slaughterhouse—well, among other things wasn't employing safe or sanitary methods. Since I was just starting out as a reporter I was apprenticing under one of the paper's more seasoned journalists. It was his story but he wanted to break me in to see if I had what it took to be a newspaperman. You know, to determine if I had the stomach for the sometimes more graphic aspects of the job.

But more than that, I think, if I could maintain an impartiality. That was the tougher of the two.

By the time we arrived cops were already at the clinic. Arrests had been made and there was a clean-up going on. Collecting evidence. The fellow I was with told me to go into the procedure room and give a reporting of what I'd find. I remember to this day what I found. A primitive abortion had just taken place maybe an hour earlier. Whoever the woman was, she'd already been taken away, and I saw what had been taken out of her and dumped into a bucket...like so much pig slop." He was unable to suppress a grimace. But he recovered, pulled back his gaze from the floor and his eyes creased. "What *this* is...that's what I saw in the bucket."

"You're certain?" Powell said carefully.

Birdlong responded with a slow rocking of his head. "Yeah, I'm sure."

Reynolds spoke numbly, his features screwed in an unpleasant expression. "But...there's no...*fetus*."

Birdlong didn't say anything. There was nothing he could say. Beyond what he'd just offered, he had no explanation.

Powell, too, went quiet. He didn't know what to think. Birdlong seemed confident and the chief had no reason at this point to question or contradict the young newspaperman's certainty.

Then—almost inexplicably, Powell's thoughts were jolted back to that night when he was last here, in the mayor's house, called out on official duty because an intruder had allegedly broken in and assaulted Warrington's wife, killing her unborn child, the fetus spilling out onto the floor, and the brutality of his crime subsequently committing the woman to a mental asylum, possibly for the remainder of her life.

Jesus Christ, maybe he, too, was starting to lose his mind, but puzzle pieces were beginning to fit together, yet in a way too incredible to contemplate.

Walter and Barbara Stromm…daughter Margaret, deceased.

Ida Krevich…son Larry, deceased.

And now Edward Warrington…only with a child that had never been born. A fetus that had been aborted through a violent attack.

Reynolds sidled over to Powell. "Gonna be hard to put a lid on this one, Chief."

Powell remained absorbed in his thoughts and wasn't listening.

"I suppose the mayor's death can be attributed to an accident," Birdlong then proposed. "No one has to know about…" He breathed out and said with a frustrated emphasis, "No one would believe it anyway."

Powell again didn't respond. Birdlong gave him a curious look and asked if he was all right.

Powell swiftly pulled himself together. "Huh? Yeah."

Reynolds and Birdlong exchanged a glance. It was obvious to both men that Powell had something occupying his thoughts. But whatever that might be, it appeared Powell was not ready to share it.

Powell spoke a little brusquely. He told the two men that he'd stay behind and wait for the coroner and the crime lab boys to arrive. He instructed both that he didn't want word to get out to the community until the medical examiner could perform an autopsy to determine the cause of death. Most importantly, absolutely nothing was to be said about what else they had found, the bloody smearing, for which there was no apparent—and certainly at this point no *logical*—explanation.

Once Reynolds and Birdlong were gone Powell started to examine the other rooms, checking to see if he could find a clue that might establish if someone else had been inside the house. To his mind there simply had to have been someone present. It provided the only reasonable explanation for those disturbing conclusions Powell had reached. As with what happened to the Stromms, Warrington's death might have been motivated by possible revenge. Whoever was responsible for these crimes was using the trauma of a dark period of the victim's past as a weapon, hoping to prey on their fear—or guilt—by planting grisly, telling evidence, a doll that looked freshly pulled from the grave found next to Walter Stromm, a pile of aborted fetal matter spilled fresh beside Edward Warrington's body. It was sick, deranged. Powell could not start to comprehend the type of warped brain he might be dealing with.

His only question was, did Ida Krevich also fit into this pattern? If some strange justice was being meted out to the parents of deceased children, Powell considered her to be the guiltiest of all since, to his mind, she had been directly responsible for the death of her boy. She not only killed but tortured the lad. Yet, unlike Walter Stromm and Edward Warrington, nothing to specifically connect her with her son was found next to her twisted corpse, except for that fresh trail of mud that also had been discovered at the Stromm house. More macabre evidence, perhaps intended to create the illusion the boy she had killed had come back from the grave.

Or…was there another key yet to be established that linked these incidents together?

CHAPTER TWENTY-TWO

Powell purposely avoided offering his theory to Dr. Arborshaw once the medical examiner arrived at the house to examine Mayor Warrington's body. It was a hypothesis with some merit, Powell believed, but he did not think that a man educated in the scientific field would necessarily agree with such a conjecture, which at most he would likely regard as crime scene guesswork. Powell had to keep his theory to himself until he had something more substantial to go on. He only hoped it wouldn't come as the result of another unexplained death.

Yet even Arborshaw was baffled by the unexplained matter staining the floor around the bed. He became more puzzled when he hunkered down to examine it.

"Virtually no coagulation," he observed as he prodded at the smearing with a cotton swab.

"Any way you can make sense of that?" Powell asked him. "Because I've been here for a good hour and I can't say how long it was before I arrived that this stuff was put here."

Arborshaw looked up over his shoulder at the chief. "*Put* here?" he said questioningly.

Powell questioned stiffly, "Can you give another suggestion as to how it got into the house? Not likely that it just seeped out of the floor."

"No." Arborshaw shook his head in bewilderment. "Naturally it will have to be analyzed, and the sooner the better. I've never seen anything like this before. If it truly is what it appears to be, it's biologically impossible."

"As opposed to anything else that's been happening in this town?"

A question that both men knew did not require an answer.

"Any guess at what it is?" Powell asked, cleverly, pretending ignorance, wanting verification of Birdlong's conclusion.

Arborshaw responded with a look that indicated Powell damn well knew what it was.

Powell surrendered the act. "Okay. And that's why I don't know if what we're looking at is an accident or a homicide."

"You're a cop. Tell me, what's your gut feeling?" Arborshaw asked him.

Powell smiled wanly. "Possibly both."

* * *

After the crime lab unit completed their forensics investigation and collected samples of the blood and tissue to take back to Breckridge for further examination, the police chief decided to bypass a direct stop at his office and drop into the diner and try to sort out his thoughts. After what he'd just seen at the Warrington house he certainly did not have an appetite, but he could appreciate a strong cup of coffee. If he knew he didn't have a long day ahead of him he would have preferred something a whole lot stronger.

When he walked through the door of Gregg's Grill, Donna Murray spotted him and gave him a wide smile. Powell tried to return it, but his own greeting was more forced than genuine. The restaurant was doing a pretty active business and almost at once Powell regretted coming inside. He noticed how the conversations quieted and the atmosphere turned tense as eyes turned toward him.

Still, he was the chief of police, protected in his authority, and would not allow himself to be intimidated.

He stepped toward the counter and boldly made an announcement to intercept the inevitable citizen queries. He didn't even want to think about the questions that would be thrust at him once the news about the mayor got out—and there was no chance that information could be held back from the public for long.

He said, "Look folks, just came in for a cup of coffee. Know you have questions you want answered but all I can tell you is the department is still investigating."

"Workin' on any leads, Chief Powell?" one of the diners asked, ignoring Powell's stalling and getting the ball rolling. "Any progress you're making that you can let us know about?"

Before Powell could try to come up with a convincing reply another voice spoke up.

"Seems like you've been doin' this investigatin' as you put it, Chief, for a long time," one of the elderly diners, a retired boatman named Les Fordish called out from his table, feeling it was his privilege to speak openly given his age and heritage in the town.

"It hasn't even been a week, Les," Powell reminded tersely.

"Lot can happen in a week," Fordish said in a huff. "And just how much ain't you been tellin' us, Chief?"

Powell bristled. "I can only give out what I know. And that's gotta be conclusive information. I don't operate on guesswork or speculation. And I don't put forward anything that might in some way hamper our investigation."

"What do you mean by 'hamper'?"

Powell opened his mouth to reply when he was cut short.

"And don't seem to be a lot coming' from there, Chief," said another gruff voice. "Y'hear stuff. You don't tell us…and then we find out you been sittin' on something else we shoulda knowed about."

"I'm not holding anything back," Powell said emphatically, though inwardly squirming at his (necessary) dishonesty. "And I wouldn't want any of you folks to think I'm not acting in your best interest."

"Catching whoever killed those sweet girls would be acting in our best interest," one of the woman customers seated at a booth said with a scowl.

"Yes, I know. But we haven't had a lot to work on," Powell said, emphasizing his own frustration with a sigh. "Virtually no clues. Nothing to help us identify this individual."

"Seems might funny, Chief, since I know a lot of us came into your office to give you a description of this fella. Lot of us seen him when he was around."

Powell refrained from mentioning that each description varied drastically from the other. And he still wasn't entirely convinced that the person everyone seemed to suspect—the transient—was responsible for the murder of the twins. Not if there happened to be a connection to these other recent happenings.

Another negative comment, this time from Bob Caffrey. "Heard your speech, Powell, at the church. Wasn't impressed then. Ain't much impressed now."

Powell shifted his weight from one foot to the other—a self-conscious gesture that he instantly wished he had avoided. He did not want to betray himself with obvious body language.

"I understand what you're all saying," he said. "But it's not going to do anyone any good taking me or the department to task."

"No one's 'taking you to task', but the people of this community would like to go to sleep at night knowing that their children are protected." A kinder tone, but no less demanding voice rose from somewhere in the back of the diner. Powell recognized it as coming from Bettina Goodwin, a widow who could find criticism with practically any*one* or any*thing* in town, but who had the uncanny ability to express herself so sweetly and innocently that one felt insulted enough to argue with her.

"Not just the children, but I'd like to sleep without keeping one eye open," said another, promptly. "No one in this community has ever felt the need to keep doors locked before."

A murmur of agreement from other diners.

Powell tried to keep the reins on his patience, but it wasn't even midday and already he was becoming overwhelmed. Repeated questions. Repetitious and not totally truthful answers. The crowd would keep at him for the next hour if he let them and still nothing would be resolved. Out of necessity he acted impulsively. Donna had just started to walk over to him with a cup of coffee when he set his eyes firmly on her and said decisively, "Let's you and me go for a ride?"

Donna looked at him, back at the customers and barely restrained herself from frowning her disapproval at the diners, each looking rife to bombard Powell with more questions, comments, theories, and maybe even downright accusations concerning the inefficiency of the town's police department, and she replied just as resolutely, "I think that would be a good idea."

She cast a requesting glance toward a co-worker who nodded that she would take over her tables.

As they drove along the coastal highway, windows open and both absorbing the relaxing salty sea air that drifted inland from the bay waters, Powell thought it proper to explain to Donna, "Asking you to come along was a spur of the moment decision."

"I don't mind," Donna said. "Though you did catch me off-guard and I might have to do some explaining later."

"Don't worry about it," Powell told her. "No one's going to argue with the chief of police."

"Wasn't the way it looked at the restaurant," Donna said, playfully shifting her gaze toward him to take the edge off her comment.

Powell responded with a mild grin. "Yeah."

Donna sighed. "Anyway, I'm glad you did what you did."

Powell turned his attention toward her. "Ask you to come for a ride?"

Donna smiled delicately. "Well, yes, that, and also how you stood up to all that criticism."

"Don't rightly know if it was criticism," Powell said with a shake of his head. "People want answers." The tone of his voice started to sound mildly agitated. "They have a right to know. Only makes it tough when I don't have much to tell them. Doubly hard when more unanswered questions start piling up. More..." He quickly stopped himself from saying anything further.

Too late. Donna wore a quizzical look. Powell had meant something by his last unfinished remark.

Powell kept his eyes tightly focused on the ribbon of two-lane highway that stretched and curved ahead. It was nearly another minute before he spoke again. He deftly changed the topic.

"I haven't been sure this was the right thing," he said, admitting, "In fact, I convinced myself it wasn't."

"That *what* wasn't the right thing?" Donna asked, hesitantly.

"Nothing against you, Donna, just stuff in my own life that I have to deal with, that I have to put into some sort of perspective." Powell felt it necessary to add, "Professional. Related to my work."

"I wasn't expecting anything more from you," Donna replied, not being entirely truthful. "I just was thinking that maybe you needed a friend. Someone to talk to."

"Been too much going on, Donna," Powell said, speaking as if he hadn't even heard her. "Trying to determine causes. Reasons. Not able to give the answers everyone wants. Because if they're there, they seem to defy logical thinking. It's like I'm treading through a backwater swamp that keeps getting deeper and murkier."

Donna turned to him, her expression once more drawn into a look of concern at what Powell might be alluding to.

Powell's own features were twisted in frustration. He could feel her focus fixed on him and he began to feel his body tense. And finally he could no longer ignore her penetrating stare. His jaw tightened and in a swift, spontaneous move he spun the cruiser off to the side of the road. The suddenness of his action startled Donna, who stiffened in her seat and stifled the gasp that had risen in her throat. And then Powell slammed his foot on the brake pedal and the car spit gravel before coming to a complete stop on the shoulder. There followed a tense quiet inside the vehicle. Powell said nothing, offering no explanation for why he had thrown the car into such a quirky and potentially dangerous maneuver.

The truth was he wasn't sure himself. But he couldn't blame her if she chose to get out of the car and walk away from him. In fact, just as strangely, he almost wanted her to.

But it didn't happen. Donna was visibly shaken, but she kept herself in her seat, drawing a deep breath that she exhaled visibly— perhaps intentionally as a way of expressing to Powell the scare he'd just produced in her. Powell was quiet, though as the silence between them grew heavier he realized he had to say something. After all, he had gotten her to come along on this ride, to help him escape from the almost claustrophobic tension at the restaurant. But what could he say that would make sense of the stunt he'd just pulled? He'd acted impulsively and recklessly and thrown her an undeserved fright and there really was no way he could explain why he had done that. It made no sense…not even to himself.

A mere surface apology didn't seem enough, and Donna had every reason not to accept his words—especially if she got the idea in her brain that he might have intentionally tried to kill her. Or perhaps his intention was to kill them both.

Powell leaned his upper body forward and pressed the palms of both hands against the steering wheel and closed his fingers over the rim, tightening them so that his knuckles whitened. He looked more distressed than his passenger.

Donna spoke cautiously, with compassion. "Are you okay?"

The last thing Powell wanted was for her to feel sorry for him.

"I—shouldn't have brought you along," he said reproachfully.

Donna tentatively reached out her hand toward him. She laid her fingers tenderly against the back of his hand, and noticed that his flesh felt clammy. Her words came gently. "You did, for a reason."

Powell lifted his face to look directly at her. He spoke his own thoughts with less affection, more pointedly. "I had to get out of the diner. And you were there."

Donna's expression softened, and her words were sincere. "I was." She paused for a heartbeat and then added, "And—I want to be."

Hearing her speak those words and the way they were delivered, genuinely, Powell regarded Donna with a different kind of consideration. Maybe it was his own naivety or perhaps an essential denial—or maybe it simply was that until this moment he had never truly known how Donna felt about him. Yet her attitude was becoming clear to him. Not in a way he expected or that he could even appreciably welcome. But neither was it a support he particularly wanted to reject. Not now. Not when he felt so many were against him as he tried to navigate his way through this ever-darkening mystery that seemed to have no reasonable solution.

But he still wasn't sure if he should accept what she was offering. He remained concerned about the potential risk to which he might be exposing her. That worry had always been one of his most pressing reservations (though he could not thoroughly convince himself that it was not merely an easy justification to avoid a potential commitment), with the outcome one he could not predict. How could he even guess how it would end? All he seemed to know for certain was that he was up against a deviant mind. A brain of sinister intention, and a character possessed of pure evil. He rationalized that *that* knowledge alone should be sufficient to preclude any sort of personal relationship.

What counterbalanced this doubt was having someone who could provide a foundation of stability. Even under all of these trying circumstances—had not the cold hand of fate intervened—Powell knew that he would have had his wife, Cassidy, by his side. He would have had to take precautions to protect her and the children, naturally. But her love and support would have kept him grounded through this ongoing madness.

"Tell me, how does one find a solution to a riddle for which there is no sensible answer?" he asked cryptically.

Donna wrinkled her brow. She wasn't sure what he meant by his question. It was ambiguous. Yet she did consider how best to reply—either honestly, or, she pondered, how he might *want* to hear her respond.

And it was then that she posed a question of her own.

"And you're asking me what, specifically?"

"I don't know," Powell admitted, responding quickly, wagging his head. He turned to her and his eyes reflected a strange, almost remote gaze. "Maybe I was hoping *you* would tell me."

Donna could see how distressed Powell was—further made evident by the slight pouching of his eyes and his drawn mouth—and for the first time since she had known him his presence made her uneasy. It seemed as if he were reacting to something even more deeply troubling than the problems she knew he was dealing with professionally. She would have felt less apprehensive if only he would talk to her outright—and not express himself through vague, esoteric phrasing. She was becoming so uncertain of this situation that she was only barely aware that her hand was beginning to inch toward the door handle.

Powell noticed her furtive movement. And that snapped him back to himself. He halted the impulsive urge to grasp her hand and pull it away from the door.

Instead he made himself speak reassuringly. "No, it's all right. I'm sorry. Just got carried away for a minute. Just too damn many thoughts spinning around in my head."

"You've just been dealing with a lot," Donna said gently. "I know it can't be easy." She was trying to be sympathetic, he realized, even though his behavior had to be unnerving.

Powell responded with a rueful smile. "You're the only one who seems to understand that."

Of a sudden, a huge tanker truck rounded the curve at high speed and the driver sounded loudly on the horn to announce its approach, the echo blaring directly into the open windows of the cruiser.

Powell tensed and his expression reflected a sudden outrage. "Sonofabitch!" he blurted, and he looked ready to throw the cruiser into gear and give chase.

Once more Donna braced herself as she saw how on edge he was. His tension seemed to be at a fever-pitch.

Powell gradually calmed himself, but his face still reflected his agitation.

"I think it would be best if I take you back to town," he said.

"If—that's what you want," Donna told him. In truth, she felt relieved he'd made the suggestion.

Powell hesitated before he said resignedly, "I've got work to do back at the office."

Donna just nodded, but her unspoken gesture seemed to express it all to Powell.

As Powell drove the sea cliff highway back into Clear Vista, the silence was pronounced. Powell regretted ever making the decision to burden the woman with a temperament that even he had come to recognize was not only starting to crumble under the pressures of his work and perhaps even the subtle encroachment of other demons, but was maybe becoming downright unstable.

CHAPTER TWENTY-THREE

Raymond Borys was an elegant gentleman, possessed of fine, proper manners, always impeccably groomed and tailored, and professionally he employed these attributes to a somber yet comforting effect. Borys was the undertaker of Clear Vista, operating the Memorial Chapel that bore his name, finely scripted on lighted glass signage over the front entranceway to the building. He served as the town's sole mortician, who enjoyed not only local business but whose reputation for providing dignified service was recognized by other communities, including the city of Breckridge.

Borys both enjoyed and was proud of his work. In fact, since he remained a bachelor with no known outside interests, servicing death was his life. Undertaking was a family tradition that began with his great-grandfather, Vladimar, who had emigrated from the old country near the start of the century. The man was a pioneer who was responsible for the immigration to America of many of his fellow countrymen. One of his great-grandson's most prized possessions was a large faded photograph of his grandfather sitting front and center among a large grouping of first generation Polish transplants. The picture was properly framed and on display inside the foyer of the building and never failed to elicit comments from customers.

Because Vladimar was so highly regarded among his fellow countrymen, clever entrepreneurs got the idea that they could profit from Vladimar's influence and decided to establish him in the funeral business. It was a wise idea that quickly proved profitable for all concerned. After Raymond died, his son took over and on it went, until Raymond Borys became the present owner. Borys considered it a privilege that he was allowed to take care of the needs of families during difficult times of bereavement and he never shirked in his responsibility. It might be said that each of his clients traveled first-class.

His establishment likewise reflected his professional approach to his business. Three large chapels and three comfortable, tastefully-decorated family rooms. During a service, appropriate low-key recorded music would be piped into the chapel through carefully concealed speakers. Naturally the funeral home presented a somber ambience, but the environment was more respectful to the departed and his or her family than it was morbid and depressing. It was a delicate balance that Borys admirably maintained.

Early that evening, in preparation of the funeral for the Loewen girls, Borys asked for his assistant Gerard to bring both caskets up from the preparation room into the chapel. The bodies had been dressed in the outfits provided by their mother and a cosmetician had carefully applied just the proper amount of makeup to both girls so not to make them appear waxen or mannequin-like but as natural as possible under the muted chapel lighting. But when the casket of Heidi Loewen was opened by Gerard for a last-minute inspection, he let out a shriek that echoed throughout the chapel.

Something terrible had happened…something that grossly and unexplainably had turned the girl's stiff if placid features into a deformed mask.

The sudden, dreadful sound that emanated from his assistant brought Borys racing into the chapel and for a man whose stoic professional demeanor was rarely challenged, his face went ivory white and he had to hold himself steady against the edge of the casket. He was in shock. He couldn't speak, but instead turned his eyes toward his likewise ashen-visaged assistant. While his words did not initially come, his expression demanded an explanation from

Gerard, who had done the actual embalming on the body, just two days earlier, after it had been released from the county medical examiner. But even if Gerard himself could find the strength to speak, the look on his face made it obvious he had no words to explain what ghastly post-mortem process had taken place. It appeared that somehow the body had suffered a terrible and delayed reaction to the chemicals used. Within the past forty-eight hours Heidi Loewen's face had become grotesquely bloated, the features no longer serene in repose but twisted in an awful grimace, one of the eyelids slightly open, fixed in a sightless stare.

With a closed casket this would not be such a crisis. A viewing, on the other hand, would be traumatic for all concerned. And the family still had not determined which option they'd prefer.

Borys understood how important this funeral was, both to the town and, of course, his own reputation. Most of the community of Clear Vista was expected to turn out for the service and since the family had no religious affiliations, the double service would be held not in a church but in the chapel of the funeral home itself. It was imperative that every detail be handled flawlessly. There could not be anything to show carelessness or irresponsibility on the part of the funeral director or his staff. And what Borys was faced with now was a calamity. Made more so by his uncertainty over the family's wishes. If they should decide on an open casket for the service Borys—even with his skills—was not sure if he could effectively repair the facial disfiguration, simply because he could not understand what had caused it to happen.

Most of the time Borys preferred to handle the embalming himself, thereby ensuring there would be no mistakes in preparing the corpse for the viewing. It was always that first sight of the body, cleaned, cosmetics properly applied and presented in clothing freshly laundered, that held the most significance. The acceptance of such by family and friends at the initial viewing would generally determine the success of the service to follow. Borys reproached himself for allowing an assistant to do the preparation on the two girls. But how could he know? He certainly had never expected such a "mistake" to occur from a licensed embalmer. As he tried to compose himself he understood that he could not rightly blame the man. Gerard had followed procedure. Whatever had caused this disfigurement was not due to carelessness. Perhaps there had been a defect in the chemicals themselves. Though what could create an adverse effect to such a horrific degree?

Throughout his career Borys had seen disturbing incidents where a cadaver might have a reaction to a specific embalming technique, most frequently through a blotching or flesh discoloration, but that could be covered up with properly applied cosmetics. In all his years of being in the funeral business he had never seen anything like this. A delayed reaction from dead tissue that somehow had become corrupted? It just could not be explained. But somehow it would have to be corrected.

He hoped that some extra cosmetic reconstruction would return the face to normal. But that would entail a long night ahead of him— and no guarantee that his efforts would prove successful.

His assistant offered to stay on to assist him, but Borys felt that he would work better alone. In truth, he was uncharacteristically nervous and he did not want Gerard to be watching him while he attempted this delicate procedure. His other concern was if the Loewen family might decide to come by the chapel this evening to view the bodies. If his work was not completed—or if he simply could not reverse the disfiguration—he would have to think of something to tell them. He told Gerard just to wait upstairs and watch the front office and to notify him if the Loewen family should arrive, otherwise he would call for him if he found the need for his assistance.

It meant a night of overtime and Gerard had already put in long hours at the funeral home, but probably feeling somehow responsible for what had happened, though Borys knew without question that the man's hands were clean, he told the undertaker he would stay.

Heidi Loewen's body would have to be taken downstairs to the preparation room. The casket was placed back on the metal cart and wheeled onto the freight elevator where it began its slow descent to the lower level of the building. Gerard helped Borys to remove the small, stiff body from the confines of the casket and place it gingerly on a sheet of plastic that was laid over one of the clean and sterilized embalming tables. Borys hastily nodded his thanks and Gerard left his boss alone to do his work. Once his assistant was gone Borys removed his suit jacket, loosened his tie and turned on the radio to his favorite classical music station, keeping the volume low. Then he studied the distorted face of the corpse. Another man not so highly trained and experienced in dealing with death would have had a difficult time focusing on those twisted features, especially with that one filmy eye peering from under its partially open lid. In truth, it did disturb Borys, but less because of her appearance than the misfortunes that had befallen her both in life and death. He lightly stroked her flaxen hair and muttered, "Poor girl. First to be murdered and now to have this terrible thing happen to you." He then dismissed his human compassion and, as he always did before beginning his technical work, regarded the corpse from a purely biological perspective.

He still wasn't sure how best to proceed. The strange swelling would have to be reduced and the features would have to be manipulated, perhaps through a careful application and molding of tissue builder, to restore a peaceful look. Borys voiced a silent prayer that his skills would be up to the task. He rolled the instrument tray over to the side of the metal table, then he turned and walked toward the large glass cabinet where his utensils and other supplies were kept. He carefully examined the items.

And then…a low moaning sounded from behind him.

Followed by a clanging, echoing crash.

Borys felt his body weaken, surrender to a chill, and against all of his will, with all of his strength, he craned his neck, turning his head to look behind him…

*   *   *

Gerard never heard the noise coming from the basement. He was just eager to get this terrible night over with. He dreaded each second that he sat in the main office, never knowing if Mr. and Mrs. Loewen might enter the building requesting to see their daughters before the next day's service. Of course Mr. Borys would have to be the one to deal with that problem and Gerard couldn't imagine how he would respond—if he was not able to repair the girl's face.

He just wished he understood what happened. He'd embalmed, successfully, dozens of bodies since earning his license and he'd never made a mistake in the procedure. While some people might look upon his work as ghoulish, Gerard considered himself an artist. He'd fixed the faces of people mangled in automobile accidents and had performed the work so well that family members initially requesting a closed casket, upon seeing the fine reconstruction work, decided to allow a viewing after all. To Gerard, that was always a great compliment that made him proud of his profession.

That was why he was certain that whatever had happened to the Loewen girl was a fluke—something for which he could not be held responsible. While there was no way he could explain it, some after death biological misfortune had to have happened within the cadaver itself.

Nine thirty-five. Much to Gerard's relief the Loewens had not shown up. By this time, Gerard did not think they would. He considered it a reprieve. And he knew that Mr. Borys would also be grateful. He decided to go downstairs and see how his boss was doing. He must be working very hard as he'd been in the preparation room for well over two hours and even the most difficult embalming cases such as car accidents and other physical manglings seldom took that long to a man of Mr. Borys's skill. Gerard only hoped that he was making some progress. Or if not, that he now might appreciate some help from his assistant.

Gerard walked down the back corridor toward the freight elevator, which was a large compartment that could hold up to three hardwood caskets. It always intrigued Gerard how quiet a funeral home was—especially after dark. It was a different kind of silence from the quiet that existed in other establishments after closing hours. It was hard to define exactly, but Gerard always perceived it as a whispered silence. *Dead air,* as it might also be called, he thought with black humor. He supposed that while most people might find it unsettling, he appreciated it. He found the silence soothing, and a calm frame of mind was definitely needed this night.

He pushed the red "down" button and the elevator mechanism buzzed and clanged to a start, then the motor hummed softly as the compartment lowered into the basement. Once Gerard exited the elevator he turned down another short corridor, and when he was about halfway along the passageway he thought he heard a strange sound. Just as quickly it quieted. He took a few more steps—and he heard it again. He knew his boss liked to play classical music while he worked on a case and his ears did detect the mild strains of some vintage instrumental composition, but the sound he heard was not part of some radio symphony. It was not really definable. Gerard got a sudden anxious feeling and found himself actually hesitant to enter the preparation room, fearful that Mr. Borys may have become distraught because he was not able to restore the girl's features.

Before he went any farther, he announced his presence by calling out gently, "Mr. Borys?"

No response, only that queer noise that Gerard could not put his finger on.

He moved forward tentatively, approaching the open door that would take him into the establishment's "inner sanctum". Then, just as he was about to turn into the room, he recognized the sound and it sent a trembling throughout his body.

He peered inside—

And to his horror he saw Mr. Borys sitting on the floor against the far wall, his body folded tightly against itself, arms wrapped around his raised knees, and he was rocking. Back and forth. He was wild-eyed, his expression contorted, drool dribbling from the corners of his lips, babbling incoherently, occasionally interspersed with childish giggling. He seemed oblivious to Gerard's presence, imprisoned as he was in what appeared to be the madness of his own mind. Whatever had happened down here had driven Raymond Borys completely insane.

Gerard's eyes scanned the room. He saw the instrument table knocked over onto the floor. Everything else looked to be in its place.

Except for one thing...

The corpse of Heidi Loewen was missing.

CHAPTER TWENTY-FOUR

A full moon—big, round, clear, yet somehow baleful—settled high over Buchanan Bay, spilling its reflection upon the black waters and spearing the smooth, even, white-capped waves that shimmered inland without quite reaching the rocky coastline. A slight breeze blew in from the bay that chilled the autumn air as if in prelude to the Halloween the citizens of Clear Vista would be forfeiting this year. Children were disappointed, of course—those who were too young to comprehend their parents' reasoning and could not, perhaps fortunately, decipher the true meaning behind their feeble attempts at an explanation.

To many of the adults, Halloween this year stood as a reflection of horror and darkness and not a night to celebrate, especially if a predator still walked among them. What better time for such a monster with an urge to prey on children to strike again? Chief Powell had his own reasons for not wanting to acknowledge Halloween. He'd had his own firsthand encounters with the unexplained, the macabre. And while he pragmatically denied that supernatural elements were responsible for all that had transpired, the spookiness of the season did make one vulnerable to less mundane explanations of such incidents. Word had been released earlier that day about Mayor Warrington's "accidental" death (no other details provided, naturally). The suspicions of many of the citizens were again put on alert, due less to the manner in which he died than how closely his demise followed the death of the Loewen girls, the Stromms and Ida Krevich. All dead within a week. And each death seeming to bring with it questions that the Clear Vista Police Department either couldn't—or *wouldn't* answer.

People began to suspect that Chief Powell knew more than what he was releasing to the public. Which was minimal.

Powell was in his office with the lights turned low, gazing out the window onto the front street. He felt a little restless, which was why he did not go home after his shift was over. But it was an odd sort of restiveness he was experiencing. Not so much due to public criticism or his aggravation at being unable to get a handle on what was happening to his town, along with the concern that he might not be able to prevent any more of these strange deaths from occurring. Tonight, what made him impatient was that he found himself receptive to a definite disquiet…an almost tangible foreboding that seemed suspended over the town. As if all that had been happening in Clear Vista had been a prelude and that the climax was still to arrive—and whatever this resolution might be, it was going to have unpleasant consequences.

Powell wasn't psychic, he put no stock in premonitions or so-called prescient abilities. About as far as he would go was to have trust in his gut. His experiences in 'Nam and later police work had instilled that reliance in him. For instance, he believed that it was simply a gut feeling that told him his wife and kids had met with an accident those fifteen months ago. His brain hadn't cosmically linked into their tragedy, nor had he received any divine message. As someone who regarded himself as a pragmatist he could acknowledge a gut feeling as a reasonable answer, and tonight as he was overcome by this unusual awareness he again tried to relieve his mind with a sensible, rational explanation for the strange way he was feeling. He was just reacting to pressures, building them out of proportion in his brain—he told himself. Only it wasn't that simple. Powell found it difficult to ignore the subtle yet persistent unease that had crept up on him over the past couple of hours—stealthily, even insidiously. The "voice" seeming to penetrate beyond his subconscious, stubbornly insistent that he recognize this ominous "message" was not merely stemming from an overworked imagination.

After too long a period dealing with this, Powell decided to take the squad car out for a patrol. Maybe he just needed to step away from the office for a while. He couldn't deny that his brain had been on overload and even his sleep over the past several nights had been compromised. Not quite total insomnia, but enough to require several major caffeine jolts throughout the day so that he could keep alert. Terry Reynolds had the night off and Powell had taken the shift of one of his other officers, so he was manning the ship solo. He contemplated calling in one of his men to keep watch on the office, and then he realized with a twinge of embarrassment that the more likely reason he'd considered doing that was so that he could have some company tonight. He was a proud man who rarely succumbed to trepidation, even back when he found himself trudging through the jungles of Cambodia, never knowing when he might be in the enemy's gun sight, and he quickly dismissed the idea. He told himself that if he could overcome real flesh-and-blood fear, there was no reason why he should let himself be overtaken by an irrational fear, which was what this *intrusion* surely was. It was nearing ten o'clock and another glance outside the window showed that the streets looked quiet and that he could handle the night shift alone.

But even as Powell made his patrol, slowly cruising down the main street and side roads that seemed uncommonly quiet he remained aware of a gloom—an uncommon yet not visible murkiness—that seemed to penetrate the typical fabric of night. He started to grow angry with his superstitious attitude, tried to compel himself to get his thinking back on track. He reminded himself that he was a logical man, even while dealing with all the recent events in town that seemed to defy everyday reason.

* * *

Caspar McGee, on the other hand, was not a logical man. Neither was he of a courageous temperament, but he remained convinced that whatever was happening in town had something to do with that black-robed figure he'd spotted those nights ago in Resurrection Gardens. When he had heard that Ida Krevich had fallen down the cellar stairs and died that same night he and Officer Reynolds discovered handprints on the grave marker bearing her son's name, he knew there was a malevolent presence at work. That was why he went against his promise to Chief Powell and spoke to that newspaperman, Mr. Birdlong. Birdlong had seemed interested in what he'd had to say, but he frankly told him he wasn't much of a believer (to put it mildly) in ghosts and ghouls and that before he would ever release such information through his paper he would need some proof. And that was what McGee was determined to show him. Tonight. If Birdlong dared to go with him. Birdlong was hesitant at first but finally agreed to meet the old man out at the cemetery after he got through with some work that needed his attention at the newspaper office. McGee had also hoped to convince Officer Reynolds to accompany him to the graveyard, but hadn't been able to reach him. The cop he spoke to at police headquarters earlier that day said that Reynolds had the night off and had planned to drive out for some well-earned relaxation in Breckridge.

* * *

Keith Birdlong closed up the newspaper office earlier than what he had told old man McGee. He wasn't putting in a late night. At least not where his work was concerned. He was sitting in his small cubicle of an office waiting for the phone to ring. He'd left several messages and was banking on getting a return call.

It concerned his former longtime companion, Chris. The fellow with whom Birdlong had shared an eight-year relationship, beginning in college, but who was the one who, at least in Birdlong's mind, ended their partnership when he steadfastly refused to leave the excitement of the big city for—as he put it—the "dullsville" of small town life. Chris liked the party scene whereas Keith's preferences were more subdued and artistic. Yet, despite their different interests and contradictory temperaments they proved a good match—until both men had to make a decision regarding their future together. There was only the vaguest compromise, as both Birdlong and Chris possessed deep-rooted stubborn streaks. It resulted in a regretful yet perhaps inevitable parting. Oh, they did briefly try to maintain their relationship from their respective distances, but both understood such an arrangement would never survive over the long term and finally they had to accept that it was over.

Tonight, sitting alone, Birdlong was suffering a troubling guilt. Maybe he was the selfish one in his decision to walk out on Chris. But then he'd always harbored a hope that Chris might have a change of heart and one day show up with his bags packed in Clear Vista. Now it was doubtful that would ever happen. He'd gotten a phone message earlier that day that Chris's diagnosis of HIV-positive had recently developed into full blown AIDS. Birdlong was devastated. The message had come from Chris's newest boyfriend, Roy, who knew about their past relationship and thought it only decent and fair that Birdlong should be notified about the grim prognosis.

Now Birdlong sat by the phone, nervously twitching his fingers, waiting for a call back from Chris. No matter what had happened between them, Birdlong needed to talk with him. He'd decided that if Chris wanted to see him—or even if he needed him back, Birdlong would go to him without delay. He understood there was nothing he could do for Chris except be there for him and help him with emotional support through these terrible days.

His eyes remained fixed on the telephone, as if he were trying to will it to ring. Even if Chris didn't want for Birdlong to see him, it was so important that they at least speak to each other, even if it was to be for the last time. Birdlong needed that connection. There was so much he felt he needed to say.

The longer he waited for the call the more resentful Birdlong became. He was furious that Chris had chosen to live the careless, sexually active lifestyle that he had. Birdlong knew that Chris had never been monogamous during their own relationship. He'd made no secret of it, and when the cruel mood came over him, he boasted of it. And naturally it bothered Birdlong, but Chris made it clear that he had to be the way he was. To perhaps pacify his partner he would always add that Birdlong was the most important person in his life— the one he would always come home to—but that he also needed his freedom. He liked to consider himself a *bon vivant*, an adventurer.

Eventually, this led to the two of them ceasing to have a sexual relationship. It was a necessary decision Birdlong made, the threat of AIDS already beginning to send waves of panic throughout the country, particularly within the gay community. In truth it wasn't much of a sacrifice. He loved Chris more on an emotional and intellectual level, as a companion. Sex had always been of secondary importance. But that didn't lessen his apprehensions when it came to his partner. His worry was that Chris's rampant promiscuity was akin to playing Russian Roulette with five of the pistol chambers loaded.

Finally the phone rang. Birdlong was so anxious he found he could barely steady his hand to lift the receiver. His mind went blank. Suddenly he didn't know what he should say. A long time had passed and things had definitely changed. He let the phone ring three times before he finally summoned the courage to snatch the receiver from its cradle.

"Hello." He knew his voice sounded tentative.

There was a long pause on the other end. Birdlong waited. He assumed that Chris might also be having a difficult time finding the right words to open the conversation.

Eventually Chris spoke. His voice was unmistakable, even if it sounded decidedly weaker than how Birdlong remembered it. His illness was apparent, but Birdlong was still thrilled to finally have made this connection after all this time. At first their talk was slightly awkward, but gradually old feelings were restored and the two chatted with the familiarity both had shared during the years they were close.

They chatted for about five minutes, recalling people they knew and good times they had shared. Never once did Chris mention his disease or its insidious progression and, while it was difficult, Birdlong tactfully refrained from bringing it up himself. If Chris didn't want to talk about it, Birdlong likewise had to respect that. But finally as Chris sounded more fatigued and their conversation was winding down, Birdlong asked if Chris wanted him to come up to see him.

There was a long pause. Before Chris could answer, a strange static came through the receiver. Birdlong waited for the disturbance to clear, but the static seemed to grow more intense. He held on the line for about a minute, growing frustrated and tense. He was just about to hang up when the interference suddenly dissipated. The connection was once again clear.

"Chris, are you still there?" Birdlong asked anticipatively.

A brief silence, and then a voice came through. It was Chris. Only now his voice sounded even weaker, faded—and possessed of a queer, unnatural quality, almost as if he were speaking in a trance.

His words were short, clipped—and startling. "Keep— away…from—the—cemetery."

"*Wha*— Chris?" Birdlong was benumbed. Did he hear him right? Was this some kind of joke his friend was playing on him?

And the connection broke. Birdlong held the phone to his ear just listening to the buzzing of the dial tone. His face went flush and his body felt weak and limp. When he started to recover, his hand instinctively scrabbled toward the phone. He lifted the receiver, hesitated, and then gently lowered it, though not quite returning it to the cradle. His jaw slackened as he considered Chris's final words.

Keep away from the cemetery.

No. It was just too impossible. How would Chris, over two thousand miles away, know that he was planning to go out to Resurrection Gardens tonight?

With his hand still poised he gazed again at the telephone. His free hand rummaged about the desk for the scrap of paper that had Chris's new friend Roy's number written on it. He then hung up the phone properly, lifted the receiver and quickly dialed the area code and the seven digits. He waited impatiently through several rings, mentally counting each one. Roy *had* to answer. Birdlong had to know for sure. He needed Roy to verify the unsettling suspicion that had overtaken him.

The phone was picked up after the seventh ring. The voice that answered sounded shaky. Birdlong introduced himself. There was a pause. Birdlong did not want to give the reason for his calling. As it turned out, he didn't have to.

Roy told him outright, "Christopher died this afternoon."

"Christopher—*dead*?" Birdlong said in a gasp. Though this news only confirmed what he had already guessed, a man possessed of a sane mind could not grasp what it signified.

"He took an overdose of pills." Roy started to sob. "I—don't know why he did that to me. He was going to move in with me this week. I was going to take care of him. I told him so…"

Birdlong wasn't listening anymore. It meant nothing to him how Roy felt, what his plans with Chris were to be. He slowly let the receiver slide from his hand even though he could still hear Roy crying.

The news of the suicide was devastating. But even that was not as startling as what Birdlong had just experienced. Never in a million years would he, a lifelong skeptic, have thought such a thing was possible. But as shiver after shiver raced through his body like an electrical charge he could not consider any other explanation than that he had been contacted from beyond the grave. No, there simply was no other way to explain it. It was no trick. No game. That *was* Chris's voice on the other end, Birdlong could never mistake it. And before the call went weird they talked about things that only the two of them could remember and appreciate. Hell, they'd even shared a private joke.

But equally as disturbing as the call itself was his dead friend's apparent warning. How was that intended? And *why*? There had to be a purpose. Although his nerves were jangled, Birdlong considered—he debated—and he finally decided he was not going to heed that advice. Now that his skepticism had been dashed, he had to investigate. Something strange was occurring at Resurrection Gardens—the old man was right—and as a newspaperman he had an obligation to find out what exactly that was.

He glanced at his wristwatch. Although it was dark it might still be early enough for him to meet up with McGee and finally get some answers.

His head was still swimming as he left the office and climbed into his chocolate brown Chevette which was parked in an alley cutoff at the side of the building. He switched on the radio for some soft rock music that he hoped would settle his emotions and then started the short drive out of town.

He must have blanked out. The next thing he knew he found himself driving a farther distance than he should… along a stretch of gravel road not familiar to him. At first perplexed, it dawned on him that there was a slight forking in the road and because his thoughts were elsewhere, he had carelessly taken the wrong turn. The road he was on was narrow with deep bordering inclines on either side and so he would have to continue on this way until he could find some sort of a crossroads or junction where he could maneuver his car around. It was dark along this road and so he switched on the high beams. The headlights speared and penetrated the blackness, dancing motes reflected in their whiteness, but the pathway ahead still looked straight and flat. Birdlong was growing frustrated after traveling a good ten minutes without spotting a suitable juncture. He needed something to steady his nerves. He glanced next to him and noticed the sandwich he'd purchased earlier that he intended to have for a quick dinner, prior to driving out to meet the old man. His fingers moving mechanically, he reached for the ham on rye and started to unwrap the cellophane. The wrapping was snug and Birdlong had to fiddle with it with his free hand while trying to steer the car along this seemingly endless gravel trail. Perhaps it was reflex but his foot had started to compress harder on the accelerator pedal as his attention wavered between the road and his trying to manipulate his sandwich wrapping.

Of a sudden his tires caught on a loose patch of gravel off on the side of the road and the car went into a spin. Birdlong frantically tried to regain control of the wheel, but he knew in those final seconds that he didn't have a chance. The car careened off the narrow road, angling down the sharp incline into the ditch and propelling Birdlong head first into the windshield, the impact fracturing his skull.

*   *   *

And so, alone, unaware as to what had befallen Birdlong, Caspar McGee summoned his courage, his resolve further strengthened with a fifth of strong whiskey and now packing his .38 revolver, and waited outside the gates of Resurrection Gardens for the newspaperman to show up. He was not eager to venture into the grounds alone after his last two experiences there. But as time passed and the hour of midnight drew near and Birdlong still hadn't arrived, McGee was getting cold and impatient. Part of him just wanted to turn back and head for home, but he was also curious to see whether he might chance another encounter with that person or apparition or whatever it was. He was just drunk enough to have the guts to take a quick look-see, just for his own benefit. He also felt protected since his pistol was loaded with six deadly bullets.

He switched on his lantern to a low beam and entered the graveyard through the main gate, where he was supposed to meet the newspaperman, unlocking it with his key and deliberately keeping it open, bracing it against any sudden gust of wind with a large rock that he carried over from the side of the road near where he'd parked his truck.

He walked through the creepy old cemetery, his lantern providing him with a lighted path along the unkempt grounds, and then he came through onto the newer section where the landscape was open and ordered, not cluttered with dead overgrowth and forgotten artifacts of the past.

As he neared Heavenly Angels, McGee felt that same trepidation begin to take hold of him. But it was even more intense and intimidating tonight. He hefted his .38, but strangely, inexplicably, it did not provide him with the confidence he had hoped it would. As if the fog clouding his brain had cleared just enough of a pathway to his sense of reason, he knew that he should not be on these grounds. It was as though he had become receptive to some *presence* urging him to turn back now. That if he dared to go any farther, if he was foolish enough to cross into that "forbidden zone" where the children were interred, he would find himself in a situation that might prove threatening to his sanity—if not his life. And if he was dealing with something supernatural, ghost or demon, it wasn't likely that six bullets or even a dozen would do McGee much good.

McGee halted and held himself steady, the lantern lowered to his side and causing a splash of light around his boots. His body started to tremble, his jaw dropped reflexively. He had gone too far. Not directly into Heavenly Angels but near enough so that the glow of the October moon illuminated the eerie activity that he was now witness to among the graves.

McGee tried to refocus his vision because there was just no way his brain could comprehend what his eyes were seeing.

They were dancing—children. A small group of children. He could tell immediately that they were...*dead* children, as they motioned about in a slow, macabre dance, the movements jerky and unsteady, upper limbs swaying in an awkward grace, as if with a coordination beyond their capability but manipulated by a supernatural puppet master. Weird, indefinable sounds emanated from the children, mostly a broken, mournful resonance much more disturbing than anything that McGee had ever heard—or could imagine, as if they were trying to intone some graveyard chant. He was too numb and his eyes too glazed to determine exactly how many there were. Neither could he distinguish any of their faces, and he was grateful for that. But he could see that they were dressed in their burial clothes, the boys' suit jackets ripped up the back, some of the pant legs likewise slit vertically. Their outfits were damp and moldy, showing the effects of long exposure to the dampness of the earth.

And most frightening of all, standing among the children was the black-robed figure. His arms were spread wide as if to figuratively embrace the undead group. *He* was the puppet master!

The moon that had cast its autumn glow upon the cemetery dance like some otherworldly spotlight faded and once more the night lowered upon the scene like the slow descent of a black velvet curtain over a macabre theatric.

McGee had been witness to a nightmare. A ghoulish black obscenity. He had seen something that neither his eyes—nor anyone else's was meant to look upon. The fright that enveloped him was so great that he lost control of his bodily functions and he could feel the urine run wet and warm down his pant leg.

He had to be out of there. Run away while he still had time.

He spun around quickly—

And found himself just inches from the black-robed figure, mysteriously appearing and standing before him, the posture slightly hunched. The figure stood silently. And now the face was visible, staring at McGee from under the cloth cavern of the hood. It was a face unlike any McGee had ever seen.

The features were human.

Almost.

CHAPTER TWENTY-FIVE

The skin was taut, pulled tightly into the formation of a skull, pale, virtually bloodless. The eyes and the mouth were of an unnatural shape. The mouth had no lips and stretched across nearly the whole of the narrow face and was set in a hideous grin, exposing two rows of large, straight but yellowed teeth. It was a grin of baleful intention. The eyes were deep-set and coal black, penetrating, and the longer McGee stared into them—unable to tear his gaze away—the more they seemed to bore into his soul, imparting a message that McGee did not want to acknowledge, but that he was unable to resist.

He did not hear the words. They were spoken to him not directly but through his thoughts. A voice that was not a voice. Although it went beyond the old man's comprehension the figure had established a telepathic bond. At first it was a vague, disconnected understanding, emerging as if from out of a haze, filtering through the protection of an alcohol-soaked consciousness and a deliberately blocked memory. But gradually the meaning became stronger and clearer and although McGee struggled against it, his will was feeble and no match for this supernatural infiltration.

He was made to comprehend why he had felt compelled to revisit the cemetery, even as he feared to do so. Why he dreaded Heavenly Angels yet could not stop himself from proceeding toward the grounds. He came to realize that it wasn't some unearthly presence that had tried to warn him to turn back this night. It was his own conscience, somehow connecting with an incident in his past that would be revealed to him at this place—at this time.

A tainted memory he could no longer suppress, no matter how hard he tried to deny there was any truth to it—

It was hardly a week ago…he saw the two little girls wandering about Resurrection Gardens—alone. He was just making one of his frequent visits to the cemetery and was puzzled why the children were out there, far from home. Were they lost? Had they maybe been abandoned? His initial reaction was to help them. But…something else came over him. A dark urge that he never would have thought existed within himself. And maybe it didn't. Maybe it was some force beyond his comprehension—*yes, that was it*! Whatever that power or spirit was, it tempted him, drawing out a compulsion that if he did possess in some dark recess of his being he had always managed to control and keep concealed—protected under his guise of a virtual town non-entity.

He walked toward the youngsters, asking if they were all right. They were tentative, even afraid. Just as were all the other children of the community, frightened of the old gravedigger. One of the girls spoke, the other stayed quiet, though looking at him with large, fearful eyes. He was only half-inebriated and comforted her and offered to help them. They were still unsure, but they seemed more fearful of being alone in the cemetery than of old Caspar, and didn't resist his promise to get them home safely. He took their tiny hands in both of his and led them to the tool shed where he promised to call their parents. And once they were inside, he shut the door.

Mercifully, McGee in this remembrance was spared the graphic details of what he had actually done to the sisters. He was made to understand that those facts were not significant. Only the consequences mattered.

The consequences…

And once the terrible deed was done the memory evaporated. It vanished entirely from his consciousness. It was as if he emerged from a blackout, retaining no recollection of the twins or what he had done. He remembered being back in the openness of the cemetery, a little confused but accepting that he'd probably just had a brief relapse from the liquor he'd consumed, as had happened to him on other occasions when periods of time just seemed to inexplicably disappear.

Along with everyone else in Clear Vista, McGee learned about the discovery of the murdered children. He shared their outrage. And when another suspect was sought following his brief interrogation at police headquarters, McGee was convinced someone else had been responsible for the crime and joined the town in their demand for justice.

And still more was opened up to him by this black-hooded figure. Perhaps the most important revelation. He was chosen to commit the killings because the deaths of the two girls were intended as a sacrifice. A sacrifice that served a greater purpose than the lives taken from the sisters. The murders were necessary. It would open a gateway so that punishment could be inflicted upon those who had brought harm or tragedy to children. Yet it would be a punishment that those guilty of these vile and neglectful acts would ultimately bring upon themselves.

They would be at the mercy of their own justice.

And Caspar McGee, though selected as the instrument for this release, also had to pay a price, for though he might not have chosen to accept the deeper truth, he, too, possessed perversion in his soul.

Against his will, McGee found himself being made to look behind him. Again, he tried to fight against this compelling force— and once more he failed.

"Damn you," he rasped.

He was staring into the dead faces of Holly and Heidi Loewen, the latter's countenance swollen and distorted, a viscous yellow fluid seeping from her lifeless eyes and drooling from the corner of her mouth, which was stretched and twisted in a death rictus.

"*Why…?*" the girls said dully, in unison. And then they both started to move forward, stepping toward McGee, their movements slow and tremulous, yet to McGee's eyes, purposeful in intent, which, he determined in his horror, was to drag him with them back into the grave, to share in whatever hellish torment his actions had condemned them.

McGee screamed and in a desperate move to end this anguish made manifest by the condemning walking cadavers—*voicing his conscience?*—he thrust the barrel of the .38 to his temple, mouthed a muted, "forgive me," and pulled the trigger.

The single gunshot echoed through the cemetery before fading into the night.

CHAPTER TWENTY-SIX

Powell had been back at the office for nearly an hour after completing his patrol when he was startled by the first loud, reverberating clap of thunder. Just seconds later the rain erupted, suddenly, without warning, discharging from the skies with a relentless intensity, hitting the earth in what appeared to be a solid, blinding sheet. Such a downpour was uncommon for the season, especially when there had been no earlier indication of rain seen or issued in the local weather forecast. It was as if storm clouds had crept up on the night skies and congealed surreptitiously to unleash their fury.

To Powell it was another disturbing omen that something was soon to occur in Clear Vista. He could no longer ignore what he was feeling. He had tried to keep sound judgment in his theories, but finally had to concede that this wasn't just a suspicion or an overworked brain playing tricks—or even latent paranoia given full rein. As he sat gazing out the window, watching and listening to the torrent of rain as it struck and rattled the glass like a barrage of pellets and slapped with a fury against the pavement, the water quickly overflowing the sidewalk and rushing over the curb to drain into the sewers, he acknowledged that this unexpected shift in the weather was a portent. It was real and true, and what troubled Powell most was that he didn't know *how* it was going to happen or precisely *when*. But he was certain enough in his conviction that he decided there was one thing he had to do.

He could not alert the entire town—it was doubtful anyone would believe him. The citizens had experienced enough unusual happenings over the past week to keep them wary, but they would never accept what Powell was suggesting. Especially since it was likely to many that his credibility had been compromised. Still, the police chief could do whatever was in his power to ensure that at least one of the townspeople remained safe, and that was Donna Murray.

A flash of lightning—a bright and brilliant electrical discharge that momentarily lit up the night skies, followed seconds later by another roar of thunder. Then a slow rumbling that sounded far in the distance, heading out over the waters of Buchanan Bay, and the force of the storm started to ebb.

Powell glanced at the office clock. It was only minutes to midnight. Appropriate, he thought grimly.

He would have preferred to first telephone Donna before heading over to her place, only he didn't know her home number. So now he would have to drive to her apartment, which was only several blocks away, and somehow convince her that he hadn't suddenly gone insane. Maybe he should try and convince *himself* of that first, he thought wryly. No, he was certain he hadn't yet lost his marbles—but come morning and he couldn't be sure of anything. The hours ahead would provide the answer.

The rain did not last long. A cloudburst that struck fast and hard and then eased into a light drizzle before ceasing completely. Powell slipped back into his police issue jacket and as he stepped from the office into the damp night chill to start out back to where the squad car was parked, he glanced up at the skies. The dark clouds were opening and scudding across the blackness of the night, their purpose done, but he also noticed something peculiar. There was a faint greenish hue to the horizon, hanging low over Buchanan Bay, off into the distance. A weird sight that he had never seen before. And while he could not be certain, the longer he looked at it, the more it appeared to be slowly moving inland.

Powell had no idea what that formation was, but considered it might be yet another omen and after he turned up the collar of his jacket he hurriedly climbed into his vehicle, slamming the door and locking it. He went to turn over the ignition—there was a *click*...another *click* and the car wouldn't start. The battery was stone dead.

It didn't make sense. Powell had just taken the car out and there was nothing wrong with the battery. He felt a chill go through his body. And then he surrendered to another reality. He was not meant to go out to warn Donna—or anyone else—of what was about to happen.

Once Powell recovered, he regained his strength, his intent, and determined that whatever this was that seemed to be working against him, it wasn't going to defeat him. He engaged this resolve by forcing himself to become angry, to utilize this resentment to his advantage. The muscles in his jaw grew taut and in an abrupt move he went to unlock the door—but once he pulled on the latch, the door wouldn't budge. He fought back a quick surge of panic and pushed against the door with his shoulder, using all of his might. But the door was unyielding, shut solid, as if wedged into the frame with cement. He next tried to lever down the side window but that too was immobile.

"Screw this!" he exclaimed. He pulled his revolver from its holster and reversed it, gripping the gun by the barrel and using the handle as a club, turning his head slightly to shield his eyes as he slammed the butt against the window, shattering the glass. He then carefully cleared away the few remaining shards of glass protruding from the window and attempted to open the door from the outer latch. But the door was still jammed. He was going to have try to maneuver his body through the window. It took some effort and he had to remain cautious of the broken pieces of glass shimmering in the pools of rainwater on the pavement outside the car, but he finally managed to free himself.

Unfortunately, he feared his troubles were only beginning. As the acceptance of the irrational overtook sane reasoning, Powell figured it was his coming to understand and his acknowledging the existence of this dark energy that had put him at risk. Perhaps it was not yet ready to have its purpose wholly discovered and, because of that, it perceived Powell as a threat. As the police chief, he was a man of authority and influence. He could not be permitted to put a halt to whatever it was that was approaching. It was something unexplainable, yet possessed of a sentient malevolence.

It might have been a crazy thought, Powell could not be sure of anything anymore. But whether or not his theory possessed substance, he decided to try and reach Reynolds and his two shift officers and order their asses down to headquarters. Let them know without taking the time to explain that they were dealing with a potential emergency. The way he figured it, all each had to do was take a gander up at what seemed to be coming their way in the skies to know that the chief's urgency and maybe even his concern and certainty that something was about to happen could not be discounted.

Powell rushed back around to the front of the office and unlocked the door. He halted for only a moment. A new awareness overtook him. It didn't seem right that the streets were so quiet. Yes, it was after midnight, a heavy if brief rainstorm had just hit, but Clear Vista suddenly had the atmosphere of a ghost town. Another weird, abstract thought, but it was as if people had either deserted the community or everyone simply disappeared *en masse*. Powell started to get the unnerving feeling that he was the only living soul in the entire town. But that was definitely crazy and he quickly pushed the notion aside. He understood he was dealing with a frightening, unnatural occurrence, but that it was imperative he keep one foot on solid ground. Still, he hurried to get inside the familiarity of his office. And once there he locked the door behind him. He stood leaning against the side wall. He was breathing loudly and beads of sweat had dampened his forehead. He rubbed his fingers along his brow and could feel new eruptions of psoriasis marking his flesh. Reflexively, without thinking, he began to scratch at those scaly patches, digging at them, until he felt a sticky wetness on his fingers. He drew his hand away and saw traces of blood. *Damn!* He wasn't aware that he'd ripped the sores open and they were not only bleeding but suppurating. Infuriated by his carelessness, he stepped away from the wall and went to switch on the overhead lights. Only they would not function. He played with the switch, flicking it rapidly, repeatedly, but nothing. The office was enveloped in a pervasive gloom, the darkness relieved only by the eerie stream of moonlight that passed through the glass of the wide front window like a spectral visitor.

Powell rushed over to the telephone. He lifted the receiver. Dead. No dial tone. He pushed down frantically on the plungers, to no avail.

His lips moved involuntarily. "What the hell…?"

If he wasn't alone in the town, it was as if something wanted him to believe he was, creating that disturbing scenario. Deliberately cutting him off from connecting with anyone else. He maintained a firm grip on his revolver as his attention scouted about the room. The office no longer seemed so familiar to him. It wasn't just the darkness or that the lights and the telephone wouldn't work. He got the weird, inexplicable feeling that he didn't belong here, as if *he* were suddenly the interloper.

And then he was overcome by a sense of urgency, equally inexplicable. The purpose of which was not made clear to him, only providing a vague message that he was not meant to be where he was.

He had to go to his house.

And while there was no reason that he could grasp for him *needing* to be there, he neither questioned nor fought against the impulse.

Because there was something waiting for him at the house. Something that he determined might provide the answer to this mystery.

He didn't bother to lock the office when he rushed from the building. He gazed into the southern skies over Buchanan Bay and, to his horror if not necessarily his surprise, he saw how that mysterious green hue looked to be expanding as it continued to drift toward the coastline.

Where is everybody? Why isn't anyone else outside to see what's happening? he thought in a frustrated frenzy.

Powell then raced to the back of the building and toward his vehicle. He had no doubt the car would start this time because he was meant to reach his house. That was intended as his destination and he would not be prevented from getting there. And as he expected, the outer door latch popped open effortlessly once he tugged at it. He slid into the driver's seat, thrust the key into the ignition, and the engine turned over instantly, purring like a kitten.

The chilly night air drifted through the broken driver's side window and so Powell flicked on the car heater to gather some warmth.

Now with the car running, Powell considered another alternative, to thwart this paranormal *poltergeist* and carry through with what he had initially planned. Drive out to Donna's place and get her to leave town with him. He debated for a few moments while the squad car idled quietly.

Just shift the transmission into gear and head out in the opposite direction, he told himself.

But as he was giving thought to that decision, he noticed how the engine started to falter. As if whatever *it* was could determine his intentions. And that indicated to Powell that if he did not follow the route to his house precisely, the car would again fail him.

Powell acknowledged that he couldn't challenge this force. And he clearly saw there was no point in resisting its influence. He resigned himself to the reality that he had no choice but to follow through with whatever destiny was intended for him.

CHAPTER TWENTY-SEVEN

Powell kept watchful as he drove through the streets toward his house, his eyes alert for any sign of life within the town. But he couldn't see anything to encourage him that all was still well with Clear Vista. None of the houses that he passed had lights turned on, either indoors or outdoors. The streets were quiet and dark—at least that was how the environment that he was so familiar with was now presented to him. But was it the reality or was this malicious influence playing tricks with his perception? Or was he himself slipping over the edge into madness? Powell felt a growing desperation as he truly could not know whether life—or life as he knew it—still existed in Clear Vista.

As he drove he questioned what it was that had come to cast this shadow over the town. And why? There was no longer a shred of doubt in Powell's "rational" mind that Clear Vista was up against some supernatural force or presence that had chosen to manifest itself in the community. Was it the result of some ancient curse? Powell pondered. He knew some of the history of the town, stemming back to when the first settlers named it Fenntown in memory of its founder. But though his historical knowledge was sketchy, Powell had never come across any significant black mark that could account for what was happening to the town and its people.

Something was reaching beyond the generations to announce its dark arrival in the present day. Yet this "curse," if that truly was what this was, had crept up slowly and pounced suddenly, like some creature of prey. Perhaps it began with the killing of the Loewen twins. And then the deaths of Walter and Barbara Stromm—and the horror they must have seen before their hearts seized and stopped beating forever. Ida Krevich, dead in exactly the same manner as the son she had abused. And Mayor Warrington, an accidental death, likely, but lying next to a gruesome trail of post-abortion fetal matter. And the significance *that* held.

He glanced at his reflection in the rearview mirror. He saw how his frantic fingering had ripped open the skin on his forehead, leaving bleeding, open wounds.

"Oh my God," he then muttered.

But it wasn't the discovery of his ruined brow that disturbed him.

What instilled in him a sudden rush of dread, what prompted his heart to instantly skip a beat, was a terrifying realization. He knew the common denominator behind the deaths of the Stromms, Ida Krevich and Warrington. He had considered it before, but not with the same admittedly distorted perception. He had investigated these incidents with the pragmatism of a policeman, believing that someone, some person with a sinister, perhaps vengeful, agenda was behind these tragedies.

Some-*one*. Not some-*thing*.

The solution was not some perpetrator of human origin. The key was the children themselves. And how they, beyond the grave, were being manipulated by this sinister presence.

Powell needed a moment to come to grips with the nightmarish scenario that had taken hold of his brain and he pulled the car over to the side of the road and braked to a stop. Once more he was sweating and his heart palpitating. Even his breathing came rapidly. More facts came flooding into his head, each leading to fantastic, implausible speculation. Taken together, as a whole, the facts presented a fantastic, implausible—but ultimately inarguable conclusion. The tracks of mud, the awful smell of decay at Ida Krevich's house. The handprints with the thin, elongated fingers found on Margaret Stromm's grave and on Larry Krevich's cemetery marker. Handprints that did not appear human and that could not have left their markings by any "natural" means.

In an instant he understood. Only he wished to God that he didn't. Because if what he was contemplating was truly so, it was too horrible, too ghoulish to accept.

He turned and lifted his eyes to the green tinting over the bay. That was where the evil resided, Powell was certain of that. The question that plagued him was, where had it come from…and what would happen once *it* reached the town?

Nothing was beyond the realm of possibility anymore. He even reflected on Reynolds fiddling with the name "Shade" to create the anagram HADES. He had joked about it even as a small corner of his brain opened to the possibility, so desperate was he to seek answers.

How much more desperate could this situation get?

How much more hopeless?

Or did Clear Vista still have a hope to escape the nightmare that slowly and insidiously was descending over the town?

* * *

Powell drove the squad car into his driveway, dried autumn leaves crunching underneath the tires as he coasted to a stop, and he waited for several moments before his fingers switched off the ignition. He tentatively tested the door latch and, sure enough, it opened without a hitch. He pulled himself from the car. The only sounds he was aware of were the distant chirruping of crickets and the return of a faint whistling breeze. Other than those minor disturbances the night remained as silent as a closed casket. The moist chill from the earlier rainstorm still resided in the air. Powell felt a dampness wrap around him like a cold shroud.

He took a quick survey of the property before heading toward his house. Although he was alone he tried not to appear obvious in his haste.

Once the door was locked and secured behind him and the main houselights turned on, creating a comforting glow, Powell felt some of the tension leave his body. His overall apprehension hadn't lessened, but for the time being he was in his own surroundings and even with the memories that often overwhelmed him when he entered the house, the atmosphere was welcoming.

His eyes fell upon the telephone and he regarded it for an instant. But first he walked into the bathroom to dry off and to address the bloody mess his fingers had made of his forehead. He whipped off his shirt which was moist and sticky against his skin and bunched it up and threw it in the towel bin. He then turned on both water faucets to adjust the flow to just the correct temperature, and he leaned his face in and splashed and gently massaged the warm water onto his brow. He repeated the procedure for close to a minute, then he lifted his head, and studied his reflection in the vanity mirror with a disgusted expression. Patches of his forehead still resembled raw hamburger. He wondered if the skin would ever completely heal with the mess he'd made of it. He patted his face dry, taking note of the tints of blood staining the soft fabric of the towel. He expelled a breath, muttered, "Fuck it," and then tossed the towel aside.

Living with a scarred forehead was the least of his worries. He put on a fresh shirt, then struck a match to a fresh cigarette and stepped toward the phone. He again considered it while he inhaled deeply of his tar bar. He wondered if the phone was operating, if he would be able to call out. He wanted to get ahold of Reynolds. But he didn't know where to reach him. Without even knowing who he might call his fingers instinctively closed around the receiver and he started to lift it from the cradle—

And then the houselights went out.

The receiver dropped from Powell's hand and skittered snake-like along the floor until the cord was pulled taut. He could hear through the silence a faint dial tone. Still, he didn't immediately reach down to retrieve it.

Because that was when he got the anxious feeling he was not alone.

That…there was also a presence inside the house. It was there, but Powell was not only hesitant but fearful to acknowledge whatever it was that had been waiting for him to come home.

"Daddy…you're home." A voice, dull and devoid of emotion, reached his ears from somewhere in the dark corners of the house.

A strained, tragic voice that sounded as if it had to struggle to get the words out. But Powell recognized the voice, even with its ghastly if passionless inflection. He also was familiar with the words, though his memory was hearing them spoken with a childish joy and enthusiasm.

The words uttered by his daughter Ruthie.

"Don't…you want…to see us…Daddy?" the voice said mournfully.

He could feel a cold dampness start to consume him, not physically but psychically. It exuded off the dank, rancid entities that were now standing behind him. The two presences that Powell could not bring himself to turn around to face.

"Why didn't…you…take us…for ice cream…Daddy?"

Powell's lips involuntarily formed the word, "No."

"We…could…all be…together now."

"*No…*" Powell mouthed again.

"Mommy, too…Mommy misses…you."

"Mommy…"

"She misses you…so much…Daddy."

And then a soul-wrenching moan…and another voice, distinctly different in tone but with the same unearthly inflection, flat yet rattled, torn from the soil of the grave.

Belonging to his son, Randy.

"Daddy…doesn't want…to look at us."

Ruthie echoed, **"Daddy…doesn't…"**

Oh God, it was true! He didn't! He *couldn't*! Because they weren't ghosts. He could almost accept ghosts. Spectral images. Ghosts were a figment of the imagination and could be dispelled. But Ruthie and Randy…they were real! And as had Margaret Stromm, Larry Krevich and Mayor Warrington's aborted child, they had come back—*physically*—from the grave.

Powell shrieked out a sudden, impulsive laugh.

Come back—*for a little visit.*

Powell felt his sanity starting to slip. He struggled to take hold of whatever vestige remained of his reason.

"Daddy…feels bad," little Ruthie said.

"Daddy didn't…want us…to…die," Randy said.

"Daddy…doesn't love us."

"*NO!*" Powell shouted tremulously.

They were taunting him, reminding him that it was his fault that they both had died that night. They were accusing him, letting him know that maybe he *did* want them to die. Because if he didn't, he would have taken them out for ice cream. He would have been driving the car. Not their mommy. Their mommy who also died because Powell didn't care.

They were getting nearer to him. Slow, shuffling footsteps. The fetid odor of their physical decay growing stronger, filling his nostrils with a sick, rotting stench.

"Tell us…you…love us…Daddy," Ruthie said.

"We'll…hug you…Daddy," Randy croaked in his dry, detached voice.

Powell had only one option. He had to run. Run from the house while even a fragment of his waning willpower could guide his move. He could not bring himself to look at them and see his children as they were now, soulless, undead creatures.

"Daddy…we love…you," Ruthie expressed in a dreary, sepulchral tone.

Powell reacted. Impulsively, with his fearful instincts gaining control, he hastened toward the front door. He fiddled with the lock then twisted the knob. But the door was sealed shut. Once again it was happening. He wasn't supposed to leave. Not yet.

Maybe not ever.

He struggled with trying to force open the door before he spun his attention toward the front picture window. A slight, desperate smile came to his lips as he stepped sideways over to it, walking with almost cat-like steps, keeping his focus only on what was in front and to the direct side of him. Yet he could feel the tug as they both tried to enforce what he believed was a supernatural will to get him to look at them. Once he faced them he knew he would be corrupted, his sanity gone forever. He resisted their energy, but just barely. His gaze skittered about the room as he searched for a sturdy, heavy object, settling on the portable television set. He edged over toward it and lifted the television from its stand. He started to laugh—a strange, almost yelping laugh. He was going to free himself from this horror and then he was going to escape this town, even if he had to do it all the way on foot. He snickered. *Even barefoot if he had to.*

But in his rush he became careless and as he moved forward with both hands grasping the television, the floor cord wrapped around his ankle in a snake-like coil and he lost his footing and his body plunged heavily to the floor, the television breaking free from his grip, the picture tube shattering on the carpet just inches from his face.

Powell lay on his belly, in pain and momentarily helpless. He thought he could hear his children's graveyard giggles growing even louder.

"No..." he whimpered, his body squirming on the carpet. He tried to get up, but couldn't pull himself upright since he had tangled himself even more awkwardly with the television cord.

Keeping his eyes averted from their approach, Powell struggled into a sitting position and tried to free himself from the cord. He was working in a flustered panic and his hands were shaking so erratically it was almost as if he had succumbed to a virulent palsy, and he couldn't seem to do anything with the cord. With his gaze cast downward he saw the two small misshapen shadows enlarge upon the floor before him.

And suddenly...his resistance was spent. He had no choice but to turn his head and raise his stricken eyes as the ominous shadows fell wholly upon him.

Two voices blending as one in a toneless sing-song . . .

"We're dead, Daddy..."

CHAPTER TWENTY-EIGHT

Earlier that night and just a few miles across town, Donna Murray found herself suddenly awake. It wasn't that first loud clap of thunder that had ushered in the rainstorm that jolted her out of her slumber, or the heavy downpour now sounding outside her bedroom window. She'd gone to bed early and had been sleeping soundly when her eyes snapped open and she was overwhelmed by an inexplicable sense of dread. And while she could not justify it, what had consumed her was a fear for Braden Powell.

She sat up in her bed and tried to make sense of why she should experience this impulsive panic. She just as quickly debated whether she should acknowledge her worry. If she should call the police station and check to see if everything was all right with Powell. Maybe that was a silly thought and one that he might not appreciate and maybe even misinterpret. Still, it hadn't merely been a dream and she'd never felt a sensation quite so distressing and her immediate decision was that she should make the call. If for no other reason than she knew she would probably not get back to sleep until she had this worry answered. Even if Powell wasn't at his office someone surely would be manning the night desk and he could either confirm or relax her concern.

She climbed out of bed and slid her feet into the slippers she kept next to the night stand, then padded across the floor into the small living room/kitchen combo where the telephone was kept. The sleep was clearing from her brain and at once she felt a little ridiculous. She stood next to the phone stand and again debated whether she should follow through with her intention. She compared it to a nightmare that seems so real and terrifying immediately upon wakening, but once the brain awakens fully, one comes to realize how irrational that fear really was. Merely a disturbing but harmless phantasm.

But then she considered how odd Powell had seemed the last time she was with him. Looking stressed, speaking in strange, complicated sentences, as if his mind was in a jumble. He had not acted at all like the man she'd gotten to know through his frequent visits at the diner—and especially not like the man with whom she had recently enjoyed a night out. Perhaps that was all it was. Worry over his emotional state had gotten her up so abruptly. There really wasn't much she could help him with there—even though she wished there was something she could do to ease all the pressure she knew he was under from the town and his own sense of duty.

Donna smiled self-consciously. She accepted that it was her own concern for Powell that caused her momentary unrest and was relieved she hadn't reacted hastily.

She turned to start back toward the bedroom and the comfort of her mattress when she halted abruptly and her body jerked back stiffly in a reflex as a gasp lodged in her throat.

Two small silhouettes, appearing as little more than dark outlines, stood in the doorway to the bedroom, blocking her passage. Both were standing still and silent.

Donna tried to stay calm. She didn't know who they were—or how they had managed to find their way into her apartment without her noticing. She shifted her gaze ever so briefly toward the main door. She had locked it earlier, as she always did, and it remained locked. She turned back to her "visitors." Their bodies were enveloped in shadow and she could not make out their faces. While their "intrusion" made no sense to her, Donna knew instinctively that whoever they were, they had come with sinister intent.

There was a prolonged silence, and all the while Donna did not flee. She managed to hold herself steady while she waited to learn what they wanted from her.

Finally, there arose an agonizing moan and the taller of the two silhouettes started to slowly raise its arm, pointing a stiff if trembling finger at her in what Donna detected was an accusatory gesture.

The voice that emerged from the mouth was only slightly recognizable as that of a child.

"He's our daddy…" it said.

Donna's jaw unhinged. She was jolted by the abnormal sound of the voice…and uncomprehending of what words were being thrust at her.

The smaller of the two then spoke. And while that voice spoke without expression or emotion, Donna could also determine a threatening intention.

"We…don't want…you." And, again, a jerky finger rose and was pointed directly at her.

The two small figures began to emerge from the shadows, their gait slow and unsteady, almost spastic in their movements.

Donna didn't want to look at them. She just knew that whatever was revealed would be much too horrible—

Why were they walking like that?

—Something that her brain would not be able to process or comprehend.

She caught just a glimpse of the pair as they showed themselves in the muted light of the hallway. In just that moment she could recognize that neither was exactly human. Both resembled ghoulish apparitions, and before Donna would allow herself to be exposed to their full horror, she spun around and dashed from her apartment, too overwhelmed with terror even to scream.

She rushed frantically down the hallway and out from the building. The brief rainstorm had ceased, but the air was damp and the streets slick and she almost skidded into a fall once her feet reached the pavement. She was hardly even aware of the weather, the cold chill that permeated the night. She ran down the street clad only in her nightgown, the further she went the more her brain grew ever more cognizant of the terror she had just experienced—and perhaps the fate she'd just barely escaped. She believed that whoever or *whatever* those "entities" were, they had come to harm her.

She wasn't responsive to how quiet and seemingly deserted the town seemed. There apparently was no one to notice a young woman rushing in a panic down the street near midnight dressed in her night wear. Donna herself didn't give it thought. Her focus was solely on running as fast and as far as her feet would take her. But gradually her strength diminished and her running slowed. She tried to keep up the pace but exhaustion set in and soon her legs went wobbly and she turned into an alleyway where she collapsed. While she sat there she started to whimper. She didn't know what she was going to do— or where she could go. The shock had been so great she couldn't think straight. It took a while but she finally forced herself to regain her composure.

Yes. Yes, now she knew what she had to do. She had to get to police headquarters. She was only vaguely aware of the strange irony as confusion continued to cloud her brain. What had gotten her up from her slumber had likely saved her life. And her worry over Braden Powell had now become a concern for herself. She needed *him* to be the one to help *her*.

Her strength returned and she got up and continued back down the street, though keeping a cautious eye open in case she was being followed. It wasn't far to go. Perhaps another block or so. Strangely, she couldn't exactly remember. The jumble still hadn't cleared from her brain. This time she didn't run, but walked with brisk steps. And it was then that she finally became aware of how dark and empty the streets looked. A quiet and stillness she'd never noticed before in all the years she had lived in Clear Vista. It was odd and unsettling, as if she'd entered a parallel dimension where everything was *almost* but not quite the same. She wrapped her arms tightly around her shoulders to brace her body against the cold as well as to give herself a sense of protection.

And then she saw it.

High over Buchanan Bay and floating inland. A strange, ever-widening green hue. A cloud-like accumulation that was both striking and terrifying, advancing against the backdrop of the sky. Donna stopped in her tracks and gazed at this anomaly with her mouth agape. She didn't know what it was she was witnessing, but once again a consuming fear engulfed her and she picked up her step and hurried onward.

It seemed to take forever before she got to police headquarters. But finally she reached her destination, and it had been just short minutes. The door to the office was unlocked and she went inside. Curiously, there looked to be no one there. And that was unusual and discomforting. A cop always had to be on desk duty to take calls unless some emergency required the assistance of the entire department. But what emergency could there be—outside of what she had just experienced? If anything, the town itself looked about as inactive as she had ever seen it. Even given the lateness of the hour.

The office was eerily quiet and filled with a heavy gloom. Between her sudden awakening, the frightening appearance of those *entities*, the irregularity she'd noticed in the sky and now no desk officer on duty at headquarters, perhaps her worry over Powell did have some significance.

Maybe. Possible. But Donna was starting to think there was more to it than that.

Something in the atmosphere just seemed…not right. Surreal, yet with a sense of foreboding. She felt no safer at police headquarters than she had at home. The sensation that crept over her was like some malignancy preparing to grab and take hold, tantamount to gnarled hands about to clutch you from an open closet.

She was cold, but the shivers that now passed through her body like a series of electric currents were not due to the chill of dampness. They came from deeper within—in response to this situation which had come upon her with a terrifying suddenness that her sense of reason failed to grasp.

She didn't want to stay here—alone. But she didn't want to return to her apartment, either. Once more she didn't know where to go. The whole town had taken on a portentous air.

Troubled by her indecision she started to bite down on her lower lip. Suddenly she bit deep, her tooth breaking the tender tissue and drawing a bit of blood. She winced. "Shit!"

And then she heard a voice.

"Donna? Donna Murray?"

It was a voice that took her only a few moments to recognize. Nothing creepy or out-of-the-ordinary about it. In fact, it signaled the arrival of a welcoming presence. She turned herself around.

"What the hell's going on?" Officer Reynolds asked as his crinkled eyes surveyed the empty office. He walked over to flick on the light switch. The overhead lights came on. Immediately.

Donna drew a heavy breath. She could have collapsed right into Reynolds's arms. But she put out an effort to hold herself firm, trying to maintain at least a semblance of calm and control in front of the young patrolman.

"Where's Powell?" Reynolds asked with a puzzled expression. Then with more emphasis, "Where the hell's *anyone*!"

Donna couldn't immediately speak. At any rate, she had no answer to give him.

Reynolds regarded her with concern. "Are you all right?"

Donna still didn't say anything, but she managed a weak nod of her head. Reynolds wasn't convinced. Her whole attitude seemed strained. But Reynolds didn't persist and let the girl express herself in her own way. In the meantime, he slid a chair over to her. She seated herself, her movements tentative and a trifle unsteady.

"Just drove in from Breckridge," Reynolds explained to her. He blew out an unsteady breath. "Didn't expect to come back to this. The whole town has…" He couldn't finish. He just shook his head in bewilderment.

When Donna could finally find the voice to speak she attempted to tell him about her strange encounter with those malevolent "children" and her unexplainable concern for Braden Powell. It was still troubling for her to discuss and she doubted Reynolds would put much credence on her ramblings. Reynolds was perplexed but did not appear dubious at hearing her words. Then, almost in unison, they commented on what was happening with the lifelessness of the town and the anomaly they both had witnessed in the skies. Although a pragmatic man, Reynolds had seen enough over the past week to accept that something beyond the ordinary was occurring in the town. Donna's own exposure had been intense and horrifying enough to convince her that Reynolds was not exaggerating in his concern.

"We've gotta get out of here," Reynolds said abruptly. "I don't know where Powell is. Don't know what's happening, but Clear Vista has gone bad."

Donna's eyes snapped wide. "We've first got to find out what happened to Braden," she urged Reynolds. "I—know now, for certain, there's something wrong."

"We could stop by and check at his house," Reynolds suggested, though it was clear by his tone that was not a decision he particularly favored given the circumstances. He added, "But I don't think we should be staying here any longer than necessary. Whatever the hell is going on, we're not equipped to fight it. And, personally, I don't want to."

"Please," Donna said, her voice pleading.

Reynolds looked torn, not able to decide between what he knew was right and Donna's own concern for Powell. With no time to waste with arguing or attempting to reason, his compassion went to the young woman.

"All right. My car's out front," Reynolds told her.

Before they left the office Reynolds took a police jacket from the rack and placed it around Donna's shoulders. She smiled at him with a vacant appreciation.

Even though he didn't think it would make any difference now, Reynolds locked the door behind them, considering the office key briefly before pocketing it. They then hurried over to his car. Once both were inside and Reynolds had the motor running, he turned to Donna. His words were gentle but firm.

"Look," he said. "I don't know if we're going to find Powell...or if we do, what we might discover. What I'm saying is, just be ready for that."

Donna gave him a brief sideways glance and a quick if absent nod.

"Do you understand me?" Reynolds repeated.

Another swift rock of her head.

That was the best she could manage. Reynolds knew he would have to accept that. How could she guarantee her behavior when Reynolds himself couldn't be sure of what his own reaction might be to what was ahead? He fixed her with an expression of concern before he threw the car into gear, spun it around in the opposite direction and headed toward Chief Powell's house.

Neither had yet to notice that a shadow had fallen against the moon, staining its silvery surface blood red.

Still, the signs were evident. As if in a fearful grouping, many of the citizens of Clear Vista had emerged from their homes, most rushing toward the town churches, seeking a religious understanding of what had come upon their community. But the doors of the churches were locked and the windows suddenly blackened. The multi-colored stain glass images appeared smudged with a deep, dark gray, made most prominent by the scratchy drawing of long, wide-spread fingers intentionally desecrating their Christian relevance. No entry or protection permitted. If an explanation for this unholy occurrence was to be sought, it would not be offered within the sanctuary of the church.

Which even to the observation of both Officer Reynolds and Donna looked hopeless as desperate citizens pushed and crowded against doors that would not open.

CHAPTER TWENTY-NINE

The horror was complete.

Powell had seen the faces of his children, what remained of their faces after the mortician's cosmetic handiwork had surrendered to the natural process of decomposition and decay, the terrible injuries that both had suffered in the crash unmasked and visible. Their bodies, dressed in the clothing they had been interred in, Ruthie's favorite frilly dress which she proudly wore to her friends' birthday parties and school recitals, and a suit that Powell had purchased specifically for his son's burial. As he sat crumpled on the floor exposed to their physical corruption, his mental faculties deteriorated into a state of incomprehension, his emotions gripped in an unimaginable terror. He had listened to their condemnation of him, that they and their mommy had died in that terrible accident because he didn't care, and that he now wanted another lady *who was not their mommy*. Who would *never* be their mommy.

They promised to hurt her before they would ever let her be their mommy. Powell numbly but repeatedly denied their accusations, but they were immune to his pathetic pleas. And as each horrid moment passed the remaining shreds of his sanity had been torn from him. And finally after what seemed an eternity of being subjected both to their decay and to their accusatory words, often spoken in unison, he could take it no longer and screamed long and hard and ran on wobbly legs from the house, out through the door that now had mysteriously opened for him. But he didn't run far. Once on the street he collapsed against the curb in front of his house. He shakily pulled himself to his knees and sat there, alternately laughing and sobbing, rubbing his hands against his scalp in a rapid and frantic motion and then starting to tear his fingers into his forehead, further ripping open the damaged flesh.

And he continued digging, fingernails now carving deep caverns into his face, pulling off the strands of skin that he pried loose with bloody hands.

Reynolds and Donna pulled up outside the house and saw Powell sitting there, tragic and pitiable. Ignoring Reynolds's urging to stay put until he could check out the situation, Donna jumped from the car before it could come to a complete stop, and she hurried over to Powell. She screamed as she failed to draw back her revulsion once she saw him. The man's face was gone, he was disfigured nearly beyond recognition with traces of the bone of his skull actually visible. His brain was shattered. He appeared barely the shell of a human being.

To her further horror Donna noticed how his hair had gone from a chestnut brown to shock white.

"*Braden...*" Donna's voice became muted.

After moments of not acknowledging her voice or her presence Powell released his bloody fingers from his face and raised dazed and glazed eyes toward her. Garbled sounds emanated from his lips, as if he were trying to form words beyond his comprehension, like an infant learning to speak. Still, it looked as if there might still be a fragment of awareness left to the man as his ruined features took on a semblance of recognition.

"It's all Daddy's fault," he said, the words tragic and pathetic, spoken weirdly in the high-pitched voice of a child—but cohesive. "Daddy let them die. They. . . they said so. They—*told me so.*"

"No. No, that's not true," Donna returned, speaking solidly, in an effort to return some reason to him.

And then Powell started to giggle as his eyes appeared to turn inward and he succumbed to what Donna recognized was complete insanity. An insanity that she recognized was his final, permanent cocoon of protection.

Reynolds stepped slowly from the vehicle, distressed by what he was witnessing. There was nothing he could do for Powell, he knew that now. Braden Powell, as he'd known him, no longer existed. He could not guess what horror had occurred this night to drive Powell to such madness, though he couldn't help thinking that perhaps his dark descent had started before tonight—back to when his own personal misfortune happened. And then compounded by those still-unsolved tragedies that had cast corruption and despair over the town.

Reynolds gently took the weeping Donna by her shoulders and lifted her to her feet. And it was then, when both stood next to Powell, consumed with fear, pity and helplessness, that it became evident that life had returned to the town of Clear Vista.

But this was made manifest in a horrific way, as a cacophony of screams and shrieks, cries and moans—some tormented, others forlorn—started to be heard. Randomly at first, isolated, then intensifying, emanating from within houses all along the street, the screams continued. It was as if some hour of reckoning had overtaken Clear Vista and homes and families were being subjected to their own individual suffering, or penance.

Donna instantly covered her ears, trying to block out the bone-curdling cries that pierced and penetrated the night like the wail of a thousand banshees. She could not bring herself to imagine what atrocities were being committed behind those closed doors and locked windows.

Self-imposed, or committed by vengeful hands.

The night of horror had begun, as it was also nearing its end.

Donna tentatively pulled her hands away from her ears so that she could speak to Reynolds. "We, have to take care of him."

But something else had happened.

It was as if Reynolds wasn't listening. His attitude changed, shifted. He became remote, almost oblivious to the girl and the pathetic Powell.

"Don't you hear me? We have to leave!" Donna shouted.

"No, it's too late," Reynolds said resignedly.

"Too late?"

"There's no place for us to go," Reynolds said.

"I—don't understand," Donna said.

Reynolds nodded. "I do," he said softly, as the sounds of distress and anguish continued to surround them, but also beginning to gradually diminish. He turned to Donna with a strange, sad smile and his words came distantly, introspectively.

"I was wrong," he confessed.

Donna was uncomprehending. "*Wrong?*"

"Not Hades, not Hell," he said. His lips pressed together in a thin line. "Not for all of us."

"What are you saying?" Donna cried desperately. "What are you talking about?" She was pleading for an explanation. Even with all the horror of this night she was seeking something that she could grasp, accept—however vague or peripheral to what was happening around them.

Reynolds focused his gaze on the blazing ball of fire that was the blood moon. There was the slight glistening of tears in his eyes. Oddly Donna could determine that those tears were neither an acknowledgment of fear or sorrow, but of an acceptance. As though he had just become receptive to a sudden and disturbingly *surreal* epiphany.

"It's the only answer." He then spoke as if reciting the words to—or perhaps *beyond*—himself, "Each person determines their own Heaven and their own Hell. No one can ever escape judgment."

Donna felt an icy grip take hold of her, even as she started to reach her own strange understanding of the situation.

Reynolds was now completely absorbed in what he was saying, to the exclusion of all else. The tormented screams and cries that surrounded him in the night, and even of Donna's presence.

It was as if he was suddenly possessed by a spirit, a force compelling him to articulate what needed to be said. Even his appearance seemed to take on a strange, otherworldly look.

He said in a subtle intonation, "We existed, and yet we didn't. Not as we thought. God help us, *this* is our reality. Nothing exists beyond here. It's all been a façade. It…*all of it* was an illusion."

Donna slowly shook her head. Her expression was troubled, still not totally comprehending his words, but fearful at their implication.

Reynolds paused before expelling a rattled breath. "Preparing us for—where we really are. Where each of us is intended to be." And then he turned to Donna and spoke to her, looked at her without really seeming to see the girl. "People can't run away from their guilt. We're still made to acknowledge our sins. Those secrets we try to deny and keep hidden, even from ourselves. And that can happen only one way." He swallowed hard before he pushed out his final words, "When we make our way through Purgatory."

Donna's eyes widened into saucers. Her face took on an expression of disbelief as she started to echo, "*Purga—*"

But then she too seemed to be affected. In some disturbing yet fragmentary way she could understand how what was happening to the town also related to her. A long-ago dark and disturbing memory she could not clearly define but one that had placed her where she now was meant to be. A shadowy recollection that she had purposely blocked from her mind.

She turned her face toward the house that Powell had lived in with his family. She understood that whatever it was that had destroyed Powell's mind and soul was behind those front doors. And she came to the realization of what that was, as she, too, had experienced his horror. Perhaps what Terry Reynolds was saying *was* the truth. There was no escape. There could be no permanent protection, no concealing of one's secrets. If that was so, and as the supernatural elements continued to take hold of the town, consuming its people like the black plague of centuries past, she had no reason to doubt him, and saw no chance for redemption.

But first she had to discover for herself that final answer. Partly curious, partly compelled, Donna summoned her courage and started to walk toward the house.

Reynolds was not even vaguely aware of what Donna was doing and made no effort to halt her. His focus connected with what he now knew was to come. Several minutes later he didn't so much as flinch when he heard her screams merge with those others that had long since reached a crescendo and now seemed to begin a slow fade into the night. He was oblivious to Donna having encountered the horror made manifest within the walls of Braden Powell's house.

Emerging from the green hue some ectoplasmic phenomenon reached with tentacled fingers into the fog that rose up ghost-like from the bay, blending with it, swirling as it lifted slowly from the steep cliffs and climbed higher, cresting the rise…and then creeping inland, the thick, miasmic mist appearing to pulsate as it rolled in relentlessly, enveloping the town and silencing the screams that had shattered the night. And when at last the fog dissipated all that remained in its path was a wasteland that gave no indication that life or community had ever existed there.

Only a solitary figure remained, standing far off and surveying the desolate landscape. A figure wrapped in a hooded black robe, a wide, unnatural grin stretching across a lipless mouth.

Slowly the malevolent grin dissolved, and as it faded the face beneath the hood changed, shifted, the features taking on many forms until finally settling on a woman's inscrutable yet serene countenance.

A woman named Mary Pemberton, who through a shadowed history and through the repeated telling of ghost stories had become a Halloween legend. But who, in truth, many years ago had suffered a tragic fate at the hands of a vengeful mob, yet whose final promise—to avenge the suffering of the children—had been carried out at a time and a place chosen by a perverse providence…

And perhaps at some time, at some place, *may be again.*

EPILOGUE

No one would ever know of the days of darkness that had fallen upon the seaside community. There is no legacy.

For people near and far retain no knowledge of any locale called Clear Vista. No memory nor vestige of such a place exists. What inhabits that site today is a depressed and deadened landscape and an old neglected cemetery whose occupants are also dead. Dead men tell no tales.

A grim area, its stillness interrupted only when the fog rolls in from the sea, shrouding the environment in a thick, swirling gray mist. The quiet is disturbed when strong winds blow in from the coast and howl dolefully across the bleak open miles, populated only by scatterings of brittle old trees and yellowed shrubbery, the sparse foliage dry like ancient parchment.

Even the old-timers who reside in nearby communities and pass the days sitting in beer parlors or coffee shops talking about nothing of significance are unable provide any background or history to the area, saying only the location had always been like that—forgotten and left to decay—for as far back as they remember. Perhaps…they are simply unwilling to offer more. To try and pry additional information from these people is futile. They are wary of such questions and disinclined to tell anything more. For while they may not admit it, they were cautioned by their parents just as their parents were told by their folks that it was better not to be inquisitive about such matters.

Some secrets must remain secrets. A distinct but nameless fear had been instilled in each generation and it was rare that anyone ventured into what came to be regarded as a genuine haunted hollow. A hollow that may or may not hold a secret and memories of a dreadful past, but where ghosts were still rumored to dwell.

The sad and lonely stretch of land known today as Murky Bluff.

The End

About the Author

Stone Wallace has worked as a professional writer for over 30 years. He has published 18 books (novels and non-fiction), short stories, scripts /screenplays and written numerous articles for North American publications. He has conducted celebrity interviews with such legendary performers as Anthony Quinn, Coleen Gray, Lloyd Nolan, Robert Stack and 50s horror director Herbert L. Strock (*I Was a Teenage Frankenstein, Blood of Dracula, How to Make a Monster*). He attended Red River College, The National Institute of Broadcasting and Robertson Broadcast Academy

He has held a lifelong fascination with the paranormal and the macabre, his early interest stimulated by the tales of Poe, Lovecraft and M.R. James. Later he discovered contemporary masters such as Robert Bloch, Ray Bradbury and Richard Matheson. And then came his discovery of Stephen King and that was when Wallace determined that writing horror fiction was what he wanted to do.

After graduating college, he wrote his first supernatural novel, the well-received **CHILD OF DEMONS**. This book was followed by the national bestseller **BLOOD MOON** and later, **GRAVEYARD**. He returned to the horror genre this year with his latest work, which he calls his most terrifying story yet.